Lazy City

Lazy City

RACHEL CONNOLLY

CANONGATE

First published in Great Britain in 2023
by Canongate Books Ltd, 14 High Street, Edinburgh EH1 1TE

canongate.co.uk

1

Copyright © Rachel Connolly, 2023

The right of Rachel Connolly to be identified as the
author of this work has been asserted by her in accordance
with the Copyright, Designs and Patents Act 1988

British Library Cataloguing-in-Publication Data
A catalogue record for this book is available on
request from the British Library

ISBN 978 1 83885 966 4
Export ISBN 978 1 83885 967 1

Typeset in Bembo Std by Palimpsest Book Production Ltd,
Falkirk, Stirlingshire

Printed and bound in Great Britain by Clays Ltd, Elcograf S.p.A.

For Ross, for understanding me

I

WINTER SEEPS INTO THE DAY through the edges; I watch it come in. I have been getting up just after six most days, or most days when I am not hungover at least, to run along the Lagan. I can feel the nights getting darker, colder and wetter, and stretching further into the mornings as August becomes September. It is one of these mornings, when I have been running for twenty minutes, maybe longer, and it is barely light out, that I meet her on the path.

The sky is pink and hazy purple, purple which has not quite turned to pink, as the sun rises. The air smells like the wet grass of the riverbank and damp tarmac. Damp tarmac, not wet. Properly wet tarmac smells sweeter; it rained yesterday but not last night.

I turn a corner and see her coming towards me down a straight stretch of path, walking in long strides. Her dog is running just ahead of her. Jesus, that dog. I make out a mangy tennis ball, gripped tightly in one of her hands. I haven't seen her since I moved out, a few weeks after coming home. She sent me one message after, to say I had left this and that thing in her house, asking how I planned to deal with it. I never bothered replying.

What to say? There was nothing to say. She was looking for a fight. I deleted that message too. Removed her as a contact, even though I know her number off by heart. A symbolic gesture, more than anything else. And symbolic for who? It's not as if she'd have known I'd done it. It was me telling myself: Done with all that. New era.

She doesn't wave at me. I can't make her face out, what expression she'll be wearing. I imagine a pleased look, a smug smile. Tight lips and a clipped voice. And what will she say? *Ah did you own this stretch of towpath now, and I'm not allowed to be here? Nobody told me.* I force myself to keep running at the same pace, to try and keep running at the same pace.

Then the dog loses it and charges at me. It's possible he recognises me, but he maybe would do this to whoever he saw out running. He is mad, like. He bounds down the path, shaking water everywhere as he goes. He must have been in the river already. He jumps up on me, throwing his entire body weight against me, soaking my leggings. His red fur is matted with mud, water and a smell of grass.

Patch, no! she shouts, as she comes running after him. *No! No! No!* She catches up with us, apologises for him jumping up.

He's fine, I say. *He's all right.* Nonchalant, as if my legs aren't soaking.

He jumps up on her, soaking her legs too, and then stands between us, panting and turning his head to look from one of us to the other and then back again. We both look at each other. Her expression, I can't read it. It could be defiant, it could be sheepish. I don't know what to say, she doesn't seem to either, even though she will have planned to come out here for this . . . what would I call it? Confrontation? Why else would she be here?

OK, right, I say. *Who told you I'd be out here?*

What do you mean? Nobody told me anything, she says. Her voice is clipped and breezy. *I've come out to walk my dog, or did you own the path now?*

I shake my head. It's a mad question to answer. But this is how these arguments are, always; both of us just being mad.

You know I knew you were going to say that, I say, still shaking my head. *I knew it back there on the path. I guessed it almost word for word.* My legs are freezing.

Patch has stopped barking and started growling. I look down at him and see he is watching a stick drifting near the opposite bank. A dark shape standing up out of the water, rippling the surface. I look back at her.

You did follow me out here, I say. I can't read her face. *What else were you doing? Watching the sun come up?*

Did I say I was here for no reason? she says. Patch barks again but she doesn't look down at him. *No, I didn't say that. I'm walking Patch.* She doesn't break eye contact the entire time, not for a second.

There is a splash as Patch jumps into the river. He swims towards the stick with his entire body below the water. His head glides across the surface noiselessly, as if it's powered by a motor. I wipe splashed droplets off my face.

This is so predictable, I say. *Jesus, so predictable.* When I hear myself say it I recognise it as one of the things I say. One of the things I always say when we have these arguments.

What, so me going for a walk in the morning is a predictable routine? she says. *Is it? Here we go, this is a new one.* This is one of the things she says: This is a new one, or that's interesting. Then she does something else she loves to do too. She says *ha ha ha.*

3

Mirthless, separate *ha*s. It's not a laugh. More an impression of a laugh.

Then I am saying she would never get up this early, except for a flight, as far back as I can remember. Why pretend she's not here on purpose? And she is saying do I think I'm the person who gets to decide when she gets up? Because I'm certainly not.

I had a life before you were born, she says. *As far as you remember is not as far as it goes.*

I look at her feet and see she is wearing stiff hiking boots. If I turn and run back, she won't have a chance of catching me. She'll have to get Patch back on his lead again anyway.

OK, right, I say. *If you came to see me, then say whatever it is you wanted to say.*

I didn't come here to see you, she says.

Patch comes scrambling up the riverbank, panting. He has the branch in his mouth. Bigger than it appeared in the water. It will have been caught on something that had held most of it down; it looks like it fell recently because it is still covered in small leaves which haven't yet disintegrated. He drops the branch between us. We both look down at him. Patch starts growling, wanting a reaction to his branch, and then lets out a single, piercing bark.

Right, I say. Patch barks again. *Well then, I'll leave you to it.* I turn around and start running, back the way I came. She calls after me. I stop and turn around.

You still have things at the house. She has to shout it.

Well, if you need me to collect them because you need the space, send me a time you aren't in, I shout back. *Leave the key out or whatever. I'll come then or send someone trustworthy.*

She shouts that I have to clear it with her if I send someone.

4

Fine, I shout. *Right. Send times, is that everything?* She nods. I take off again and don't look back.

I run back along the towpath towards Botanic Park, past the block of new-build flats with big windows looking onto the river, which always have multiple rental and sale signs up outside them. Today I count three for rent and two for sale. Everyone says it's because river rats from the Lagan climb up through the pipes and emerge from their toilets. I don't know if that's true. There aren't many cars or people out; too early.

I run past the bridge to Ormeau and up to the park. There's a white flag with a red cross and a red hand of Ulster, overlaid on the cross, flying on the lamppost on the other side of the bridge. Union Jacks fly from lampposts outside the housing estate on the embankment too. Red-brick buildings, against the green of the river bank and the blue of the mountains.

What was that all about? I wonder as I run. I think of Patch and his stick and the phrases. *Do you own this path? This is so predictable.* Or did she say it that way? Was it quite like that? And the bigger question: What was she up to? You could say checking on me, you could say she cares. But then, as I will think to myself often, why be so weird?

And the argument, did I start it? Maybe, but she did come out to the path, which is why it started. Cause and effect. Thinking of cause and effect is a form of regret. But then, I can regret the way something went without necessarily feeling guilty for my part in it, I think.

I get to the park and the gate's unlocked. Great. This morning is looking up. I run laps around the flower beds. Roses wilting for the autumn, leaves on trees turning yellow. I can see them opening the university library as I run my third, fourth lap. Lights turn on in the glass room above the canopy of the trees. I only see one other person, a man with grey hair poking out from under a tweed cap, walking his dog.

The way it went, why does it always have to go like that? I could make it different, maybe. I could not say the things I always say, not react. But then, it would have to be who changes, who fixes things, and only so much of this is my fault.

Does everyone have these relationships they sort of live in the wreckage of? It's hard to know, and hard to ask anyone. Hard to describe, for a start. But also hard to ask because the idea of asking, of describing it, is so exposing.

Hard to describe because I don't even know what's going on half the time. Like, what was she up to, coming out to the path? What was my mum up to, following me out here like that? How did she even know where to find me?

2

ANNE MARIE HAS TAKEN THE boys to her sister's holiday house in Donegal this weekend so I have the house to myself until Monday. Her sister is there with her too, with her children, and Anne Marie's mother has come up from Dublin. Mother, that's how she's always referred to. They'll go on walks on windy beaches with long, tough grass and eat oysters and the children will wear wetsuits and do watersports.

There is a list of chores to do while they're away. Things I don't usually have time for. Deep cleaning the inside of the oven. Organising the piles of clothes which live permanently in the laundry room. Using an old toothbrush to scrub the build-up of black slime from between the shower tiles. Dusting.

Anne Marie made a point of saying not to worry about doing everything, and certainly not to do anything extra. *You should have some time to put your feet up too*, she said. *And obviously treat the house as if it's your own place and have whoever over.*

I wouldn't though, have whoever over. I wouldn't risk upsetting our arrangement by testing the boundaries of her hospitality like that. In the current circumstances I wouldn't have anyone other than Declan round for drinks, and it would very much be for drinks with dinner. That's the plan this evening.

I move six bottled beers from the laundry room to the fridge before I start to cook. Declan will be here in about an hour. We'll eat and then go to Madame George's, the bar where he works, for more drinks. He's not on tonight and his boss Tony lets the staff there drink for free, more or less, if they're not working. Maybe we'll buy a few drinks out of politeness, or because it's both of us we might bring a hip flask of rum and just ask for free cokes.

For dinner I'm making a curry; working mechanically through the steps of a well-worn recipe from my student days. Condensation frosts the inside of the windows as I cook. The sweet smell of onions and spices frying fills the stainless-steel-and-green-wood kitchen. Green, but tasteful: pale pistachio. Pistachio cupboards punctuated with gleaming, understated, energy-efficient appliances. On one wall a giant, numberless clock with thick black hands. Beside it a wooden sign that says COOK, another that says HOME.

Towards the end of the recipe, at the simmering and stirring stage, I go upstairs to wash the smell of cooking out of my hair and get dressed. After I shower and dry my hair, I kneel to do my makeup in front of the mirror in the room I sleep in. More bronzer than I would wear during the day. Grey eyeshadow with black eyeshadow layered over it, and dark eyeliner, but no eye makeup more extravagant than that: Madame George's is only a bar.

I inspect my cheeks for eyeshadow smudges, and then I pull the skin at the outer corner of my left eye taut and let it go slack, examining it in the mirror, looking for creases. Trying

8

to decide if any I can see are real or an effect of my foundation. I smile at myself in the mirror, watching the creases deepen.

Then I wipe residual eye shadow dust from under the same eye with my thumb. I decide to leave my lips bare.

The home system makes the bell sound as I finish pulling on my tights. It will be Declan, I know it will be Declan, but I go to the hall to check the video feed anyway. Anne Marie says to always do it, even if you think you're sure who it will be. *It will be the one time you don't check that a burglar will knock you out of the way,* she says. *He'll push you over and charge into the house. That's how it is with these things. Always.*

As far as I know Anne Marie has never been burgled, but the home system is the thing to have now. It represents progress and refinement. And, I have to admit, its presence does make the threat of burglars seem prescient, so I do always check the feed anyway. In the camera I see Declan standing on the doorstep, checking his phone.

I let him in and he follows me into the kitchen. *Thank you for cooking, darling,* he says. *Smells lovely in here.* He's polite enough that he'd say that whatever it smelt like, I think, but I still smile. He asks if he can do anything to help as he opens drawers, looking for forks to set out.

When we sit down to eat, with two bottled beers and a plate with a large naan bread, torn into pieces, on the table between us, he tells me about the trouble with his new flatmate. She moved in last month. A friend of a friend who seemed fine in small doses, at parties and drinks, but who has turned out to be a nightmare to live with. *She's bad in the normal ways, like,* he says, shaking his head and picking at the foil coating his beer

9

bottle. *Messy and whatever. Inconsiderate. Leaves every pot and pan she uses in the sink to soak for days, and then you lose the head and end up washing it yourself. Borrows your charger and locks it in her room. All the rest of it.*

But she's grating on a personal level too. *She uses strange words as well,* he says. *But on purpose, like in a way that you can tell she wants you to think she's a character?*

I laugh. *Like what?*

I don't know, he says. *Fabulous is the new one.*

I laugh and say that's not a strange word and he laughs. When I'm talking to Declan like this there is always lots of laughter. Sometimes because something is funny. But often more to signal our comfort in our gossipy, slightly conspiratorial, way of being together. We have a huge catalogue of shared jokes and reference points, accumulated over years of friendship; we met in sixth year, through friends on a night out. We were immediate best friends back then, at different schools so slightly exotic to each other, and we didn't spend enough time together during the day to bicker. He stayed when I left, and the urgency of our friendship dwindled in the intervening years, but the ease of it never changed.

It's the way she uses it, he says. *She uses it too much. Do you know what it is?* he says. *She's annoyed me so much now everything she does winds me up.*

After dinner Declan wants to smoke so we sit in the garden. The pristine, recently remodelled garden. Anne Marie had men in landscaping over the summer. The project finished the week after I moved in, in July, and would have started, I realised recently, just after Anne Marie's husband Gerard moved out in March. Out of the family home and into a new-build flat near the Cathedral Quarter with the girl he was having an affair with.

She is younger; I gather younger than thirty. But that might be an exaggeration, one of those things that gets said to make a bad situation sound worse, more transgressive. Thirty does have a weight to it, the sense of a boundary. Anne Marie doesn't say much about it. I still don't know who decided he should move out, if he was thrown out or made the decision himself. But he is a solicitor so nobody needs to worry about money, at least. A new garden for the new era.

In daylight this garden is too much. So pristine it reminds me of a mini-golf course. Glossy even. But in the dusk the bright colours are greyed, shadows add depth to the plasticky finish. We sit on the wooden patio chairs with our bottled beers.

Don't you think it feels like being in a film set out here at night? I ask Declan as he rolls his cigarette.

He laughs. *I know exactly what you mean. Or a theme park. It feels like we've gone into a cordoned-off area at something. That grass even looks like someone's hoovered it.*

We finish our beers catching up on gossip: a new competition Declan has entered a painting into; what we expect the crowd to be like tonight; news of the life events of people we vaguely know, engagements, courses, jobs. I watch him pick the entire foil casing off his beer bottle between cigarettes, shredding it into a pile of silver curls on the patio table.

Declan goes inside to get us another beer and when he comes back out he's had a call from his boss, Tony, to ask if he can work later after all. Someone else has texted in sick. He's offering time and a half, and Declan could do with the money. Declan told him we had plans tonight and Tony said I can have free drinks. He also said it's not busy, we'll be able to chat.

I ask if we have to leave right now and Declan says no. Not yet, we don't have to be there till ten. We can drink here for a bit longer. We can get a taxi too, and Tony will pay Declan back for it.

Sure, OK, I say. *Yeah, why not.*

It will be good craic I think, he says. *He'll owe me for this too, I bet nobody else answered the phone.*

By the time we are trying to get a taxi we have each had four bottled beers. Not quite drunk, but on the way. Or maybe Declan has had five. I start to count the bottles lined up on the kitchen worktop but get distracted by Declan swearing at his phone, at the taxi app. He squints at the screen in the bright light of the kitchen.

When he gets one and it arrives we bundle into the back. The driver asks us if it will be a big night. Declan laughs and says he's working, actually. *Yous are mad*, laughs the driver. Declan and I both cackle.

Declan turns to me. *Oh here, I meant to say*, he says. *Guess who I saw earlier?*

I say I don't know, he says to guess. I say I really don't know. He says have one guess. I ask what gender the person is and he says that will give it away. I say then I really don't know and he says guess. I guess my mum.

What? He laughs. *No. Why would that be gossip?*

Well, I. It doesn't matter, I say, shaking my head. *Right, I guessed. Tell me.*

Mikey, he says.

Oh right, I say. *Yes, I wouldn't have guessed that.* I try to keep my voice light. Not to change the mood here in the back seat of the taxi. The warm, easy mood.

12

I don't want to sound as surprised as I am. Or as surprised to be as surprised as I am. I didn't know he was back; he didn't say. But. He doesn't have to. It's not as if we have an arrangement, or ever have had.

Anything concrete. Neither of us has to tell the other anything, really.

Declan is saying he asked about me and he knows I'm back. He has come home recently, for a placement in a hospital. He's living with his parents again to save up, hoping to move back here permanently if it goes well. He's going to buy a house, maybe not imminently, but in a little while. He has savings, he has a plan. *Yes, he always wanted to come back, didn't he?* I say. *He was always going to do that.*

You're annoyed, I can tell, Declan says.

I laugh. *I didn't say anything. I said nothing.*

He raises his eyebrows. *I know. Exactly.*

I laugh. *Well, maybe. He didn't say he was about. Same story.*

I'm sure he will, he says. *I don't know how long he's been back.*

We'll see, I say. *I'm not annoyed. You know. Did I ever tell you he sent me an email, when it all happened?*

No? What? Why an email? he says.

I don't know, I say.

Declan asks what it said and I say I can't remember exactly, it was condolences. It was polite. Not even polite, that's the wrong word, it wasn't formal. It was a good thing to do, I guess. It was strange, at the same time.

The driver shouts back to ask who we're talking about. *What's this gossip then? Somebody's boyfriend?*

3

MADAME GEORGE'S ISN'T BUSY TONIGHT; Tony did say
it wasn't. It's a small bar. One room with two areas,
both around the same size, which feel almost like two separate
rooms because of the difference in floor level between them. In
the raised area there is a small stage, and bands or DJs play there
when they come. People dance in that area, around the stage,
when it is that kind of night. In the lower area there is a collection of circular wooden tables with a few chairs each, and then
the bar and barstools. The bar is on the same side as the door.
It's the first thing you see when you enter.

Tonight there are two tables of people. At one, a group of
friends, students probably. Three girls and two boys. They aren't
dressed for a night out, there are tote bags over the back of their
chairs, rather than handbags, and they're mostly wearing jeans and
trainers. One of the girls looks to be telling a story, making shapes
in the air with her hands while the others smile. At the other
there is a couple who are maybe in their mid forties. The woman
has short, dyed red hair and the man is wearing glasses with thick
black rims. She is showing him something on her phone. At the
bar there is a man with dark hair, sitting by himself by the looks

of it. The place is almost empty, really. But it's so small it doesn't feel it. Even a small crowd gives the feeling of a buzz in here.

Tony greets Declan at the bar, thanks him for agreeing to come in. *Right, good to see you.* He nods in my direction but doesn't make eye contact. He always interacts with me in this gruff, formal manner. He's wearing bootcut jeans, brown leather shoes and a black shirt. The same outfit he seems to be wearing whenever I see him, with the shirt always half tucked into the trousers, in a way where you can't tell if it's intentional or not. He has a shiny, red, freckled face and very dark curls and eyelashes. He stands with one hand on his hip, causing his silver belt buckle to protrude under a slight paunch, as he and Declan talk about logistical issues. Stock and the rota.

I hear him repeating that we're allowed free drinks as I take a seat at the bar. *The place is hardly heaving,* he says. *But don't go mad, like.* I leave two stools between me and the man sitting there and drape my jacket over the stool on my other side. The man turns to me and smiles and raises one of his hands like a wave, or a salute. I return the smile.

So, do you work here too? he says to me, nodding towards Declan behind the bar. I can hear he is from somewhere. America, maybe. It is not the most natural introduction. He said it too quickly. I guess he's a tourist, maybe, or here for work and wanting to have a conversation with a local, an authentic experience.

No, sure I own the place, I say. *I'm just in supervising him for the night. Making sure he's on his best behaviour.*

He tilts his head back in a slow nod. He opens his mouth slightly and I can see his teeth are bright white, very straight. He has all his hair. Dark brown, almost black but not quite. Light brown eyes. A healthy, sandy tan. He's good looking, in a polished way. If you were describing him to someone you'd have to say he was good looking. He licks the inside of his lower lip.

Well, it's a great place, he says, looking around at the tables, then back to the bar. *It's cosy.*

I tell him I was joking, and he laughs. *Right, sure*, he says. He sounds relieved, maybe a little confused. But strange, dry, slightly rude jokes are the authentic experience. Then, so is slightly jarring warmth. I find myself filling the awkward silence that follows with too much backstory, explaining how we were going out tonight but then Declan got this text, even about the free taxi.

A welcome can look like so many things, depending on the place. Breezy, affable small talk and guarded pleasantries erected as a kind of fortification against closeness. Or brittle, spiky toughness which can quickly give way to shared confidences, quick loyalty.

So, you guys are from here, I guess? he says.

We are indeed, I say. *We grew up here. Are you visiting?*

What did you say? Visiting? Yes, visiting, he says. *Well, working here, not a holiday, or not only that.*

Then he moves across the stools to the one beside me, in a deft swinging motion. His feet barely touch the floor. *Sorry, do you mind me moving down to this stool?* he says, as he pulls his drink across the bar. *I can hear you better.*

I can't exactly say no now he's done it. Or I could, but to do so would seem needlessly hostile. Go back to your seat and we'll both drink alone, thank you. And it's not even like I think we should sit separately.

But we could have come together gradually; this seems forced.

No, I don't mind, I say, smiling. *So you're visiting here? Is this your first day or what?*

He laughs. *Do I seem that fresh?* he says. *I got here a few days ago. Wednesday morning your time.*

Declan comes out from the store room, carrying a stool for himself, and sits down behind the bar. He asks us what we're drinking. I get a beer, the man asks Declan to recommend something local and I smile behind my hand.

Declan gets the drinks. I turn around on my stool, towards the man. *So where are you from?* I ask him. *The States?*

That obvious? he says, smiling. *Yes, I am. I'm American. I'm originally from Boston.*

He says his name is Matt Taylor. One of those names which is so generic it's almost remarkable. He is teaching a course at Queen's. *So it's actually Dr Taylor, technically,* he says, smiling and looking down at his lap. *Although it's not like I use that title, really.* Teaching doesn't start until after half term; he got here early to give himself a few weeks to settle in and let the jet lag wear off before class starts. He says class instead of lectures.

I sip my beer as he talks. I notice I'm not really interrupting, except to say *yes, right, I get you, wow, really*. Short affirmations to show I'm engaging with what he's saying. Declan is the same. It's the way he's talking; there's an energy to it, like a coiled spring being let out of a box. Not that he's droning on, really, more like he's delivering a speech.

One of the girls from the group of friends approaches the bar, holding her bank card. Declan goes to serve her. The man turns on his stool, more towards me, and continues with his story. About how he has moved from New York, where he had been teaching. And that getting that job, at that university, had been very competitive. It was hard to convince them to let him go, he explains, even for this one term.

17

So you were a big deal, were you? I ask.

What? he says. *Oh well, I don't know about that. I had a good standing in my department, I suppose.*

I smile.

He nods. *Right: It's a joke?* He laughs. The skin around his eyes creases. Or, really, the slight creases that are there already deepen. I can't tell exactly what age he is; he's not old but he's old enough for his face to have set in certain places. Maybe late thirties. *I had that coming,* he says, holding his hands up, still laughing. A warm, contagious laugh. I start laughing too. *I didn't mean it like that. I meant it like, well,* he says, moving his hands in the air as if he's rotating a football. *I don't know what I meant.*

No, I'm only wondering why you left? And decided to come here instead? I say. The girl Declan was serving leaves the bar with her drink and Declan joins us again.

Good question. The American laughs. He pauses. *Well, I'm writing a book too. I've wanted to for a long time. I needed to do some research here at some point. It seemed like the perfect time.*

What, some Troubles thing, is it? Declan asks.

What's that? the American says.

As in a book about the Troubles? I say. *Like a history or politics book?*

Oh right. Yes, I see, he says. *No, it's fiction, it's a novel.* He smiles again and looks down. What does looking down like that mean, I wonder. Bashfulness? Evasiveness? *It's English I teach, by the way. One of the characters lives here.*

Declan and I glance at each other. He is frowning slightly, his brow is furrowed, as if to say: *Why has he stuck a random character in Belfast?* That's what I'm thinking, anyway. I shrug at Declan and turn towards the American, and it's obvious he's seen us exchanging this look. I smile, as if that cancels it out.

18

He laughs. *What's that look for? You looked at each other there.*

Oh no, says Declan. *It's nothing. We're wondering what gave you the idea to do a character from here. Or I was. It's a good idea though!*

Sure, it's a fair question, he says. He explains how he studied in Dublin for a term, years ago now, and became interested in the history round here. That's where he first had the idea. It has grown in his head since then.

The door opens behind us, letting cold, fresh air into the bar. I feel drunker, suddenly. I add everything I have had to drink so far up in my head. Two beers here. Four before? Five? A group of girls, maybe late teens or early twenties, enter in a huddle. They're wearing skirts and heeled boots and one of them is wearing very red lipstick. They arrange their bags and jackets around one of the empty tables and two of them approach the bar.

Here, I need to get this, says Declan. *But that's class that you're doing a novel.*

The American smiles, says thank you.

Declan moves down the bar and the man continues talking, just to me now, but he doesn't make eye contact, looks into the distance. *It's been something I've wanted to do for years*, he says. *And then this opportunity came up. Well, it seemed like the time. Finally.*

I nod but don't interrupt; again his delivery has taken on the speech-like quality.

He goes on. *And there were some things going on in my personal life too, so it was a good time.* I look at his hand and there is no ring. But he must mean a girlfriend, or a boyfriend. What else is there to go on in your personal life?

The girls have left the bar and Declan joins us again. I ask him what age they were, did he card them, and he shakes his head and laughs. I ask for a rum and coke; the American says he'll have one too.

Declan makes the drinks and the American asks us what the crowd is like in here, usually. The novel and personal life conversation seems to be over. I say it can be busier, usually young-ish but not teenagers. There's a lot of teenage drinking here but they prefer to wear high heels and go to nightclubs. He laughs at that. Some older people too, like older couples who like to go to gigs, that kind of way. Or very old men drinking by themselves. That's a thing you'll see a lot in bars here, even ones where the crowd is mostly young. Old men with white hair drinking by themselves. *I don't know if you've noticed that? I say. Have you been about much?*

He laughs. He hasn't noticed that. Although he hasn't really been here long enough to have gone to a lot of bars. And the jetlag means he's kept a weird schedule. He has been to the Ulster Museum, but not the whole way round, just to the Easter Rising area. Declan asks if he saw an exhibition by a certain photographer which is there at the minute, but he didn't. He took a black taxi tour. He means to go to the Giant's Causeway but he hasn't got around to it yet. I get another rum and coke. He gets one too and then gets up to go to the bathroom. Declan opens a beer.

Shall we stay open for a bit later, what do you think? Declan says to me. Or is he melting your head? I'm quite enjoying chatting to him.

I laugh. *No, I know what you mean. He's all right craic, isn't he?*

I check my phone. It's after half twelve. The bar is supposed to close at one unless they have an act in playing. It's in a residential area. But it's not uncommon for there to be a lock-in.

Tony often does this; the people who come regularly expect it and the prospect of this happening is one of Madame George's main selling points. Everyone can stay but nobody is allowed outside to smoke; as far as I know none of the neighbours have ever complained. It's residential, but a lot of student houses.

The students are keen to stay, people that age always want to stay up all night. Declan lets them buy a bottle of vodka to share between them and prices it as five drinks. The group of girls are the same. The American seems thrilled by the prospect when Declan explains it to him. His eyes widen. This would definitely count as the authentic experience. You'd never get this in a tourist trap.

I am drunk, but aware enough of my drunkenness to get a glass of water. Declan is asking about New York, what it's like, saying he'd like to go some time. The American is talking about how expensive his rent was, how inescapable it is, how it has spread to the rural upstate areas, even. *There are literally no neighbourhoods which haven't been full-scale gentrified*, he says. *We're talking nothing. Does not exist.* He swipes his hands across the air for effect. Declan nods but I can see he is finding it boring, his eyes are glazed. He wants to hear about the good bits. We know about gentrification, we even have that here. But how to ask? You can't just say, stop talking about your rent, it's boring.

Anyway, it hardly meant he couldn't live there. His area was nice, he says, convenient to his work. They got a good deal. But it was hollowed out. Almost every restaurant or bar had become a chain. Worse than that, there were barely even any of those, instead endless chain coffee shops.

This bar, you know, he says. *You don't get places like this. You know, it's more. It feels. It feels.*

Authentic? I say.

Yes. You know, here, he says. *It's much better here, in that sense. It has kept a sense of itself.*

I sip my drink. Is that what he's doing here? Trying to get back to the way it seems like it was before, before chains and apps and gentrification and expensive rents even in rural towns upstate. Because I'm drunk I want to tell him it won't work, if that's what he's doing. There is nowhere you can go to get away from it. That's the whole world. It's no different here. We have the chains. Worse than that, because not having chains felt like a form of deprivation for a while, we're still excited instead of depressed by them. I want to say it, but I know I want to say it because I'm drunk. Drunk enough to think it but sober enough not to say it.

I tell him he doesn't have to worry about chains too much here, we're always the last to get them. He laughs.

More drinks. Rum layered on top of the end of drinks. Sometimes water but not enough. He asks what I do and I say I'm a nanny, kind of. *Declan is an artist though*, I announce. *You should ask him.*

Declan laughs. We talk about that for a while, about art school and bar work to pay the bills and entering competitions and applying for fellowships and grants. The fact there's no clear path, that it's one of those industries where people know people and things work that way. The fact there's less opportunities here than other places. But it's cheaper to live here. Besides, Declan likes it. It's good for his work. That's the main thing.

We call it a night before four. When we open the door to leave, the wind stings my face. It's frosty out now, a kind of translucent covering over everything. The three of us stand in the street huddled in our jackets.

Declan is going the opposite way so we say our goodbyes. He says it was nice to meet the American. *Thank you for the sparkling company, my darling,* he says to me before he heads off. We always say that when we're very drunk, I can't remember how it started.

The American points vaguely up the street and says he is heading in the same direction as me, so we head off together. He talks about where he's staying. A family's basement flat. They did it up for the mum's dad to live in after his wife died, then he died two years later so now it's rented out.

What about you? Do you live with friends from college? he asks.

I remind him I'm a nanny. My living situation isn't that different from his, except I'm not in the basement and I have to help with homework sometimes.

He asks if I like it. I cross my arms over my jacket to keep the cold out. I tell him it's all right, I get on with Anne Marie well enough. It's a comfortable situation. I get time to myself during the day.

He says he meant the job. *I mean that sort of is the job. There isn't really much to it. I don't know.* I laugh. *I haven't been doing it long enough to hate it. Is that an answer?*

He asks what I was doing before. I don't know how to explain it, but I can't blame him for asking. I could not have said the bit about the length of time. Not made that cryptic comment. That's on me. I tell him I was studying, doing a course. I decided to take a break for a while, I wasn't sure if it was for me any more. I dropped out but I might go back. I'm still deciding.

A seagull squawks overhead and I look up to see it gliding across the sky. A white crescent sailing against the black.

Right, I see, he says. *I'm guessing it was postgraduate, based on your and Declan's age. And him having already finished?*

That's right, I say.

Yes, some people find that jump difficult, he says. *I remember that from my own Masters and PhD, a lot of people dropped out. Probably the right decision to get some perspective.*

Sure, exactly, I say. We're coming towards Anne Marie's road. He laughs and tells a story about someone from one of his various degrees who effectively ran away. *You know, he stopped coming to class and then someone found out from Facebook he was living back in Hong Kong*, he says. *He didn't tell anyone. No supervisors, nobody.*

Yes, that was me, I say. *Just like that.*

He laughs. I want to move the conversation away. I say I've liked being back. Declan lets me share his friends. *He never went away so he has more of a life here, I guess*, I say.

How come he didn't move away? he asks.

I mean he's never said as much, I say. *But I think maybe partly to stay close to his dad.*

Declan's dad moved here by himself when he was young; he got a scholarship to study physics. He was very academic, would win national competitions and all the rest of it. From a tiny village with no running water in Sri Lanka. Queen's wasn't the best university he could have gone to but it was the one which paid all his fees. So he ended up here, in this strange place with its sectarian divisions and odd, traumatised people. Where, at the time, there was barely any immigration, for obvious reasons. Not so different from where he'd left, but a richer country. That's something.

He met a girl from East Belfast studying religion. She is really that Protestant. Has cousins who would march in the Orange Order on the twelfth, although her brother never has. She doesn't see them a lot. Her parents go to watch the parade but just for the day, treat it as a family day out. They don't stay for the bonfires. And she's a kind person. Works as an RE teacher. He works at the university. Years later here they still are, with Declan. The dad sends money back. I don't know more about it than that, I don't know exactly who to. Just that he sends money back. He has brothers and sisters still there but he never seems to go back. Long flights, important projects at the university, and bad months to get back, turn into bad years and then decades.

But I don't say any of that. It's not my story to tell.

His dad moved here by himself, when he was young. And you know, Declan is an only child, I say.

He asks where Declan's dad is from and I say Sri Lanka. *Oh right, oh yes, no, I see, that makes sense*, he says. I smile at that. Nobody from here would pretend they hadn't noticed that Declan isn't white.

Our conversation has lulled as we're coming to the end of Anne Marie's street. I could start it up again, ask another question, then suggest he comes back for a drink. He'd probably say yes. And if he didn't, it's not like I'd have to see him again. But the idea of tomorrow morning. More talk, more backstory. His bright, spring-like energy filling my room. Even tonight, I have this image of his white teeth flashing under the spotlight in Anne Marie's kitchen.

I say it's my street, and so goodbye, more abruptly than I intend.

Right, sure, he says. *Of course.* We both awkwardly thrust limbs forward. For . . . a hug? A handshake? Our eyes meet and for a terrible moment I think we might both step forward and crash into each other, like when you're trying to get past someone on the street and you both keep going the same way to avoid each other.

4

WHEN ANNE MARIE AND THE boys return from Donegal on Sunday night she says she is very impressed with how clean and tidy the place is. *Well, this is fabulous. Absolutely fabulous*, she says, beaming, when she opens the fridge to get milk out for her tea. It is a sight to behold. I soaked every shelf in antibacterial solution overnight to remove even the most stubborn, years-old patches of slime and grime. Even the vegetable crisper, one corner of which had long been sacrificed to the fetid mess of a spring onion which had frozen after rotting. The shelves are now ordered by food type, and nothing, even any of the sauces, is out of date.

She stands back, looks at me and says fabulous again, and then looks back to the fridge as if she can't believe her eyes. An exaggerated reaction. Too much, perhaps. But I still feel a surge of pride. It strikes me that Anne Marie might be the best boss I've ever had. And she did step in and give me this job, when things weren't going so well living with my mum back there; she's a decent person at the end of the day.

The boys are upstairs already, exhausted from a sailing lesson. So tired they didn't even complain when Anne Marie took their phones to lock them away in the safe for the night. A post-divorce initiative usually met with fierce resistance. She got the idea from another parent who said a doctor recommended it, to make sure phones are not the last thing they see at night or the first thing they see in the morning.

A doctor. Nobody here calls psychiatrists psychiatrists or psychologists psychologists or counsellors counsellors. Just like nobody says mental health or addiction or trauma. People say a doctor, or he always drank, or that someone is on the spectrum. So often the spectrum. Their children, people they go on dates with, dads definitely. There is a certain librarian who everyone always says is on the spectrum because he wears the same two cardigans on rotation.

I follow the boys up the stairs to check they are brushing their teeth. They are both standing by the sink, with white foamy mouths and slack arms. Too tired to hold their toothbrushes firmly. When they finish and walk to their rooms, Rory turns to Calum and points his hands in a fake gun shape at him. *Pachaw*, he says meekly. As the younger brother, eight to Calum's ten, it's Rory's job to be a pest, but his heart isn't in it. Calum ignores him.

Back in the kitchen Anne Marie is drinking a glass of white wine. I ask her if it was a good break and she says it was good that her mother came because the boys bickered so much on the drive up she almost lost it. I don't know what that would mean, Anne Marie losing it. But I nod and laugh.

You know. She took them out for dinner one night, and I sat and I read my book, and you know what? I have never known peace like it, she says. *I have never. Never.* She laughs. *But you know, they're always on their best behaviour with her because it's all treats with*

27

Granny. She lets out a shrill laugh. The sort of laugh which is intended to make a statement seem softer, less pointed, but often has the opposite effect.

I want to ask her if she told my mum where I was running but it's not a good time. Between homeworks and cleaning and dinners it isn't a good time all week. It gets to Friday and the boys are having dinner with their dad. They'll stay there for the weekend. Anne Marie has planned to go for a cocktail in a bar in town with her sister. It is at the top of a new skyscraper hotel, which is supposed to be the highest bar in Belfast now. Sort of like being the tallest tree in a grazing field, and I imagine the view will be strange, more than anything else. But it's the new place to go.

We are drinking wine in the kitchen before; I'm meeting Declan later too. Anne Marie's telling me about the latest argument with her sister's old man neighbour in Donegal. He wants to install a fence and is trying to insist she pays for half of it. I could ask her about my mum now, but it still doesn't seem like the right time. I put it off again.

As one week blends into the next I forget about it. There are other things to think about. Laundry. Helping with the homeworks. The new chores Anne Marie sometimes wordlessly adds to the list, which make me worry I've not been doing something properly. *Dust pipes behind toilet! :)* was the latest. And they were dusty when I went back there but is that something you're supposed to know to do?

As I run along the Lagan one morning I'm thinking I should really just ask. Every time I run now I think of that strange meeting. It comes back to me. I try to put it out of my head. Breathing in the cold air, which seems colder every morning now. I concentrate on breathing, try not to think of her, when I see someone coming towards me. Her again? It must be. For god's sake.

The figure draws closer as I keep running, deciding whether to turn back. When I can see it more clearly I realise it's a man. I sigh in relief, tripping up my breathing. Just another runner I haven't seen out before.

I carry on running and, when he is closer still, I realise it is the American man from the other night. He starts waving. There is a considerable stretch of path between us at this stage so we're forced to keep running to clear the distance, as if towards each other.

Small world, isn't it? he says, when we stop. We're both breathing heavily. I'm conscious of the fact I'm sweaty. The cold air makes our breath dance in front of our faces. He is very pink and fresh looking, like he has shed an old layer of himself. *You're one of the only people I know here,* he says, chuckling through breaths. *And what are the chances of bumping into you out here?*

Not sure about the world being small, but this city's tiny, I say. *You can't hide from anyone. You'll find that out soon enough.*

It's great out here. So peaceful, he says. *The man who owns my flat suggested it as a good place to run. I didn't know I'd have the trail to myself.* He laughs.

Yes, this is not a 5 a.m. run kind of place. Or even a 7 a.m. run kind of place. We're lazy. I smile.

A lazy city, as well as a small one. He laughs. He laughs, I think, because I have told him what he wants to hear. That this is a place with no early mornings. No late nights in the office. No productivity. No burnout. No late capitalism.

I ask about the jetlag. He has beaten it. *Just about,* he says. He is back in a routine. He needs routine. He will start teaching soon. These last few weeks have felt like a holiday. He needed one. But he is ready to get back to real life now.

I ask when he started out this morning and he says about half an hour ago, from the carpark entrance. *The Giant Rings, I think it's called.* He points behind him. The name is slightly off but I know the field he means; it's a field with a giant ring in it. I'm confused for a second, about why he would have started there; it's not close to where he's staying. Then I realise he's clearly not staying as close to me as he said he was the other night.

Giant's Ring, I say. *There's just the one. So, wait? Did you move? Or are you staying same place?*

Oh no, same place as before. The flat in the basement of that house, he says. He looks confused; he doesn't know what I mean. Then his eyes grow wider and he tilts his head back. *Oh, of course*, he says. His voice sounds higher but maybe I am imagining that, projecting a symptom of embarrassment onto him.

Yes, when we walked back the other night that was actually a bit up the road from me, he says. He laughs. *Yes, because I said it was. Right, yes.* He goes on into a big explanation of how he thought he knew where he was going but he didn't and didn't think to check, or want to check and seem like he didn't know where he was going.

We have been standing still for long enough for the cold to feel sharp; I blow into my hands.

Yes, he says, nodding at my hands. *Cold. We should get moving, I guess.*

It was good to run into you, I say.

He looks like he is going to take off, his legs are poised to run, but then he stops again. *Actually, I was going to say*, he says. *If Declan is working this weekend, maybe I'll come by? Unless that would be really annoying for you two, having to explain everything to an American again.*

I tell him it wouldn't be annoying but I don't know what shifts Declan is working. They get changed all the time because Tony knows he can work whenever.

Well, do you want to take my number and give me a text when you're going to be there? he says.

Sure, let's swap numbers. No bother.

He thanks me again for us being friendly the other night. As I run off down the path I think about whether or not I will tell him when Declan is working. Maybe. I will definitely reply if he gets in touch.

The sun comes up as I run. Grey and pink over the Lagan Meadows with the big trees clustered together in patches, which look like a forest from the distance.

5

I T IS A FRIDAY NIGHT, and Declan and I are sitting in a booth in Keenan's with a group of people we have known, or vaguely known, since we were teenagers. Keenan's is a pub with four floors, each one full of a varying quantity of old men with scraggly beards and brown leather jackets, teenagers and people who started drinking here as teenagers. The teenagers tend to dance on the top two floors while the old men nurse their pints downstairs. Anyone else you'd have a rough chance of bumping into on any of the floors.

The huge size of the place means you don't really notice the varied clientele. It's full of dark, shiny wood and the floors are glittery black. The decor references Irishness, but Irishness in the sense of down South. There is Guinness paraphernalia everywhere but no Gaelic tops, no framed pieces of paper with Irish surnames written in Celtic font, no pictures of politicians or affiliated figures.

The way it's worked out with the seating at our table, I'm trapped beside Joanne, in a conversation about the new-build flats she has been to view this week. She is going to buy one this year. She stayed here to study, lived with her parents the whole time and did geography because it was undersubscribed and offered a bursary for good grades, and so, during her studies, she saved up almost enough for a deposit around here. A few years of teaching later, still living with her parents, and here she is, deposit in the bank, viewing the new-builds. About to have it all pay off.

I heard this story from her tonight, before her phone was produced for pictures of the new-builds. But I've heard it so many times before too. We've known each other for years, but our level of conversation never seems to progress beyond this. Over time I've started to think there is a type of person who, no matter how much time you spend with them, you never seem to get to another level of knowing them. And you get to have the feeling that you could be stuck on a desert island with them for years, still talking mostly about the weather.

That's what Joanne is to me and probably me to her. When she tells the story tonight I respond the same as always, saying it was shrewd and sensible and she did well. When I'm thinking: But at what cost?

The new-build photos she shows all look the same. White walls, plastic windows and tiny kitchens and bathrooms with compact appliances; a white plastic shower unit squeezed into a corner by the toilet. She zooms into the photos to highlight positive aspects of each one. Her nails are neatly filed and painted peach. *This one has a separate living area and kitchenette*, she says. *Good space around the bed here.*

The worst of it is that I can hear a better conversation happening just to my left. A boy called Shane telling a story about the chaos caused at the burrito bar where he works because they issued a voucher to students. *It was fucking madness, they swamped the place*, he says. *A queue the whole way down the street. All brandishing their phones with their sticker up on the screen.* He is close enough that I can hear everything that's being said if I tune in, but the way we're positioned I'd have to fully turn my back on Joanne to join the conversation properly.

Everyone in that conversation seems to be laughing, enjoying themselves. I'm searching for a polite way to reorient myself away from Joanne and the new-builds; I down my drink and get up to go to the bar to facilitate it.

Our booth is a few metres from the bar and, as I get up, I see Mikey standing there, by the bar. He is looking straight at me, his hand raised in a static wave. I feel panicked, caught out. It makes sense he would be here, this is an obvious place for him to be. Still, I'm . . . unprepared.

I head towards the bar. I wish I knew how long he had been looking in my direction. I want to know if I've been sitting hunched over, making unflattering facial expressions. And then I wonder if he would have said hello if I hadn't seen him, or slipped past, glad to go unnoticed. And then I worry it looks like I'd seen him and got up for the bar as a pretext to say hello.

I smile, trying to look friendly but not too eager. Surprised, but pleased. But not too pleased.

He looks the same as always. Square jaw, fair hair, slate-coloured eyes, slightly crooked nose which looks straight from the front. Solid, manly. He is smiling too, friendly but not too eager.

Up close his eyes aren't slate. They're light blue with a bit of yellow around the pupils. Dark yellow against the black, like a wasp. I know this but it surprises me every time, the way they turn from dark to light like that up close, the warm yellow stripe.

You're looking great, he says. *You're looking very well. Sure, will we do a hug?* His hug has an authoritative weightiness, maybe it always does. He smells of the men's perfume he has always worn, lemon laundry detergent and old cigarettes. Woody, stale and fresh at the same time. Same as always.

The bartender slides his drinks across the bar, a pint and a glass of something clear and fizzy, and extends the card machine. He taps his phone to pay.

I say it's great to see him, that me and Declan were talking about him the other week. He has heard I'm staying at Anne Marie's, he says. His mum told him. *You know her sister Maureen and my mum are tight?* he says. Again, I feel caught out. How could I forget that connection? One of those links through which gossip here spreads, web-like, to far-flung corners.

Yes, I say. *Yes, I am. It's going well. We're getting on well.*

It's a nice house. It's a good set-up. He smiles, raises his eyebrows slightly.

What does that smile mean? About Anne Marie's house? I know how he knows it's a nice house. There was a summer weekend when I was sixteen and had been babysitting for families on Anne Marie's street long enough to be trusted and recommended to her as a housesitter; Calum was just a baby, too young for a babysitter, and Rory wasn't even born yet. Housesitting was a coveted role, like babysitting, but without the work. That summer weekend, he came over. We accidentally smashed a bottle of nice wine in the kitchen, not recognising how nice it was. But we never got caught. That was the summer I worked in call centres so I could buy thrift-shop clothes and drink in bad nightclubs and spend a week in Europe; a summer when it sort of felt like I could do whatever I wanted and never get caught. And now I'm half back there, in the possibility of it. That feeling I thought I'd forgotten. Like time has split in two and I'm in both halves at once. But was the smile supposed to do that or was it just a smile?

Yeah, it's a good set-up, I say. *A great set-up. A good size. Lots of rooms. Sorry, I meant lots of room. But, lots of rooms too.*

He laughs. I do this. He always makes me do this. I talk rubbish, blather on.

What are you drinking? he says. *I'll get it.*

Rum and coke, but it's all right, I'll get it. I turn to the bar and order. Protesting because I'm flustered more than anything else.

Ice and a wee lime? says the bartender.

What? I say. *Right, yes. Thank you.*

He sets about making the drink, shovelling ice out of the plastic bucket on the counter behind him, under the spirits. I turn to Mikey and ask about his placement. It's going well. Of course it is. He asks if I've finished my course. Not quite, I tell him. I'm supposed to go back next September, almost a full year from now; I have a while yet.

That's a smart idea, he says. *Go back with a clear head.*

The drink appears and he taps his phone on the card machine, laughing. *Too slow*, he says.

I'm about to start the back and forth about how I was going to pay when we're interrupted by a girl I recognise from around but don't know. She has very long, shiny, static hair and is wearing the high-waisted black skinny jeans which never seem to fall out of favour here, where trend cycles are elongated to the extent they don't need to repeat. She takes the glass of fizzy liquid off the table.

Here's where you are, she says to Mikey. She nods and smiles at me. I nod and smile back.

Sorry, I've been ages with your drink there, he says. *I've bumped into some old friends. This is Erin.*

She looks at me for a few seconds. Then back at Mikey. Then at me again. There's a look on her face; her eyes narrow slightly, then widen.

Oh god, you're that person, she says. Then she sort of . . . gasps? And then she covers her mouth with a hand, as if this might somehow stop her from having said it. She has a tiny button nose.

What do you mean? I say, smiling. *Which person?*

I'm so sorry, she says. *About your friend. I saw on the news.* She touches my arm and looks at me with wide eyes. They shine with reverence and horror.

We both know that's not true, about the news. There wasn't anything about me in the news. She might have seen what happened on the news, but not my link. The truer story will be that someone from around here told her that someone from around here had a link to that particular story, and then she went trawling around my social media for more information, for whatever she could find. Telling herself this served some higher purpose than nosiness. Nobody knows anything because of the news. I mean, come on.

God, sorry, that was rude of me, she says. *That was really awful.*

That's all right. Don't worry about it, I say. I smile at her. She drops her hand from my arm but not the look, the wide shining eyes.

It was terrible, she says.

I feel goaded, as if I am being searched for a reaction I'm disappointing her by not giving.

It's completely fine. Don't worry about it, I say. I smile at her.

She nods then. *Are you back here for a while now, then?* she says.

Again I feel I'm being searched, not for a reaction this time, but more information. Interrogated, almost.

Yes, I'm back at the minute, I say.

She nods again. And scans my face with her eyes. Neither of us says anything else for a few seconds; I glance at Mikey and he is wearing a forced-looking smile.

Are you working here? she says finally.

Yes. I pause. *I am.*

Where? she says. One last try, for what? Information, a resolution, a reaction?

I look at Mikey and his smile has transformed from forced to strained. I can't tell if it's because of me or her.

Have you been out for a while? I ask her.

What do you mean? she says.

Have you had a few drinks already? I say. Mikey coughs.

No, I haven't. Sorry. I was only asking how you were doing. She clasps her purse to her chest. She looks stricken. Pity quickly turns to defensiveness, anger when it's not met with the desired response. And I know what the desired response is, and I could just do it. But to live on such a short leash, just to avoid interactions like this? It doesn't seem worth it.

Sure, well, thank you, I smile. *Thanks for that. Anyway, it was good to see you both, it was nice to meet you.*

Mikey says yes, it was; I don't meet his eyes. *We'll get on now and leave yous to it,* he says, nodding towards my table. *Let's get a coffee this week when you're free? I'll give you a message in the week?* he says to me.

Sure, I say, clipped and formal.

I sit back down in the ratty velvet booth beside Declan.

38

Who was that he was with? he says, nodding over my shoulder in the direction of the bar.

I don't know, I didn't ask. I shake my head.

Hmm, he says. *No point, I suppose. Leave her to it. Sure he'll only be someone else's problem next week.*

I laugh and finish my drink in a few sips. That interaction was sobering. But Declan's right. What else should I expect? I go to the bar to get us another round as they ring the bell for last orders. People are talking about getting coke, going back to Declan's for an afters. I consider it but I'm sober enough to know I'll regret it tomorrow. I'll offload on someone I barely know or send drunk messages and wake up ashamed of myself.

I walk back to Anne Marie's to sober up. By the time I get back up the road I'm so clear-headed I could probably drive. I drink two glasses of water and take all my makeup off. *Think how good you'll feel tomorrow,* I say, smiling at myself in the mirror, as I work diligently through every step of my moisturising regime, not just the basics.

My ears ring furiously in the silent bedroom when I lie down. I turn to one side then the other and I can't get comfortable. My phone lights up on the bedside table. A message from Mikey appears on the screen. **Any afters?** I shake my head. This? Really? The idea that I might reply is so abject it's almost funny. I pick up my phone. I haven't technically opened the message; he won't know I've read it. I could turn my phone face down on the table, go to sleep, treat the whole thing with dignified detachment.

I open the message so he will see I have read it, then lock my phone without replying. It flashes again, a few seconds later. **I don't have Claire with me, dw.** That one makes me laugh.

At him? Myself? Again, I open it and don't reply. A few seconds later: *I'm not seeing her either btw. Long story. I'll explain in person.* Well, of course, he isn't, he's never seeing anyone. It's always a long story, or there's more to it, or it's not exactly what it looks like, on a technicality.

I open the message and this time I start to type a reply. *A long story? That's not like you . . .* I delete it, holding down the backspace button. Start it again. Hold the backspace button down again.

Shame stops me. Shame at the idea of leaving proof of how territorial I had been. The way it went earlier tonight, well, he can't say for certain that I acted jealously. I didn't do anything, I would say, what did I do? I was polite, I made small talk. We would get tangled up in an argument about whether I really had been asking how drunk she was. Anything subjective can plausibly be denied.

But a snide message. There it would be, in the cold light of day. Proof I was jealous and territorial and lashed out because of it. And what else would that say? That I was invested in our relationship, the idea that we have some loyalty to each other. That I was, would have been, am and would be.

I set the phone down on the floor, screen down this time. My hands are damp; my face has gotten hot, gone red. I lie down and pull my duvet over my head. In the dark, alone with my jealousy. The desperation in that jealousy. I consider picking up the phone again, sending a message to say I'm not out, I went home, inviting a reply asking to come over. I don't, in the end. Not out of self-respect, but because of the effort involved in getting up and putting makeup on again. There it is. This is how I feel, apparently.

6

IN THE MORNING THERE IS another message from Mikey. *Can I call? It's easier to explain*. I read it and rub my left eye, then my right eye, then both eyes together, and then my whole face. As if, if I kept rubbing, I could sort of rub myself and my hangover and these messages away. I remember the *God, you're that person*. Oh god, oh Jesus. That person. I slink back down under the covers and lie there, in the blue light of the phone.

I set the phone down on the bedside table and go down to the kitchen for a glass of water, maybe a paracetamol. In the hall downstairs, on the way to the kitchen, there are open suitcases everywhere and beach towels and sunscreen and swimsuits. They're packing for the half-term trip to Portugal. God, that crept up quickly. I pick my way over the suitcases to the kitchen. Anne Marie is sitting on the sofa in the corner of the kitchen with a notebook in front of her and a pen, a cup of tea balanced on the edge of the sofa.

Oh, hello, she says when I enter the room. *What time were you in last night? How's the head?* She laughs. She goes on about how she thought I was one of the boys, and how they need to bring her down their underwear and socks and everything else she's written down for them on their lists. She starts to read items out from the list in front of her, asking if she's forgotten anything obvious.

I didn't think my head was too bad, thought the hangover was manageable, but I can tell already I'll be too hungover for this all day. I let the tap run cold, drink one glass of water, and fill another to take up to my room. I say I'll send the boys down.

In my room I check my phone again and I have a message from my mum saying I have to come and collect the things next Thursday, in the afternoon. *The things? My things.* She will be in to supervise me. This is technically good, I tell myself. Anne Marie and the boys will be away, I can sort it all out before they get back. There won't be any awkward questions about why I suddenly have all my things here. No awkward scene where I arrive back in a taxi with all my worldly belongings and Anne Marie starts to panic that she'll never get rid of me, that she's taken on a squatter. No awkward conversation where we have to talk about it all in subtext.

Still. It's only technically good. It's not actually good. It's one more thing. One more thing I would rather not have to do. One more example of what it's like to be *that person.*

I need to go out, get out of the house. I shower and dry my hair, put mascara and peach lipstick on with blue denim straight-legged jeans, a black polo neck, a black coat and a scarf for good measure. I don't know how cold it is but I want to be out all day. I don't revisit the kitchen before I leave, closing the front door carefully behind me so it doesn't slam. I don't want to be accosted and requisitioned for an errand.

I walk to Botanic park, around the flower beds and the tropical ravine. I don't go in though. I keep walking, out of the park and past Queen's and down Botanic Avenue. I don't stop till I get to the big church behind the department store in town. I don't remember what it's called because it's never been my church, so I have only a passing relationship with it, and because it is named after one of the saints with a forgettable name. Mark or Paul or something. Saint Something's. I like a lot of other churches better, but there's never anyone I know in this one, or never has been, anyway.

It is a large, grubby and very ugly red-brick building with mesh cages over the stained-glass windows, maybe left over from the Troubles or maybe because it's in town. The inside is ugly too; full of the gaudiest memorabilia. I enter through the big metal doors at the back and, just standing there, without even walking around, I can see a statue of adult Jesus, painted yellow-gold and affixed to a large wooden cross; more than three statues or tapestries of the baby Jesus with the Virgin Mary; a tapestry of a snake hanging down from a tree to whisper into the ear of a disciple, probably Judas Iscariot; purple velvet upholstery on the altar and the altar server's chairs; and a glittery mosaic tabernacle. Beyond what I can see, the place is full of crevices which are themselves full of this kind of thing; brimming with ugliness. Like every Catholic church I have ever been to, around here anyway, there is too much red and purple. Too much bright gold. But it's peaceful.

The feeling of peace is always the same, in any church. Outside, the noise is endless. Cars driving and honking; people walking, talking and shouting; traffic lights constantly beeping; phones ringing; the rain. Inside, the silence is peace. And there is the dark, rich smell of incense, like burning perfume, and the blurred candlelight in the darkness. These things, too, are a kind of silence; they help you think in a certain way.

I always tell people who grew up here I'm Catholic. They know what that means. I tell people who didn't that I'm Catholic but not religious. Some of them know what that means, but not everyone. It doesn't matter what it means, anyway; it's not true. It would be truer, probably, to say I'm religious but not Catholic. Not quite right, but truer.

I know what's wrong with the Catholic Church. I don't like most of the rules but I like the ceremony of it. And there is a feeling I used to get, sometimes, when I was young and religion seemed more real, as if there was something more. Something joining the things that happen together, or something more between us; I can't explain it any better than that. Whether I'm religious or not, whatever I think about it, I grew up with that feeling so I can't forget about it, and maybe that's all religion is, anyway: having that feeling or remembering the feeling of having it.

The prayers I remember too, and when to sit and when to stand. Or the prayers I remember when I'm at mass, in a group. I can't say them by myself from memory. But there are certain lines I think of sometimes: when everyone would speak together and we would say, *Holy Mary, Mother of God, pray for us sinners now, and at the hour of our death*; when we would turn around to the people in the pews beside us, and behind us, and shake hands and nod and say, *Peace be with you*; when the priest would speak and we would follow and say, *I believe in one God, the Father Almighty, maker of Heaven and Earth, and of all things seen and unseen*; and then, when we would say, *He suffered death and was buried; on the third day He rose again*; and then, *He will come again*

44

in glory, to judge the living and the dead. And, *I believe in one, Holy, Catholic and Apostolic Church.*

I never knew what Apostolic means. I'm not sure I know what the rest of it means, either, but the words are something to me. Even if it is only nostalgia, that's something.

I dip my right hand into the little gold tray of Holy water by the door, let the cold of it coat the tips of my fingers, and touch my forehead, the centre of my chest, then my left and right shoulder. *The Father. The Son. The Holy Spirit.* The place is empty. I sit in the third pew from the back with my head bowed and think about how strange it all is.

That I don't have my friend to talk to. That this terrible thing happened and nothing changed. Not even me, really. That I dropped out, moved back, lived with my mum again, fell out with her again, started working for Anne Marie, became Anne Marie's housemate even, and still, in a way, nothing changed.

That whatever has happened I still get up in the morning, work, eat, go out drinking, meet people and talk to them about their lives, tell them about mine, or lie to them if I don't want to tell them about mine, and, at some point, go to bed. That, whatever else happens, time moves forward; every day the sun rises and it sets, and some days it streaks the sky with orange and pink, or it shines through the trees in such a way that the light looks like a single yellow-green line and I forget for a while, or even for a second, that anything bad has ever happened. How strange it is to be *that person.*

I remember where I was when I found out, and the odd, cold way the message was delivered. It was after a day in the lab. I was on the way home, queuing in a corner shop to buy onions, bananas, maybe other things I can't remember, opening and closing different apps on my phone to pass the time, and a notification came up on the screen to say someone had posted a photo in one of the group chats.

It was a screenshot of a mass email from the university, outlining what had happened in clipped, formal language, because it was on the news already, and the university had, as they said, a duty of care, and a responsibility to pass the information on to us themselves. They sent it to everyone but I had never set the university emails up on my phone so I got it by screenshot. It was so banal in its formality I can't even remember exactly what it said. I haven't looked at it since.

I remember reading the name and feeling this churning, lurching sensation in my stomach. My face was very hot. The hand that I was holding the basket with was shaking. I put it down and walked out into the street and looked up at the sky. For what? What did I think would be there? I felt like I might start running, as if my body didn't know how to respond, but would do something like that on instinct. I never cry but I made a terrible, blunt noise, more a roar than a scream, and I saw someone on the other side of the street stop and turn to look at me. It was a manly, feral noise and I remember feeling shame, on top of everything else, for being so unfeminine, for not crying in the normal way. Ridiculous. Why the fuck do I care if somebody on the other side of the street thinks I'm not grieving like a woman?

I stood there, not knowing where I should go, what to do; there was nowhere for me to go, really. The hospital? Which one? And to see what? She wasn't in a coma, and I wasn't family or anything like that. I didn't even have any of her family members' numbers.

I thought, briefly, of calling her phone, in case a family member, or somebody at the hospital, was looking after it, waiting to answer it in case someone like me needed to call, so they could tell me what to do. But almost immediately I knew there was no point. Why would anyone be doing that? And what if someone did answer and they didn't know who I was? How would that feel?

I couldn't go to our flat; I needed to get away from where I was standing, where I had been standing. I looked at my phone again and there was a notification to say someone had replied to the screenshot in the chat. I opened it.

OMG. WHATTTT.

I instantly locked it again, then unlocked it and turned the phone off. That was a terrible response. I can see, now, it's because those words, all kinds of words like that, have been overused, misused, so much that they don't mean anything any more, rather than the words themselves being wrong. They were expressing shock and confusion, which was an appropriate response. It's just that when everyone talks like that all the time it makes that way of talking unserious.

I walked a few metres down the street to a bus stop and got on the next one that came. I didn't even check what number it had on the front of it; it might only have been going a few stops more, but it wasn't, luckily. I needed it to keep going and it did. There was only a handful of other passengers and I sat in one of the front seats on the top deck, so I wouldn't have to look at any of them and think about how they hadn't got the same news as I had, and hate them for it.

I don't remember what I was thinking, or everything I thought about. I do know I had some strange, guilt-inducing thoughts.

About how it really could have been anyone else, someone who meant nothing to me, and how much better that would have been. How I always thought if anyone I genuinely knew died young it would be drugs. Not even a proper overdose but an accidental one. Or like when you hear about a friend of a friend who took a valium to get to sleep while on coke and it made their heart stop. Or a bad pill, or something. It happens. I thought about who, out of everyone I knew, I would have thought would die young, or could. I thought about my shopping basket, holding my space in the queue.

I thought about calling someone and then I didn't know who that would be, and then I kept thinking about how I didn't have anyone to call. And maybe I did and I only felt that I didn't. Kate would have called her parents, maybe. If it was the other way round.

I looked out the window at red and beige townhouses and realised I was heading towards central London and I felt giddy, hysterical. How strange. What a strange thing to do, to get on a bus like that. When the bus stopped I almost went drinking, or for a drink, but I didn't. I crossed the street and took the same route back, to where I had been, near the flat, and I spent the last bit of that journey taking ten deep breaths in a row, over and over again.

When I got off the bus, across the street from where I had been hours earlier, I turned my phone on. A barrage of notifications. I listened to a voicemail from my supervisor at the university, who said I couldn't go back to the flat, it was cordoned off for now, and I had to stay in university accommodation for the next few days, and I had to come to a certain building to organise this. There were missed calls from friends but the other voicemail messages were from numbers I didn't recognise so I ignored them.

I ended up having to stay in that accommodation for a week while the people, the officials, did whatever they needed to do at the flat. One of them brought a suitcase of my clothes over for me, but they didn't ask in advance what I needed, and I remember thinking it must have been a man who packed it because there were three pairs of high heels and two going-out dresses I hadn't worn in years. I left them in a pile in one corner of the room, and maybe it was those things, relics from when I was eighteen, nineteen, in a student room, that made me think, almost constantly, about when I had first moved over.

There were drinks with different friend groups that week, and groups of people going to sit in someone's kitchen and share memories. But I kept thinking that nobody had as many memories as I did, or the same ones. And someone would tell a story and mix up the order in which things happened and I would feel so frustrated and start talking over them to set it straight. *I know what you're talking about but it wasn't like that*, I would say. I kept thinking about how I hadn't had anyone to call. Everyone I knew seemed like an acquaintance.

One of the days I met with her parents in a coffee shop and it was as if none of us could bear to say anything that wasn't small talk. Her dad listed different addresses where we had lived, and described what each area had been like, where the pubs were. And I said things like yes, or that this or that place had the cheapest pints. They're nice people but they had their own grief; there wasn't anything we shared beyond the basic facts of what had happened.

When we left we exchanged phone numbers and email addresses and I walked around in the sunshine after. I thought about how normal they were, to have something like this happen. Her family are all so normal. Her parents are getting divorced, or they were at that time, maybe not any more, but even when they were, it was all happening in the most straightforward way possible. There was a lot of talk about how they could maintain a functional relationship, since that would be the best thing for everyone else.

They're very English, really. Modern English. They have family video calls and group chats, an annual reunion, and they all meet up for a big day out when it's one of their birthdays. If they need to go to therapy, they go to therapy, or at least counselling. English families do that.

They aren't the sort of family you get all the time over here, where you suddenly find out you have an aunt nobody has ever mentioned, and everyone pretends that's not a weird thing to discover, or acts as if it was something you had always known about when you know you didn't; or where people just stop talking to each other and carry it on for years; or won't divorce no matter what happens, how many affairs someone has or whatever else. It didn't seem fair for something like this to happen to them. It seemed incongruous.

Then, after it all, after that week, I went back to the flat and acted almost as if nothing had happened. The university said I could stay in the room they had found me for as long as I needed, I didn't even have to pay, and I knew that they would have meant it, that they would have been terrified of the prospect of a bad news story, and so would be as accommodating as possible. But I told them no. I said my flat was where I lived,

I needed to go back sometime and putting it off wouldn't do me any good.

And I went back and pretended that, or at least externally behaved as if, everything was normal; I did it for weeks. I got up in the morning before eight, got dressed, went to the lab, ran models and recorded the results and changed variables and then re-ran the models and did those steps again. I had lunch in the canteen, made cheap instant coffee in the communal mugs, always stained pale grey on the inside, and sent emails. I didn't cry the whole time, not even when I was alone, not once. I told everyone who asked that I needed to keep busy. I was doing fine, or at least OK, but I needed to keep busy. And nobody pushed it, as far as I remember, but maybe somebody did and I am being unfair.

But that feeling I'd had, that everyone I knew was an acquaintance, that I was alone, didn't go away. Instead it seemed to swell, like something being blown up inside me until it pressed against my lungs, the back of my throat, and the space behind my eyes, and became unignorable. And I had another feeling, or a thought: that what had happened with Kate is the way things are now. Not only for me, but in a bigger sense too; that, now, the things you would never have imagined could happen, will, and whatever way you thought things would go, is not the way things are any more. How do you ever get over that? How do you go back to the life you were living? What meaning can any of it have?

For those weeks, I got up every morning and went to work in the lab and came home and it never felt normal. Then one evening I walked the whole way from the lab back to the flat. I'd never done that before; it took almost an hour and a half. It was bright, it didn't feel like the end of the day. I remember it was uncomfortably warm and I wasn't dressed for it. I was wearing wide-legged black jeans with a leather belt and the strip of skin where the belt met my back was damp with sweat for almost the entire walk.

In my room, at the flat, I stripped down to my underwear, left my clothes in a pile in the corner of the room, dragged my suitcase out from under the bed, and started folding the clothes hanging up in the wardrobe into sausages and slotting them into the suitcase. When I had packed everything I wanted, I showered and booked a ticket for a rail and sail the next day, with the first train on the way to the ferry leaving Euston after six.

Maybe it was only on the ferry that I truly understood what I was doing, or maybe I didn't let myself think about it properly until then, in case the logistics made it seem impossible to leave. Either way, it was only when I was standing out on the deck, holding on to the slimy railings and watching the water below me churn, that I thought about things like calling my landlord, letting him know I'd left, trying to get out of the lease; telling my mum I would be back later that day, fracturing the silence over our latest argument, whatever that was about, explaining what had happened, even though I knew she must have known; letting everyone, or even anyone, know I'd left, even just by posting in any of my various group chats; or emailing the university.

My legs have started to go stiff on the wooden bench. These things, this church furniture, is always so dreadfully uncomfortable; I suppose that's the point. I shift myself forward, lean back and look up at the cross hanging above the altar, and Jesus pinned there, with his arms spread out and one leg folded neatly over the other.

I remember it was only on the ferry that I cried. I don't know if it was the sea air, or the water, the grey starkness of it. Or maybe because I felt anonymous, or because it was only then, with some distance, that it all hit me. That journey had always been something I seemed to do at the start or the end of things. The end of terms, the end of the year. Maybe that was part of it too.

Whatever it was, I sat on one of the grubby velour benches in the area partitioned off as a cafe and bar and cried in an ugly, barking way. I cried until I felt like I might be sick, and kept crying, retching. The person sitting nearest to me, a middle-aged man in a faded black felt coat, came over to check on me. *Are you all right, love?* he said, something like that. I told him he could fuck off, and shouted at him for staring at me, even though he hadn't been. I went on, saying everyone was always staring at me, that nobody would ever leave me alone even for a minute and I didn't need his concern or anybody else's. I wasn't making any sense. He was kind enough to apologise and go back to his seat, where he pretended to read as I cried and cried.

Poor man, he was only trying to help. I hope he knew I didn't mean any of it; I didn't even know I was saying.

What problem did I think I was solving by leaving? What did I think would happen back here?

I look up at Jesus on the cross. There's another line from mass I think about sometimes. *He was crucified for our sins under Pontius Pilate.* More for the name Pontius Pilate, which I have said so many times it has no meaning beyond the sounds any more. I don't worry, really, if I'm a sinner, or about eternal damnation, Hell or anything like that. Part of it's that we were never taught about religion that way, we had a priest who used to come to our class at school and say things like you would never go to

53

Hell if you asked God to forgive you. We weren't taught the Old Testament, it was all stories like the Good Samaritan. The soft sell.

The priest who came to our class had a big red face and a single clump of white hair with the same texture as Brillo pads. It stood up from his head as if it was completely solid. I remember wondering how his hair would respond to a hat: if it would sink under the weight of it, or remain erect, a thick layer of padding between the hat and his head.

He used to say things like, *Jesus is your friend who looks after you.* And we could ask questions about anything to do with God. And we would all sit and think about the same questions. The obvious ones. How are God, Jesus and the Holy Spirit one person? Why does God let people die? Why does he let wars happen? Why do people get sick? Can Jesus see you naked?

Or I assumed we must all be thinking about the same things, anyway, because the questions everyone would ask were the same ones I had. That's one of the things you can't ever really know for sure. None of us would have admitted it. And if someone asked something stupid or weird, we all would laugh, as if we weren't thinking it ourselves but were too shy to ask.

I lean back in the pew and look up at Jesus. Glittery face and hands, howling and nailed.

Were we all thinking the same things back then, Father? Did we have the same questions?

Its expression doesn't change. I smile.

So Mikey, again, Father. Back to that old mess. Bad idea, isn't it? What would Kate say about that?

The face stays as it is; the hands stay as they are. I smile and bow my head again.

Kate would say I'm being stupid. That's what she thought about this whole situation. The length of time it went on for, the back and forth of it. But then she would still talk to me about it. We would talk about it.

Is it bad to think about this? To sit here and think about what my friend would think about this boy? Is that the wrong way to grieve? Disrespectful? Weird?

Then, does it matter if it is? One of the things about Kate was I could talk to her about things. Everything. There is a distance between everyone. With her, there was less distance. Or there seemed to be, the way I remember it. Her manner helped with that. She was less suspicious of other people than I am.

I never asked her about the distance, if she felt that way too. There are certain things you never say to someone because you don't have the words to say it, or because you feel like you might change something and not be able to change it back. But I wish I had now. I wish I knew how much I would miss that time. Maybe there wasn't less distance and it only feels that way now. I wish I knew if that was true too.

I sigh and look up at the tapestry Jesus. The howling face.

Was there really less distance, Father?

The glittery face continues to howl. I smile and bow my head.

I think of respect and guilt and sinners. I don't know if I have the constitution to really worry about being a sinner. I don't have a lot of shame; maybe I was born that way. I think about when I used to go to confession and I would make things up. It's not even that what I was really doing was so much worse than the things I would confess – well, sometimes it was, but it was my own business.

I look at Jesus on the cross again, his warped face, as if he is shouting. His feet tucked neatly together. *Is this the way I was born, Father?* Nothing happens, of course, and I smile and bow my head. *Forgive me, Father, for I have sinned, for being selfish, lazy, having a bad temper, lying to other people and myself, being stubborn and not treating other people the way I would like to be treated.*

I stand up, stretching my legs out, and walk over to the metal station where the candles are. You can pay for them with an app on your phone, as if the Catholic Church doesn't have enough money. I light two, one for my friend and one for everything else. On the way out I dip my hand into the little dish with the Holy water and bless myself again. *The Father. The Son. The Holy Spirit.*

I push the big metal door open just enough to let myself out and it closes behind me slowly. It doesn't slam. I walk out into the street, the noise and the rain. There's everything. Too much of it. I look up and there's an aeroplane in the sky. The whole world. *God help us. God help all of us.*

I check my phone on the street. A missed call from Mikey. And a message saying let's get that coffee later in the week. A sign?

I hold my finger over the call button but I can't bring myself to press it. I don't trust my voice to not do something strange on the call, crack and cry, or say something angry about last night. No, a message is safer.

Sorry, missed your call. I'm out running errands. Yes to coffee!

Np. When? Which days work?

I don't want to say, well, really every day. All the time. Mornings, afternoons and evenings are all options.

Mornings are good for me, I write. Aloof, mysterious.

The mornings he can do are Monday and Thursday. I reply that I have a work commitment which I can't move on Monday – technically true. And that it strictly needs to be Thursday morning; I'll be busy in the afternoon. He says, sure, fine, great. Thursday morning it is.

7

ON THE FIRST DAY OF the holiday to Portugal I have a trial shift at a coffee shop, an outlet of a big chain. I applied months ago, before I moved in with Anne Marie, and never heard anything back at the time. Then last week they sent an email inviting me to try for a new opening, at a different branch nearby. I replied yes. I sort of have a job now, but depending on the hours I could do both. And I only sort of have a job; the arrangement with Anne Marie is temporary, dependent on goodwill and circumstance.

It's raining as I walk down to the shop, heavy rain lashed sideways by a strong wind. Struggling against rain like this with an umbrella, battling to keep it from turning inside out while rain gushes in under it, is always futile, so I brave it in Anne Marie's hooded pink raincoat, the hood continually blowing back off my head. I arrive with soaking hair and damp socks.

The manager, a woman with yellow hair tied back in a ponytail, takes me into the back room to explain the company ethos and the role. *Each neighbourhood store should feel like just that, a neighbourhood store*, she says, reading from the brochure. She has to raise her voice to be heard clearly over the beeping and sloshing of a suite of dishwashers. There are five screens showing footage from all over the shop, including the room where we are currently standing. *That wee one looking at my room isn't for me*, she says, tapping the screen which currently shows us both standing, looking at the screens. *It's for my boss, if he needs to check what I've been up to.* She smiles as she taps. Maybe she noticed me looking at it, or maybe it's simply the first question everyone asks.

I won't be working on the till today because they won't invest in training me to that extent unless they decide to hire me, she explains. I will be on the shop floor, tidying whatever people leave on their tables into a grey basin, bringing it into the back room and loading it into the dishwasher. Disinfecting the tables after. *And just be fast, and be smiley. It's dead easy*, she says, brightly. She gives me my basin and a cloth with disinfecting spray. *I'll do a spot check of the bacteria level on the tables with my UV pen during the shift, so be sure to give them a wee clean.* She brandishes the pen at me.

The policy for phones, she explains, is that we aren't allowed to take them out on the floor. *And that's the company policy across all the outlets in the whole world, not just something I have come up with for this branch*, she says, smiling. The policy says any shift shorter than five hours will have two breaks of ten minutes each, and if these are exceeded, the time is deducted from the next break, but this can only happen three times before there is a meeting to discuss it. The policy says to smile a lot but not talk too much to customers. The policy says if metrics in key performance indicators are not met in a given week, there may be a meeting to discuss why, at the manager's discretion. The policy says if there are three meetings for any reason, then employment may be terminated, at the manager's discretion.

I march out onto the shop floor with my grey basin and pink disinfectant spray. On the first table there is a cup half full of liquid that smells like it's probably hot chocolate with an orange peel and a tissue stuffed in on top of it, a stirring stick broken into small pieces and a saucer. I organise the debris into the basin and spray the table. The rest of the four-hour trial passes similarly, although the mess people leave is creative. A cupcake case turned inside out and mashed into the table. More stirring sticks mutilated in different ways; one has been shredded finely lengthways. Sugar poured into pyramids with the shredded sachet beside. Torn-up receipts floating in cold coffee. Tiny acts of aimless destruction.

At the end of the shift we sit in the room with the dishwashers, and the manager holds an electronic device in front of her and asks how I found my shift. She nods, smiling and tapping the screen, as I say I found it interesting and challenging to learn the ropes, and that I enjoyed interacting with customers. The yellow ponytail darts around in the air as she nods and taps at the screen. Then she passes it to me; there are forms for me to complete.

Even if I don't get the job, I will be paid for my time today, at the rate of half my pay if I were employed. I have to fill out an invoice on a system; there are temporary passwords for me, and then I should receive payment in a month. If I do not receive payment within thirty working days of filing my invoice, there is an email address for me to lodge a complaint. It will respond within six weeks. *Now, only use that email for an invoice which has been filed but not paid*, she explains.

Now, we'll be in touch, she says. *Not me, but the company. And you have to fill out feedback too, which we give to the regulator. You*

60

do that before we get in touch. It was brilliant to meet you. She extends her arm for a firm handshake.

In the evening I get the email with the feedback form. I fill it out positively. The way it's set up, with me sending it back first, it seems obvious I have to. When I have completed and submitted it I get a text a few minutes later to say my job application was not successful. They are not able to give further feedback because of the large volume of applicants.

I try to sign in to their system to fill out my invoice and my temporary password doesn't work. I email a complaint to the address she gave me with the subject heading `Invoice Password Not Working`. I get an automated reply instantly, telling me their software has detected that my query is not related to a filed but unpaid invoice and so my email will be deleted. I fold my laptop closed.

The coffee shop is still open. I call and there is a menu with buttons to press for different kinds of query. I listen up to number six and then hang up. I could go back in person and ask. I picture myself trying to explain the issue, that it wasn't to do with me forgetting the password, or anything like that, but rather the impenetrability of the system, while the yellow ponytail dances through the air. It simply doesn't seem worth the trouble.

Without the routine of my normal chores, my week in the house by myself passes slowly. Anne Marie sends pictures from Portugal a few times a day: her book on a sun lounger beside a pool, one of the boys eating a watermelon, her sister half hidden under a floppy hat. When I get a holiday picture I go outside and take a picture of a puddle or autumn leaves and reply with a crying face. *That's some Tuesday*, I'll say. *Holding up OK here.*

I look for other jobs, things in call centres and shops, but without focus or urgency. I gesture half-heartedly to myself at making, or changing, longer-term plans: I draft emails to my course supervisor, dropping out permanently, saying I'll be back next month, asking can I transfer course, and I save them all as drafts of different possibilities. This feeling of trying to plan around so many variables, and the ways I might possibly feel, is like plotting a course along a shifting surface. By Wednesday evening I am bored enough to spend more than an hour getting ready to meet Declan at work, where a student comedy night is taking place.

I sit at the mirror in Anne Marie's bathroom, curling my eyelashes, applying mascara and then using a different mascara with a different brush to apply more mascara to each eyelash individually. I use three shades of grey eyeshadow. Bronzer, blusher and highlighter.

My phone lights up with a message from Declan. *Your man from New York has come in.* I open it. *We're chatting at the bar now. When are you coming down?*

Ah, have you told him I'm coming? Don't!! I will explain. I'll be down soon.

Lol you're always scheming. I won't. Dw, he's said hello and ordered a drink. I glance up at the mirror and catch myself smiling down at the phone. I reply.

Lol!! Yes. I'll explain. See you soon.

I look at myself in the mirror. Too much? Maybe, although it's probably dark enough in there that he won't notice.

I send the American a message. *Hi, sorry for the short notice, I'm going to head to Declan's bar this evening because I've found out he's working. No pressure to come but thought I'd let you know :).*

Hello, nice to hear from you, and thank you for thinking of me. I'm here now, as it happens. I'll see you soon :).

Ah nice, Declan should be starting soon I think.

8

I OPEN THE DOOR TO Madame George's in the middle of one of the comedy sets. A boy, could be twenty, with hair swept back and to the side and fixed in place with shiny gel, is telling jokes about sectarianism and the stereotypes we have for each other. About how Protestants love to pay for things you shouldn't have to pay for, like say you go to a private beach by accident. And how Catholics are so shifty about authority, we speak in code around home monitoring systems. Not the most original material, but it's true that Protestants would be too happy to pay for the beach. I stand at the back until he finishes, when I clap along with everyone else. Then I head towards the bar, where the American is sitting talking to Declan.

The place is busier than I expected, warm with bodies and laughter. Every table is crowded with people and there are extra chairs scattered around, and more chairs around the stage too. His was the last act, it turns out. People start queuing at the bar for drinks, and along the wall leading up to the bathroom door as I sit down.

How bad was it? I ask the American, tilting my head towards the stage. *I just caught the end there.*

He laughs and says it's not the worst he's ever seen. He did this type of thing at school himself, he's seen worse. He's probably done worse. He laughs at that, looking down as he shakes his head. In fondness at the memory, or embarrassment? I'm scared to find out. His comedy days appear to signal the depths of an earnestness of spirit I had already sensed and started to feel vaguely menaced by. The less said about those, the better.

I ask what he did today. He had class. And before that, things to prepare for class. He was thinking of going to see some graffiti but didn't get time, it was dark too early.

I was also going to maybe see the Titanic museum sometime, maybe this weekend if I get time; he says.

Oh no, I say. *Oh, you don't want to be going there.* I explain about it being a terrible tourist trap and too expensive. *Everybody says that*, I say. *That's what everyone says, ask anyone.* Declan joins us again, the queue having abated, and joins in berating the Titanic museum. In truth I've never been, and I don't think Declan has either, but you have to say it's terrible; that's what everyone says.

All that tourist stuff in general, Declan says. *Don't get a taste for it now.* He laughs. *All that shite.*

I get a beer. They're not free tonight; the place is too busy. Declan and the American start back into the conversation they were having before I arrived, about the American's writing. His process. He says he writes lots of notes about the characters, the relationships they have with each other and their interests, that kind of thing. *I mean, I'll need to have all that finished before I really make a start with it*, he says. *You can't rush it.*

No, painting's the same, Declan says. *It takes as long as it takes.*

The American nods and says yes, but distantly, the way you might say brilliant about something a child was badgering you to look at. I glance at Declan, but if he read that yes the way I did, his face doesn't show it. *Anyway*, the American says. *Yes. Sorry, this might be very boring, talking about work like this. So what were you doing before you came down?* He smiles at me, then at Declan, but the question is for me.

I scratch the foil collar of my beer and smile. What to say? That I spent all day sitting about, and then hours getting ready? *Yes, work. Errands, things for work. For the house,* I say. *Things for the house. Nothing interesting.* I'm unsettled by my own clanking rustiness at socialising, by the fact I couldn't even think of a vaguely interesting lie, but I smile through it. A forced, apologetic smile. The worst thing I could do now would be to grimace. *God, I sound boring,* I say. *Work is so boring, I guess. You're right.*

There's something. Something to respond to, at least.

He laughs. And then starts on about how it depends on the job, whether it's challenging and stimulating. How, with something like academia, while it's not what it was, it's still using his brain every day, using his degrees. The speech-like quality returns to his delivery as he moves onto the downsides of office jobs, sending emails all day, moving things around on a spreadsheet. I down my beer and order another. The curl of foil I have picked off the bottle neck rests on the table between us.

I watch his face as he talks. His white teeth flash when he laughs. He has dimples, very long, dark eyelashes and a square jaw. There is something compelling about his face, but his earnestness is disconcerting. He is better looking than I am. Or is he? Are we really just different types? Don't sell yourself short, Erin, I think to myself.

Objectively, he would be better looking than me. But objectively doesn't account for different tastes, for people not tending to like what they're supposed to like, or what you'd expect. And would he even be, objectively? Who would make this objective judgement?

I excuse myself to go to the bathroom. There's no queue and the room is empty. I set my bag down beside the sink under the mirror and check my face. In the severe blue light of a durable LED bulb in a room with black walls I look like I am wearing a lot of makeup. *It's a bad light,* I say. *Don't sell yourself short.* I open my mouth to inspect my teeth. Straight-ish, white-ish, like always. There's nothing wrong with them, really.

I take my phone out of my bag. There are emails, notifications for social media and notifications for messages. There is a message from Mikey. I can read the first few words without opening it. *Hi there, can w.*

I open it. *Hi there, can we move coffee to a bit later in the afternoon? Sorry about the short notice.*

I roll my eyes at myself in the mirror. Later in the afternoon, when we never said the afternoon, and in fact I specifically said it couldn't be. This sort of last-minute change of plans, issued via a cryptic message. Always this. I shake my head and smile at myself in the mirror. Why am I still doing this? It's almost eleven too; I could have been asleep. Unlikely, but I could have been. And then I wouldn't have got it till tomorrow morning, which would have been . . . even more inconsiderate.

I can see he is online. *What time were you thinking?* I type. *I have something I can't move in the afternoon.* I send it. *Sorry if I hadn't said that before*, I add, knowing we both know I did say before.

Sorry for the late notice, he says. *It's something for my mum, she wants it done in the morning. Could we do 12?*

Not really a reply to what I said. I lock my phone and open it again. *Well, I have to get stuff from my mum's house in the afternoon, close to 12. You know it's difficult to change plans involving her so let's move the day instead.* I send it as one long message. More formal, maybe. His status changes to typing. I watch for a few seconds and then lock my phone and put it back in my bag. This conversation, this back and forth, could go on all night. And where will it get us? Either into an argument or circling back to the original plan after god knows how many messages.

Back at the bar I order a rum and coke. *And I guess for me too*, the American chips in, then he wordlessly pays for both drinks.

He and Declan have been talking about comedy again. The American is calling it a very raw form of storytelling. Declan says it's very dorky, doing student comedy. He laughs at that and looks down at the floor again. *Anyway, hold that thought*, the American says. *I need to use the restroom.* He squeezes my knee as he gets up.

Declan smiles and continues smiling, watching over my shoulder, waiting till the American has gone into the bathroom and closed the door. *So what's going on there? What was going on with the texting earlier?* he asks, one eyebrow raised. *Would you go back with him, do you reckon?*

Maybe, I say. *I don't know. I don't know if it's on the cards.*

Oh, it is, he says, laughing. *He's dying for a story, sure. You can tell. He'll probably put it in his book.*

I laugh. *Do you think it's real? The book? Like, do you think he's actually writing a book?*

Maybe not, Declan laughs. *It sounds like he might be in the research stage a wee while yet, doesn't it?* He winks.

This is the thing when someone talks a lot about doing something, isn't it? I glance over my shoulder to check he's not wandering about, coming back to his seat. *Why do you think he left his other job?*

God knows. Something personal? I mean, he might have been sacked? He wouldn't say to us, would he? We both laugh. *Maybe he slept with a student or something!*

Would it be that? It wouldn't be something like that, I say. *He's too young to be properly punished for that, surely? Like fully sacked. It would be a slap on the wrist or something?*

Who knows! Declan raises both eyebrows and does a comedy shrug. *A position of power, isn't it?* He glances over my shoulder. *Anyway, Joanne was showing me a lot of houses she is looking to buy on her phone; you have to see them. These new-builds, all the exact same house every time. And she goes through photos of every fucking room and you have to say wow about all of them.*

I nod. *Yes. I do remember her showing me something about a breakfast bar that folded down into a regular table. Like it changes height slightly for different meals.*

The American touches my leg again as he sits down. *Who are we talking about?*

Someone me and Declan know.

A friend?

Not quite a friend. Someone we know. Declan laughs. *A member of a friend group, I guess.*

Declan explains how it is when you live here, that there are places everyone goes and where you see everyone, so if you know someone reasonably well, and especially if you have friends in common, then you have to really not like them to not interact. *Like you'd have to be known as enemies, even.*

He doesn't say – but how would you explain it? – about the network of brothers and cousins and women who live down the street, the way they know things about you, and everyone else, and how they tell everyone the things they know and you can't go about or do anything without everyone knowing what you've been getting up to and asking you about it when they see you. The information exchange. How that feels intrusive, nosy and personal but strangely anonymous, at the same time. As if all you are is these discrete pieces of information that have been gathered about you. The way you can never really leave it, because you can think you have, but then one day someone will hear your accent and ask what school you went to or your surname and then they will start telling you whatever information they have. And you'll want to know too.

I get another rum and coke. The American is talking about community, about how he feels he doesn't have a community in the same way. He went to a boarding school that wasn't near where he lived, and while the families who sent children to the school did know each other, and many did similar jobs so would see each other in that context, there wasn't really any shared geography.

Most of the people he knew as a teenager only meet up at reunions, and maybe certain groups would plan to see each other, but that's difficult because everyone lives in different cities. The people from that time he talks to the most are those now working in academia too.

My family are, like, classic WASPs. He laughs. I'm drunk enough to find that funny.

70

What actually is that? I ask. I've seen it before but I have no idea what it means.

White something Protestant? Declan says.

Anglo Saxon. The American laughs.

Well, I'd be careful telling everyone you're Protestant round here. Declan winks, an exaggerated conspiratorial wink, and laughs.

When the bar is closing we stand up to leave. The American trips trying to extract his left leg from his stool and sends it clattering to the floor. *Oh god,* he says, laughing. Then he tries to walk, not realising his legs are still entangled in the stool and it sort of drags behind him like a jockey still saddled to a startled horse. He turns and looks helplessly down at it. We're all drunk.

Outside it's frosty, a freezing night. The ground is wet and moisture hangs in the air. There's no rain but it feels like it could start any second.

Declan huddles inside his jacket as we say goodbye. He thanks me for the sparkling company and walks off down the road, leaving me and the American standing in the street.

So, he says, looking up at the sky, then down at the ground, then back at me. *Are you planning to walk back?*

I was planning. I laugh. *You can't pull the same trick as last time. Remember, I know where you live.*

I was actually planning to ask more directly tonight. Shall we get a taxi and have another drink at mine?

I'm not sure if we need another drink, but, sure, let's go back.

The granny flat has its own door at the back of the house, but we have to walk around the house to get to it, crunching over gravel. *Shh, shh,* the American keeps saying, in the whisper people

71

do when they're drunk, which somehow feels louder than a shout. *Quiet, they're sleeping. The family are sleeping,* he says. I can see my breath, given shape by the cold, hover in front of me as I walk.

The front door of the granny flat opens straight onto the living room. He turns on the light as I close the door behind us and the room is suddenly very light. Startlingly bright. I feel drunk, blinking as my eyes adjust to it.

The place isn't the tidiest yet, I'm still unpacking. You know, he says, waving a hand around the living room. I follow him into the kitchen where there is a lidless plastic takeout container on the counter, empty except for a few congealed noodles and a green pepper. I turn away and find myself looking instead at a pizza box, folded and balanced on top of a stainless steel bin. The kitchen light seems very bright too.

I walk back out to sit in the living room while he starts to make drinks. He shouts about gin and I say yes. I sit down on a sofa in the middle of the room. I don't want to go poking around but I can see into his bedroom: it looks fairly big, a lot of room around the bed, clothes on the floor. I think for a second about Joanne's new-build, the one which had a good amount of space around the bed, and smile.

His suitcase is open on the floor by the sofa with a pile of books stacked haphazardly beside it. I can see deodorant, an open wash bag and a belt. I start to picture him getting ready earlier, choosing one belt and trying it on and looking in the mirror and then choosing another, remembering to apply deodorant just before leaving the granny flat.

God, it really has been a while. I had forgotten about this part of going back with someone, when the lights are too bright and you suddenly know too much about them, what they do during the day, what they did before they came out, whether they look after themselves, if they did their dishes earlier, what toiletries they leave sitting out because they use them all the time. The terrible, unsexy insight into a near-stranger's grooming habits. Sometimes you'll notice an outsize version of something, an enormous value-size tub of Vaseline, say, or an old-fashioned product, like talcum powder, and then all you can think of is what that signifies. I lift the suitcase lid with my foot and fold it closed.

It's too quiet, too. This part of the night always is. But then if someone puts music on, it's still too quiet, and whatever music there is has too much meaning attached. The problem with this part of the night is how to move to the next part without saying, well, will we have sex now, or what? And you are almost too drunk to have sex but you have to have another drink anyway, to set the mood. Or you have to look at someone's books, or another collection, to make conversation. Or some men start talking about their dads, or worse, their mums.

He shouts in from the kitchen, apologising again for the mess. I look around again and spot a plastic bag with an empty crisp packet, a sandwich box and a bottle inside it. They had been hidden under the suitcase lid. I lean forward and lift the bag handle with one finger; I lift the suitcase lid just enough to deposit the bag and its contents inside. *It's not even that messy!* I shout back. *It's fine!*

He comes back with the drinks, not quite cold gin and tonics, and sits down on the sofa. *I haven't had a chance to totally unpack,* he says, gesturing around. I take a sip of my drink and it makes me feel nauseous. I'm too tired to talk and drink for much longer. I lean over and start kissing him. He bites my lip and I bite his back. I start to pull off his shirt. *We should go in the bedroom*, he whispers, touching my neck.

In the bedroom he starts to take off his trousers, standing by the bed. He fumbles, and starts pulling them off without pulling the zip down, then pulls them back up to do the zip, then half trips stepping out of them. It's not the most appealing display, but it's been months. He's a good-looking guy and I'm here already. Besides, does anyone look suave taking their jeans off?

He lies back on the bed, and when I see his entire body I can tell he is out of shape. The slight softness to his frame doesn't match the broadness of it. He doesn't look bad, but I can tell this isn't exactly what he looks like when he looks the way he wants to, or probably when he pictures himself.

I kneel beside him and he pulls my t-shirt over my head. We kiss again and I start to pull his underwear off.

Will you suck my dick? he whispers in my ear. I'm surprised by the timing. There has barely been any build-up; I still have my jeans on. But I'm probably too tired and drunk to get wet enough to have sex anyway.

I run my tongue along it and put it in my mouth, and he starts groaning so quickly, making such a deep, almost pained sound, that I wonder when he last slept with someone. He probably masturbated earlier today. He's hardly had a lot else to do. But being touched by another person for the first time in a while is a different kind of pleasure. *Fuck. Fuck*, he says. *That's really good.*

He says the things everyone says, which they all learned from porn, which I know because I did too. *This is so hot. Your ass is amazing. Does that taste good? Fuck. Yes. Keep doing that with your tongue. You like this. You like the way my dick tastes.* Maybe he wouldn't talk like this if he wasn't drunk, but we probably wouldn't be here if we weren't drunk.

I know it's cheesy and embarrassing, aggressively heterosexual and unenlightened, but it turns me on anyway. That's what it's designed to do. And I started watching porn with this kind of talk, maybe even these exact sentences, when I was too young to know it. was cheesy and unenlightened and I just thought it was hot. I still think it is. That's how desire works. You have these impulses and feelings you started having before you knew the context or how to think about them, and when you know the context you keep having them anyway. That's why it's so fucked up, often. Maybe I even started having sex like this before I knew this kind of talk was cheesy and unenlightened. Do teenagers know things like that?

He tells me to stop for a second. *One second, I'm really close,* he says. I am wet enough now. We could have sex. But I want to keep going, until he is right on the edge. Maybe it is inertia; or the noise he is making, the longing and loneliness in it; or maybe I have an idea he might say to someone after, a friend or someone, that I give great head, whatever that would mean to me; or maybe it is because I haven't done this in a while. Whatever, I keep going. He groans. He doesn't tell me to stop again. He starts to spasm slightly, and I pull back just as he cums on his stomach, the grey slime seeping into his stomach hair.

I didn't realise you were so close, I say.

He laughs. *Me neither,* he says. *Lie back and let me touch you.*

Fuck, you're so wet, he says, as he pushes two fingers inside me. *You're thinking about me fucking you. You're thinking about my dick*

75

inside you. Yes, that's what you want. You want me to fuck you. You wanted me to fuck you earlier in the bar, didn't you?

He is going slightly harder than I would like, but only slightly. Not hard enough for me to bring it up; maybe if we slept together again, or the time after that. I come pretty quickly anyway. He lies back and I turn to face him.

Sorry I came so quickly there, he says. *Honestly, I'm so drunk I'm surprised I could even get hard.*

I don't know why men always say that but they always do. I tell him don't worry.

I go to the bathroom and use a white bath towel and hot water to take the worst of my makeup off, staining it black and orange. He can wash it tomorrow if he notices.

9

I'M WOKEN UP BY A dull, pulsing pain behind my eyes. There is a sweet, rotting taste in my mouth. The pain almost feels sweet too, sweet and sickly like bruised fruit. I should have had some water last night before I went to sleep. Even one glass blunts the worst of a hangover. I'm thirsty as well as nauseous, maybe still tired too. I can't tell past the nausea. The room stinks of wine even though we didn't drink any. Putrid alcohol always smells like wine.

I turn to see what he is doing: if he is lying awake, waiting for me to wake up, or on his phone. He is asleep, facing me. His mouth is slightly open, but he isn't snoring or even breathing heavily. He still looks handsome. His teeth look very white; the bed sheets are new but they seemed greyed in comparison. His pillow isn't under his head; instead he has slept with his body wrapped around it, like an animal clinging to a tree.

My phone is on the floor by the side of the bed. I pick it up and it won't turn on. I get up to look for a charger.

In the living room I find a canvas bag full of different cables and adapters, lots of duplicates. I imagine half of them won't work. He seems, from what I've seen so far, like the sort of person who would pack a bag of broken plugs in his suitcase and cart it around, to another continent. I try three potentials before I get one that works and my phone shows a green light to say it's charging.

I get a glass of water and stand drinking it, looking out the window in the kitchen. The gravelled floor of the garden is right below my eyeline. If anyone was walking around out there, I would see the bottoms of their legs, and if they bent down, they could look in at me. I can't really tell what kind of day it is, other than that it's not raining. I can't tell what time it is from the light.

A coughing sound comes from the bedroom. I go back in and he is sitting on the edge of the bed, slightly hunched over, holding on to the bedframe to steady himself. *Good morning*, he says. *God, I feel terrible.*

I ask about painkillers.

I unpacked those already, I think. He laughs. *For situations such as these.* He stands up and starts moving stacks of paper around on the bedside table before rummaging around in the pile of clothes on the floor.

Mornings like these are always full of bad jokes, mine as much as anyone else's. Nervous laughter and half-hearted innuendo. It would be awkward, or I would find it awkward, if we weren't still slightly drunk. That sweet-mouthed morning hysterical state where you could maybe legally drive, just about, but you wouldn't do a job interview. It really has been a while; I had forgotten this bit. The morning after. The smell of alcohol, in the room, on my breath, on both of our breaths. The warmth and the sweat. Sometimes you might have sex again. But once someone has left the bed, probably not.

Aha! he says. He removes a strip of plastic and silver foil from the back pocket of a pair of crumpled blue jeans and holds it up in the air triumphantly. He passes it to me.

I take them to the bathroom with a glass from the bedside table and fill it up with water from the sink. I take two, swallow them, and look at my face in the mirror. There is grey under my eyes. Actually my entire face sort of looks grey. But . . . not too bad. Not as bad as I expected. Maybe it only seems that way because I'm still drunk. My cheek bones are pronounced; they flare out slightly, below my eyes. I have a strong jawline and hollow eye sockets. There is no softness to my face. It's sort of the opposite of heart shaped with vibrant, plump cheeks. I can look severe.

I am not quite symmetrical, although it is hard to see exactly how I'm not; you can just tell. The way it is for most people. My lips could be fuller. My nose is small enough; it could be straighter. My teeth are crooked and, in the context of present company, yellow-ish, but not obviously so. Someone else might get adult braces but I probably never will. I have big smoke-coloured eyes, dark hair and a light tan. I smile at myself, slightly drunkenly, raising my eyebrows suggestively. Nobody would mistake me for a model or an actress. But I'm doing all right. I have looked worse than I do today.

I wipe away the makeup that has gathered under my eyes, using the same towel I used last night, and go back to the bedroom to get dressed. He has put his trousers on while I was out of the room, the black jeans and black leather belt from last night, but no t-shirt. I look at him for a few seconds. He looks better standing up; I suppose who doesn't? Solid and substantial. He catches me looking at him and smiles over at me.

He says he has a headache. *Man, I feel rough*, he says. *God, I have felt better.*

Right. Yes. The same, exactly the same. You know, I think it was the mixing drinks. When we had all those different drinks. That always gets you, doesn't it? That's what I always say when I feel awful because I drank too much. Or that it was because I started on beer and then switched to something else but came back and ended on beer. Or red wine was the culprit. And then the other person might say that it's the same with gin, if you mix it with anything. Or that tequila never gives you a hangover, you can drink as much as you like.

He just agrees. *God, yes. That last beer*, he says. *We didn't need it, right? Nobody needed that.*

I laugh. I ask him the time. *I have some bits and pieces I need to do today. Some things I need to sort out in the afternoon.*

He says it must be some time after nine. *Do you have time to eat? We could get a coffee? I don't know when you need to go.*

Whether this offer is extended out of obligation, loneliness, friendliness or a romantic impulse to prolong our encounter, I don't know. I don't know what I want it to be, either, but I have time to kill and I would only drink a coffee by myself anyway.

I tell him I might be sick if I eat. *But, sure, let's get a coffee*, I say. *There's a good place near here. A lot of places, actually.* He gives me a look I interpret as quizzical. I laugh. *For the mums. All the mums round here, to pass the time during the day.*

He showers and I get dressed. I put mascara on using my broken compact mirror, balancing it on the counter top in the kitchen. It's the only makeup I have with me. I open his fridge to see if he has any soft drinks. I need the sugar. The painkiller isn't working yet; my head still aches, like my brain is mushrooming outwards, exerting pressure on the inside of my skull. He has bottled beers, some arranged on the shelves and some still in a plastic bag on the bottom shelf, a small plastic tub containing a white sauce and some limes. I close the fridge, pour another glass of water and check my phone.

A great cascade of notifications greets me when I turn it on. Messages in group chats, even the ones I have muted; things people have posted on different platforms; messages from Declan; spam emails; real emails; a new notification for an old voicemail message; a birthday notification for someone I had a one-night stand with years ago and haven't spoken to since; an alert to say I missed my alarm this morning, as if I wouldn't know, as if I'm not the person living my day; messages from Mikey.

I slide most of them away, tutting and shaking my head. *Go away, go away*, I mutter absently. I open my emails before the messages from Declan and Mikey, half-drunkenly smiling to myself at this gesture towards a professional life I don't have. There are things I subscribed to by accident, or because I was given no option not to. News website updates. Advertisements for sales. One real one, from the coffee chain. I open it and it says I lost my password so I should fill out a separate form, embedded within the email, with my bank details and personal information.

The amount of money I am supposed to be owed for my training day is already filled in. It is slightly wrong, but not by enough to be worth doing anything about, and the email says not to reply to this address anyway. I'll fill it in later.

I slide the emails away and open the conversation with Mikey. There is a stack of messages. Coloured bars full of text, all different lengths and widths fill the screen. Short messages, long messages, paragraph breaks, missed calls. I skim-read them.

Sorry. I didn't know you had something you couldn't move, let's stick to same time. I'll sort changing it with my mum.

Genuinely, I'll change it. I shouldn't have organised both on the same day.

One missed call.

Hi, I wanted to say I'm genuinely sorry. I read back over our messages there. I want to make it clear that I wasn't trying to mess you around. I was looking forward to catching up. I am now free at the time we originally said and I'll keep that free.

Two missed calls.

Those were all last night. Hard to know exactly when I left the bar, but most of these were probably sent before. If I'd checked these last night, would I be here this morning? Probably not. But then, if it was so easy to change this new plan of his, why did he have to complicate things in the first place?

I start to wipe my left eye and then remember I have mascara on and stop. I read the most recent messages, from this morning.

Hi, can you let me know what's happening, if we are doing this morning or not.

Yes or no?

I can see he is online now. I start typing a reply. I could call, it would be easier. But American Matt would come crashing out of the shower in the middle of it. *Oh, who's that on the phone?* he would shout, in his eager way. And then Mikey would shout down the phone, *Who's that you're with?* I rub my eye again, remember about the mascara again, and stop.

For god's sake!!!!! I'm only back here because you messed me around last night! I type. I hold my finger down to delete it.

Hello! Sorry about this, I type. I add the exclamation mark so it sounds breezy, like: God, hi! He reads it instantly. His status changes to say he is typing. I start typing again, quickly.

So sorry, this wasn't intentional at all!!! I got drunk with Declan. My phone was out of battery.

For most of the night.

I thought we weren't meeting any more so I didn't think to check it.

He reads them instantly. Could they read as passive-aggressive? I type another message.

Genuinely, genuinely!!

Again he reads it instantly. Again his status changes to typing. Watching this status, waiting for a reply, is making me jittery. I put my phone down to let it charge before I leave and go to get changed. I check it again before we leave the flat.

Dw, let's sort another time next week. Call me this afternoon when you're free.

Fine, fine. Good. For a second I wonder how he knows I'm not free. But maybe he doesn't mean it like that.

Outside it is sharply cold and bright. I could tell it wasn't raining from the basement kitchen, and now I can see it won't today: the sky is bright blue and endless, unmarked by grey or white. The winter sun – well, this is an autumn sun but it hangs

83

like a winter sun – is very low in the sky. It glints off the car parked in the drive, a white flash. There are crumpled, papery orange leaves scattered over the gravel. I wish I had sunglasses to wear; the light is applying extra pressure to the pain behind my eyes. The painkillers have still not started working.

We are only a few streets away from Mikey's parents' house. I knew this last night, or I must have done, but I didn't think about it properly. I feel furtive walking to the coffee shop, as if he, or worse, his mum, might see me from across the street, or drive past in the car. Or a friend of his mum's, and then she would say to his mum and they would all talk about it and someone might even say to Anne Marie.

We go to a coffee shop with a big window at the front. Really, the entire front is one big window. I suggest sitting in the back. *Sure, if you get a table, what do you want?*

Just a coffee.

What type?

Just a black one. I don't take milk or anything like that. No sugar.

He comes back with the coffees, one black and one frothy in a wide cup. The table lurches slightly as he sets them down and some of the liquid jumps over the edge of my cup.

He asks what I have on later. *Are you working, or something to do with the children you look after, even?* I tell him they're on holiday this week. I'm too hungover to remember if this contradicts anything I told him before. *But later, it's an errand I have. I have to collect some things I left with my mum when I stayed with her recently.* I'm too hungover to lie.

Oh right, I didn't know she lived here. I don't think you said that. Or did you? There is a look on his face, as if he is putting the puzzle pieces together.

84

Well, where else would she live if I'm from here? I know I sound snappy, unnecessarily so. But I'm hungover. But then, so is he.

I tell him I didn't mean to snap. *Sorry, sorry if I sound short. I'm hungover. You mean to ask why don't we live together if she lives here, or something like that? Or that's what you want to know?*

He laughs. *Well, I don't know if I was asking that. Sorry if it's something you. I mean, it's your business. I didn't mean it in a nosy way. Honestly.* Again he laughs and kind of puts his hands up, as if I have a gun trained on him. I have to laugh as well.

I explain that we tried it when I came back and it didn't work out, which is basically true. *In an ideal world I would rent a room somewhere*, I say. I tell him I moved back kind of suddenly, that it can be hard to find a room here at short notice, and then the situation with Anne Marie sort of appeared and it was a good temporary solution.

He says it all makes sense. *I didn't mean to probe*, he says. We sip our coffees, sit in silence for a few seconds. I ask him what he will do for the rest of the day and he says he doesn't have plans. He might unpack if he feels better later. I nod. *Yes, good idea*, I say. He says he still feels like he is on holiday so it is hard to work up the will to unpack and move in completely. He will do it though.

Yes! Holiday mode. I know what you mean. I cringe listening to myself: since when do I say things like holiday mode? I have the feeling that we've used all our conversation up, front-loaded things by getting the small talk out of the way too early.

We sip our coffees and stare at the door in the silence that follows.

I cast around for other things to say. Only terrible options present themselves: Well, do you like music? So, are you a middle child?

Do you play any sports then? For a second I remember his body, the unexpected softness of it.

How's the head? he asks.

I smile at him, grateful for the intervention. I can see his coffee is finished. *Terrible! Crap, awful,* I say, smiling. *I'm working up the will to go back and shower in a minute.* I drain the end of my coffee. *Will we head on then?* I say. *If you're finished?*

The cups rattle on the table as we stand up. *After you,* he says, gesturing to the door. I lead the way out of the shop. Out on the street we both stand, blinking at each other, in the sunlight.

Right, I say. *Well, thank you.* I add: *For the coffee.*

Of course. Yes, he says. *Well, I'll see you around. I'll send you a message. I have your number.* He holds his phone up and jiggles it around in the air.

Great. Yes, me too, I say. *Well, goodbye.*

He extends a hand, seemingly on instinct because he quickly drops it again. I could initiate a hug but I suddenly sort of don't remember how they work, which way the arms go. I nod at him and he nods back.

Yes. Great, goodbye, he says, and turns to head back to his granny flat.

10

I ARRIVE AT MY MUM'S HOUSE with my suitcase, empty except for a roll of bin bags. I ring the bell until I can hear her banging around inside and the dog barking. I still feel slightly drunk, hysterical, as if today isn't quite real. But my headache has gone. Thanks to the coffee or the painkillers.

I tidied myself up, too, when I went back to Anne Marie's for the suitcase. I showered and then sat in her dressing room, just off the en suite, to blow dry and straighten my hair. I spent longer on my makeup than I have in a long time, even than last night, layering creams with shimmer and a green tint under my foundation and dotting highlighter over it. I curled my eyelashes. You'd never tell I'd been out last night.

I see her as a grey blur through the translucent door pane, swelling like an ink blot as she approaches. She looks me up and down when she opens the door. She is wearing black jeans and a grey polo neck, I imagine to make the point that she hasn't made too much of an effort. But I can see she has straightened her hair.

You rang the doorbell for too long, she says. *Once is fine. I didn't know what was going on. I thought it was the police, or god knows what.*

I only rang it once, I say.

But just one short ring is what I mean, she says, shaking her head. *When you ring it like that, holding it down like that, it could be the police or anybody.* Again she shakes her head. *I wouldn't know what was going on. It could be anybody.*

Endless potential responses cross my mind, with their endless arguments in tow. Why would it be the police? I could say. When you knew I was coming today, at this time. I could say, How many seconds over the appropriate threshold was I? How many exactly? I could reach over and hold down the bell again.

Our arguments have a primordial quality. One of us says something or gives a certain look and it's like an ancient signal has been activated. The other responds with a pointed remark, or their own certain look, and we're off. Sniping, insults. Both clambering around in the wreckage of a lifetime of old arguments and unresolved issues. Picking bricks up out of the dust to throw at each other. Not today! I tell myself. A reaction is what she wants.

Right. Of course, I say. *I'll bear it in mind. One short ring.*

She looks at my face and shakes her head. *I haven't sorted any of it out. Obviously it was not my responsibility to do that,* she says, pointing at the suitcase and then turning and gesturing back into the house. *It's upstairs in the room you were staying in.*

Yes, of course I wouldn't expect you to do that, I say. *Thank you again for arranging this.*

I follow her up the stairs and trip over the same raggedy bit of carpet that has been tripping us both up for over a decade, longer even. A strip which has come loose and now sits like a flap, curled back on itself, on the third step from the top. I tut to myself. She could definitely afford a new carpet; she could probably fix this issue by cutting the flap off with a pair of scissors, even. But instead she chooses to spend every day for the whole rest of her life tripping over it.

In my room she turns to face me but doesn't meet my eyes. *That's everything there.* She extends her left arm, as if she is doing a safety demonstration on an aeroplane, to point to a pile spread haphazardly over the floor. The entire rest of the room is bare. Even the bed has been stripped. For effect? I wouldn't put it past her.

Brilliant, thank you, I say. She looks at me as if she is going to say something. I notice there is more blue under her eyes than I remember. More grey in her hair too. The change seems sudden, but the picture I have of her in my head will be from years ago now. And she is almost sixty, an age when the passage of time starts to show as clearly again as it does when you're very young.

The pile is bigger than I expected but I have the bin bags. I can see baby toys and clothes, things I didn't even know she had kept. She must have gotten them down from the attic. I could ask why but it seems like an obvious trap.

Great, I'll start packing then, I say.

I don't have time to help you, I'm working today, she says.

God, I'd forgotten it was a weekday. *Yes, I know you're working,* I say. *Obviously you're working, it's a weekday. I know it's a weekday.*

Please don't snap at me. She smiles for a second. I shouldn't have said that obviously. *I've already done you a favour putting it all together. After the way you acted.*

The way I acted? That's what we're calling it. Right. That's what we're calling the strangeness of me coming back, after Kate, expecting a refuge of some sort, warmth, and finding things

89

between us as fractured and cold as ever, as distant and unforgiving. But it doesn't just mean that, does it? The way I acted. It means barely speaking to her after I left for university, and arguing with her when I did. And getting to do a lot of things she never did and then seeming not to make the best out of it that I could have. Being one side of these endless arguments over nothing and not knowing how to fix it. Although she doesn't, either. And then the fact I was born before her life had settled down, and made it so it never could. Having a dad who couldn't be less interested. Not filling the space left by everything else. Going out all the time with friends when she was always so lonely. Being selfish and free in a way she never was. Now grieving in a way she feels she never did.

The way I acted is things I've done, and the fact of me existing, this terrible, unresolvable dynamic, and everything that came before it. The way things are, the way they were. Everything: it's too big.

What do you mean when you say that? I say, taking the bait, knowing full well that's what I am doing. *Which way did I act?*

I would love to have someone else's house I could just turn up at, she says. *Eat their food and treat them like dirt. Come and go whenever it suited me.* She says it with real venom. Startling venom. This is how she is. So calm, so controlled. And then, so angry.

Me too, I say. *I would also like that.* I tell her I hate arguing with her because she always acts crazy.

Here we go, she says. *I'm crazy. I'm crazy? And you come back, no job, sitting in the house all day getting yourself worked up over the news. Leaving without saying anything. And I'm crazy?*

I don't know what to say. *My friend died,* I say. It doesn't sound right. It's true but it doesn't sound right. It's too small. All the things we were going to do. The way things were going to be. *You know that*, I say. *I have a job now*, I add, feebly.

She doesn't look at me. She snorts. I don't know if she means it to sound like a snort. *You aren't the first person to have had something bad happen to them.* Now her brother. A brother in a bombing is always the trump card. I don't know if it is objectively worse than Kate. How would you measure? I know how she would do it. He is family, so points for that. And my uncle, before I was born, so it would be selfish and cold of me not to allocate more points for that. And younger than her, and she was younger than me when it happened, so more points for that. Whatever, it's a conversation, an argument, I'm not going to have. I could say: Neither are you. Or I could say: You know what, it was a long time ago. Or I could say: Yes, and? Are you ever going to move on? Or: I'm sorry I can't give you what you want.

But I don't. *Right, OK*, I say. *I'll get on with this then.* In a voice with as little emotion as possible, no detectable snarkiness.

She looks at the pile and then at me and leaves the room. I hear her walking downstairs, creaking on certain steps I know will creak. The cheerful robot music of her computer turning on, or being logged into, or whatever. The robot voice, as fake as mine just sounded. *Hello, welcome back, what is your first task?* You can hear fucking everything in this house.

I put the books and shoes into the suitcase. I start stuffing the toys into bin bags. A monkey with gingham pads in its paws, a purple fleece dinosaur, a clown with strings of yellow wool for hair and a wide smile. I don't recognise half of them, more, even. Part of me wonders if she went to a charity shop to get extra toys, to drag this whole thing out. But no. She wouldn't do that. Would she? Probably not.

I fold the last of the clothes and zip the suitcase up. Patches of floor have started to appear amongst the pile. I am making good progress. How long did I dread this for? And now I'm doing it and it's really not the worst way to spend a few hours. I open a box and find more clothes, mostly pyjamas and t-shirts and leggings which are so old they have become pyjamas too. They can all go in the bin.

At the bottom of the box there are more soft toys. A red dinosaur, a green alien I remember from a film, my spotty rabbit. I hold the rabbit up. The white rabbit with its long floppy ears, red spots, black glass eyes and missing foot. The white rabbit which is grey now, maybe was always grey. Which I used to sleep beside at night and read stories to and which I would tuck in when I made my bed in the morning, so he could sleep there during the day.

Which lost its foot when my mum hid it outside as a punishment for something when I was in primary school. And then I went out looking for it and she locked me out for hours. And it was raining, so much so that my clothes were soaking and droplets ran out of my hair, and then down my face. And what was that even a punishment for? I think about doing that to Anne Marie's boys, even if they had done something bad. I wouldn't.

I called her a bitch for that, when she let me in, and she slapped me. *You fucking bitch*, I screamed. And she grabbed my shoulders and pushed me back against the kitchen wall. And I kicked her. And then. Or was there something else next? Well, whatever happened next, soon after that I was curled in a ball on the floor and she was hitting me, again and again, with the metal hoover pole. She always takes it off to hoover and crouches on the floor with the hand-held bit because she says the suction works better that way. *Mum,* I remember I was saying, through sobs. *You're going to kill me.* Over and over again.

Then there was the crack. The plastic join in the pole cracked. A flat noise. We both heard the sound and thought it was me. She was stunned at herself. She shouted that I had to get out, as if I needed telling twice. And I did go out, out the front door and running down the street, but where was there to go from there? No money for the shops. Too ashamed to go to a neighbour. No other family. I was crying so much at the bus stop a woman gave me a few quid and I took myself for hot chocolate. A treat.

When did those episodes stop? When I got bigger. The brutal truth of it is I got bigger and older. Big enough to look after myself. Old enough to conceive of the darkness behind something like that, the depression and torment under cruelty, much more frightening than the act itself. Fucking terrifying.

The handful of times I went to counselling, when we got a few sessions for free through the university, I could tell the man found these incidents disturbing. A young guy, wearing grey skinny jeans and black-rimmed glasses. They're not supposed to show a facial expression but he did. I never went back. To be looked at like that? To relive that? No thanks. I never speak about it with her, of course. Post-conflict is when everyone is just trying to get on with their lives.

Kate knew my mum was difficult. I remember being drunk or on coke and saying that she would have been unpredictable, violent sometimes. Kate would bring it up again sober. Not the next day, but she would ask how Christmas would be. Or if I'd heard from my mum recently. We spoke about the silences more.

Kate found it hard to imagine, she said, the length of time these silent stretches went on for, how impenetrable they were. Her own parents would never do anything remotely like that. I remember her saying: *I mean, it sounds like utter madness to me, she sounds totally mad.*

I was grateful for that, the opportunity to commiserate over how strange it was. Also, just that space to talk, if I wanted to. Many people go to great lengths to avoid considering grim experiences, as if they may be contaminated by even acknowledging certain aspects of reality. They will say it sounds terrible, ending the conversation as quickly as possible, or unwittingly act as if you've transgressed by telling them; wincing, appearing disgusted.

Kate was curious about people, generally; that was one of the things I liked most about her. And I felt like she could understand certain things, even if she hadn't experienced them: a consequence of her curiosity maybe. *Is she dangerous, do you think?* she said once. *To you, I mean.* We were drinking green tea on a Thursday night, slightly hysterical having sat up too late, talking about everything under the sun. Almost the same feeling as being drunk.

She believed me when I said no. And that I felt more sorry for my mum than myself, which is true. *I understand why*, I told her. *And I can feel sorry for her. Forgiveness is trickier.* She nodded, said that was a good way to put it.

It's forgiveness that's truly complicated. And there is this instinct, this blind anger that surfaces and seems to take over in certain interactions.

I throw the rabbit across the room. It bounces off the wall and barely makes a sound. I look at it lying on the floor. I want to throw something that would make a bang, cause a scene, break. I want to go downstairs and scream in her face. *Maybe I was bad, but you were fucking worse.* I could smash dinner plates against her kitchen wall or drag her work computer onto the floor.

I picture the living room. Her computer station. The sofa with a throw over it the exact same colour as the sofa fabric, so that nobody ever sits on the real sofa fabric and leaves a mark. She has never had any pictures or anything up on the walls, only a mirror. There is a little table for magazines. I don't think I've ever seen her read one. There is a vase that sits on top of that table. She got it at an art fair years ago, for flowers. As if she buys those. It's a regular ceramic vase, but she loves it and she'll find it hard to replace. Actually, it will be impossible to replace. I open the suitcase and squash the rabbit in on top, with his arms folded across his body. I zip it closed.

I can hear her downstairs as I sort out the rest of the debris. Her chair rolling around the floor, her muttering things at the computer occasionally. Coughing. *Shut up, you stupid woman,* I mutter to myself.

I check the taxi app. It says one could be here in twenty minutes. Enough time. I order it and watch the map on my phone, to check it is on its way. I don't want it to take longer than that. I drag the suitcase downstairs and leave it in the hall. I follow with two bin bags. I am on the way up the stairs to get the last one when I hear her shouting up the stairs after me.

What? What are you saying? I lean over the bannister. She is standing in the hall, with her head cocked to the left and her right hand on her hip.

These bin bags are not being left here for me to deal with, she says.

95

I say I wasn't doing that. *Obviously, I am taking them with me. Just the fact of them being bin bags doesn't mean I'm dumping them. I only have one suitcase.*

It's not up to me to organise another suitcase, she says.

I say, *Sure, thank you,* and check my taxi. Ten minutes.

I hope that's everything that was up there, she says. I tell her to go and check, my taxi won't be here for a few minutes. She marches up the stairs, performatively loudly. Clanging and banging. I carry the bin bags to outside the front door; nobody will lift them sitting there for a few minutes. I leave the suitcase in the hall and step into the living room. The vase is still there, empty as it always is. A few minutes later she comes back into the room.

Yes, that looks like everything, she says. She is looking at me in a strained way. Her face says she is annoyed there is nothing to tell me off about. Maybe something else too. It's a look I can't quite place.

I ask her how she knew where I was running. She says I didn't tell her I was leaving. I say we weren't speaking anyway and ask again who told her. She looks to the side and then down. I say if she doesn't tell me I'll find out anyway.

She looks up at the ceiling and then down again. *I used the tracking app thing on your phone.* She doesn't look up. *It was linked to mine from when you stayed here.*

You linked them, you mean? I say. She doesn't say anything. I tell her you're not supposed to use it for that. *For tracking people without asking them. For stalking?*

Well, she says. *Well. Why does it work that way then? Why does it let me do that if you're not supposed to do that?*

I look at the ceiling. My phone makes a tinkling sound. *Right,*

96

my taxi is here, I say. *You can pretend all you like, but you know as well as I do you're not supposed to use it without asking someone.*

I walk past her to the hall and drag the bin bags out to the car. The driver opens his door to help and I say it's fine, I have one more thing to get. I throw the bin bags into the boot as he closes his door.

I walk back into the hall and drag the suitcase onto the doorstep. She is in the living room shouting out that she was hardly stalking me. I walk back into the living room. With the suitcase outside I will be able to run down the path and pull it into the taxi with me before she reacts. I say it is stalking and she has to take me off the app. She says I'm being dramatic.

Delete me, I say. I walk over to the vase and pick it up.

Put it down, she says.

Delete me, I say.

Put it down, she says. *You're being dramatic.*

I'll say it once more, take me off the app.

She shakes her head. I throw the vase against the living-room wall and it smashes. She screams and covers her face even though she's nowhere near it. She is shouting and I run past her and slam the door behind me. I quickly drag the suitcase into the back seat with me.

Great, that's everything, I say to the driver. As he drives off, I turn around and can see her standing on the path, waving her arms.

I I

At Anne Marie's I haul the bin bags and the suitcase up to my room and lie on the bed. It's so quiet here, in this house. The ceiling looks so white. I let my eyes follow the plaster moulded pattern that borders the ceiling, tracing knots, all slightly different from each other, and crevices where cobwebs have formed in certain places.

That tends to have been how our arguments go. Then the silence, for weeks or months. And then someone will have to apologise. Generally, in historic terms, this will have been me. Although usually out of strategy rather than remorse, as a way to access resources. Her car, her food in the fridge, her house, even. All the rest of it.

Round and round it goes: the predictability underscoring the pointlessness of it. How is it that I can describe this pattern so clearly and still be caught inside it? Is this the normal limit of what knowledge can do? The normal gap between knowing about something, understanding it, and really changing the way you feel about it? Or is it a more personal failing?

Hard to ask anyone else. Even Declan. I doubt I'll tell him about today; I have the feeling that I'm leaning on him enough already, these days, without going into all this too. And I can't really think of how I'd bring it up. It's hard to describe, for a start. But also hard to ask because the idea of asking, of describing it, is so exposing. Like asking someone, or forcing them, I suppose, to lower a light down into the gloomy recesses of your soul and bear witness to all the warped, ugly, underdeveloped things crawling around down there. Like asking someone: So tell me, are you as monstrous as I am? Or: How monstrous do you think I am? If that's not the same question.

I sit up with my back against the headboard and take my phone out. I look up how to unlink us on the tracking app and the first three guides I can find have more than ten steps, and sub guides with even more steps for different types of phones. One has a thirteen-minute-long video. Right, fine. I'll take the tracking off later.

I can't sit here. The house is too quiet. The bin bags look messy; it's depressing. I'm not unpacking now. It's been enough for one day. I get up and walk down the stairs and out of the house, closing the door quietly, although I don't really know why. Out on the street I turn left and walk. The sun is blazing and the sky is bright blue. When I get close to the river I can smell the water, the wet grass pressed into mud on the bank. I walk along beside it, breathing it in. Fresh dampness on a bright white day. It's a beautiful day to feel terrible; what a waste.

I cross the road, away from the river, and walk up one of the sloped streets. A street that looks like a messy stack of red-brick terrace houses, balanced precariously on top of each other along the slant of the road. Each one is run-down in a slightly different way, from years of students living in them and the landlord never bothering to do repairs between tenants. Paint peels off doors and weeds grow out of the cement between bricks. I find myself walking faster and faster.

When I get to the top of the street I cross the road and open the gate to the mini orchard surrounding a grey stone church building. I have only been in here once before, years ago. I barely remember it. There are signs on the door about choirs and Scouts for boys under fourteen and the rest of it. I push it open and walk straight to the front pew and sit down with my legs stretched out in front of me. I don't bother with the Holy water; I walk straight past it.

The nearest Jesus to where I am sitting is not on a cross. He is a statue with long reddish hair, a blankly smiling face, gathered white robes and one hand held up like he is directing traffic. His head is cocked to one side, as if he doesn't look simpering enough without that extra detail. Very ugly and plastic-looking, although I don't know what he is actually made of. Painted in pastel colours. Smaller than me, but not so small as to be a mini statue, just as if he is a five-foot-nothing man, which is worse than a mini statue. Really, so ugly.

I bow my head and think about what my mum's life has been, what that generation's lives were. Or I don't really; I can't think about it. It makes me too sad, too guilty. That there was a time, not long ago, when young men here, younger than me, little boys even, would shoot each other, kill each other, because of all this. That nobody has ever really got over it. That it was hardly much better for the women. That it was worse, in fact.

I look up at the tilted head, the faded pastel face, with its brainless smile. Beaming out at nothing. The paint around its mouth is chipped on the left side. *And what did you do about it,*

Father? Did you do anything? Ever? Of course not. I bow my head again.

They were fighting for something better than what they'd ever get. Not only a united anything, or a real vote, the right to work, housing or socialism. But freedom. Which might mean too many things to too many people to ever be more than an abstraction. Or might be a simple thing that we've become too complicated to want or even recognise.

Whatever, freedom was the dream. Maybe it always is. And when you get it — well, you never get it, but when you get close, when you get peace, you find out that life is a job in the civil service, maybe, if you're lucky. Or at the regional office of an accounting firm based in London if you're luckier. Kids you can't talk to because they grew up too easy. A pension plan where the employer pays less than a quarter of the amount you pay yourself from your salary. A car that breaks down almost exactly every six months as if it has been programmed to do that, which maybe it has. A phone with too many ways to talk to too many people. You find out nobody believes in anything. You're not supposed to believe in anything. You're supposed to shop and save up for a deposit for a house and pay your mort-gage and have kids who you do your best to make sure never have to worry about anything. And then you resent them for it, but you're not supposed to, or maybe you are, because whatever you give them, whatever you do, they always seem to want more. Everyone does. And you're supposed to live till you're a hundred. You're supposed to want that. Whether you have cancer, dementia or whatever else.

And then you find out it isn't doing any good. None of it is doing any good. The civilised life where you get a good education so you can work and shop, and you see something you want so you save up for it, and you are always trying to reach another level of stability or comfort, or however you frame the accumulation and greed of being civilised to yourself, is destroying everything. The entire world. Forests burning. Diseased animals. Extinct animals. Floods. Ice melting. Poisonous air. Waste and destruction everywhere. You find out stability is destruction. Peace is violence. But then violence is also violence. So where do we go from that? How can we live?

I look up, again, at the stupid statue. The stupid, placid, pastel face. The closed, smiling eyes. The unnatural peach colouring. The luxurious cheapness of Catholicism. The worship of idols. *Of course you don't have the answer, Father. There never are any answers from you. Never anything from you. Your stupid fucking face. Eyes like little crescent moons. Well, fuck you.*

I look away. I think about how my mum used to say *God's a Prod* every year when it didn't rain on the twelfth of July, if we were speaking. Seemed like it never did. It was a joke or a saying, but maybe it was serious too. Or maybe it was a way of trying to say that we don't take any of this too seriously, which we always seem to be trying to find a way to say, and which we probably wouldn't need to say if we really didn't. *God's a Prod. Well, Father, if he is the Protestant one, if it's not you, if it's him. What did he do? Nothing.*

There were so many times we weren't speaking. I don't remember them all. Not even half of them, probably. Or why they started or ended. And even when we are speaking, why there are things I can't, or won't, say. *Why can't we talk about anything? Why are you so cold to me? Why does nothing that happens to me seem serious to you? Not even Kate. Not even that. Why are you never happy or sad for me? Why do I always have to be the one who says sorry? How much of the way things are between us do you think is my fault? Do you accept that any of it is yours? Do you even realise that almost the whole time we've known each other I have been a child and you have been an adult?*

What would be the point in starting any of that? I wouldn't get any answers. I know how the conversation would go. Denial, obfuscation, strange accusations and dramatic descriptions of my own faults, the things I have done wrong over the years, the ways in which I'm disappointing. As if I don't know. Thinking about it makes me feel so completely furious I could rip sections of my own hair out, straight out of my head, or charge at the altar right now, like a bull, and punch it.

I look at the statue. The hand held up in the air, looking like it is stopping traffic, or waving at courtiers from a balcony. *Father, what am I supposed to do when I feel like this? What am I supposed to do with her?* Anger takes so much energy, takes it all out of you, and when it's gone there's only sadness.

I think about when we used to go to mass sometimes, me and her. She didn't like to go too often. She said it was because she was a single mother and the Vatican disapproved of that, and that other families looked at her, but I thought, I still think, it was more that she saw herself as rebelling in some way. Against her family, or the culture of religion here, or just the idea that this was what people did. How would the Vatican even know about her being a single mother? And she always said it that way, specifically about the Vatican. As if it was The Man. When we went, we were always late and she was always wearing jeans. That was probably a rebellion of some sort too. But then, she still went. And when someone died or was in hospital, she would light a candle. And probably for a lot of other things I didn't know about too. You never know the things somebody else is holding on to in that way, that they need to light a candle for. Who would expect to find me in here now?

Really, Father, that's the most fucked-up thing about it all, isn't it? The way she still went. The way I'm here too. The way none of us can let it go, can really say it doesn't mean anything. The way you give me nothing and I still come to talk to you. The way I still need to talk to you.

I look at the altar. A cross hangs above it, but with no Jesus nailed to it. Just a cross. I think about my friend, about coming here for her. What else would I do? How else would I think about what has happened? Is happening? How would I say goodbye? There's counselling. Learning about unhealthy patterns in your behaviour and how to put things in perspective and develop better coping mechanisms. Maybe that works for some people.

Maybe that's all you are, Father. Grief and the past, patterns of behaviour and coping mechanisms.

I bow my head. Is it just grief? That's not why I came here today. I came because I was angry. It's disrespectful to pretend otherwise, even if only to myself. I was so angry, too. Because of my mum. Because of how exhausting it is for us to not know another way to be with each other. Because of the years of stiffness and coldness. Because I can only feel sorry for her or empathise with her in the abstract. In reality I lose it, I can't help myself. Because you get used to living with dysfunction, with a bad situation, and then a new bad situation happens and it becomes unbearable, as if it is all happening for the first time again. Because things seem to be easier for a lot of other people. Maybe they aren't; they probably aren't.

I come here when I'm angry, to have space to let go of it. And sometimes I come here, or I have come, because I'm lonely. Or lost. Or stressed, or hungover, or on a comedown, or both. Sometimes I find myself wandering in somewhere, to some church, to sit in the quiet for a while, just to think. For no reason at all. To light a candle. I look at the stupid statue again. Well, however stupid it is, I'm the one sitting here, looking at it. I smile and nod at it.

Maybe you're a habit, Father. Maybe that's the best word for it.

I slide to the end of the bench to leave.

When I open the doors at the back and find the winter sun still bright, white against dry orange leaves scattered on the path out to the street, glinting off parked cars, making me squint, I know it is the afternoon but I feel like the day is starting all over again.

12

As the afternoon turns to evening, I keep busy with a list of the things I have to do before Anne Marie comes back.

By now, having worked my way through the kind of chores that get done once every six months, I have reached the part of the list with the kind of chores that nobody has ever done. There is a bundle of clothes in a red wicker basket that she has said should be ironed and folded and put back into the basket in a neater way.

I start with a shirt. I pull it taut across the board and push the iron over the fabric, watching each section disappear under one side as a mass of deep veins and emerge from the other as a slick, flat plain. I try not think about anything else. Such a simple motion, so clear what you are doing, that you are making an improvement, and then you are finished. Almost no work is like this, I tell myself.

Repetition turns to monotony about three shirts in and I find myself abandoning the basket, hoping Anne Marie won't probe beyond the new top layer of neatness, to look for information about American Matt on the internet. He is not easy to find.

The name Matt Taylor is too common. I look through more than twenty Matt Taylor profiles, on various social medias, with their location set to New York and then Boston, and none of those who have themselves as their picture are him.

I close the tab. I search his name and the name of his university. His staff profile page comes up. It says he is currently on secondment to Queen's, so he was telling the truth there. He wasn't sacked. The picture is old; he is younger. There are two email addresses listed: one for the university and a personal one.

I use the email address to find the real Matt Taylor. The profile is mostly private. The only thing I can see are the pictures he has used as profile pictures. The most recent one is a cartoon. It was changed to this about four months ago. The picture before is of him and a woman with shiny dark hair and very shiny, very white teeth, exactly like him. Matching smiles. He is wearing a shirt, trousers and a blue tie with no suit jacket. She is wearing a blue dress with thin shoulder straps. Dainty white sandals. A different blue from his tie, but only slightly. They are standing in a manicured garden with stiff hedges and a gazebo in the background. Guests at a wedding, maybe. I hover over her image, willing a tag linking to her profile to appear, but it doesn't. I enhance the image. Clicking and clicking, making her bigger and bigger until her face is blurry. Her features are small and symmetrical. Dainty. She is pretty. Straightforwardly pretty. Parents want you to end up with a girl like this. And the boys would say you'd done very well for yourself, and slap you on the back. Metaphorically, at least. The kinds of boys he knows. So, what happened? I look at the whole image again. I make him bigger.

Did you cheat? Lie? It wasn't her who ended it, or initiated the ending, or you'd be sadder, wouldn't you? Were you one of those boys, growing up, who looked preppy and went around with that social group because you almost felt like you had to, but you listened to music they would think was weird and you read poetry in your spare time, which they would definitely think was weird, and you always felt, deep down, that it wasn't your world and the real you was going to happen sometime, when you got away from all of that, but then every place you went it was the same, and you never grew out of it, and one day you decided you had to go out and make your life your own life? Is this you doing that? Or does commitment scare you? Because it means getting old, and not being young. Or because of what your dad was like, or your mum? Are you a seven-year itch guy? Did it get boring? Or maybe you are sad, maybe that's why you're here. Why you haven't unpacked. Why you don't seem to look after yourself. You do seem lonely.

I make him small again. I click to the next photo. It is from years ago, with two friends, the same kind of guys as he is. Healthy, clean. The next one is with the same girl. Years ago, now. They are sitting outside at a white table set with three white plates brimming with salad leaves, wine glasses and a bottle of white wine. There is a swimming pool in the background. A little one. Like it's someone's house or a holiday home. No other tables around them. Definitely not a restaurant. Whose is the third plate? A friend, a parent? Their teeth look especially white; they have tans.

This is part of the story. A breakup with the girl with matching teeth. His long-term relationship ending. I'll tell Declan. I'm glad to have the information and I feel tarnished for having done what I did to acquire it. I make her face bigger again.

I pick up my phone and open my message thread with the American. The tone of them. The friendliness. The keenness. What to make of it? It arouses this feeling. Suspicion? Pity? Not quite. And, I mean, I can hardly pity someone for wanting to talk to me. Not while keeping my self-respect intact. But us meeting like this, speaking like this, it's as if there's been a mix-up. Not that he's out of my league, exactly; more that we're playing different games. I have this feeling of, what do you want? Maybe to get laid. Maybe only that. But do you really need to be so friendly and eager for that to happen?

The thought forms or makes itself known — I have a sense that it formed the very first time we met and I forced it away, not wanting to consider the unflattering fullness of it: We are meeting like this because he is at a low point in his life. That's where his interest comes from. Desperation, really.

What to do with this thought, now it's here? Hard to tell if this is my low self-esteem or a cold brush with reality.

And I mean it's not that I consider myself unattractive, exactly. But who do I consider myself attractive to? Not men with bright white teeth who went to boarding school, played varsity sports, and write novels. Well, have fantasies of writing a novel. No, more like men who would performatively exempt themselves from team sports at school, who have ideas of themselves as rebellious or as people nobody understands, who maybe get into fights sometimes. If there's a sport involved? Boxing or running. It's as if they can sense that we share something. A grottiness of spirit.

Mikey doesn't have that grottiness, it's true. On the surface at least. But he seems to be holding the core of himself slightly out of reach; that's part of his appeal. Aloofness always holds power, even if you're not sure whether it's justified. And there is the sense, with him, that underneath it all, the real Mikey might be just like me. If I could only get to that part of him. Delusional? Probably. But he could be.

The American, on the other hand, seems to hold nothing back, which makes his motivations oddly more opaque. People in general are just not as straightforward as he presents himself to be.

There is a pristine kind of femininity men like him seem naturally connected to. Women who are always organising group holidays, and have a natural, wholesome rapport with parents. Kate wasn't like that, but she could be a bridge sometimes. She understood those women; they liked her. Women who always smell clean and have things like nice notebooks to write in, and a refined skincare regime. They don't wear too much makeup. Women who can make me seem, comparatively, low and squalid. Do I even mean that in a bad way? Couldn't I get a manicure if I wanted to? Don't I, in that sense, choose my squalor?

I close the messages with the American. I scroll to the messages with Mikey. I read the ones from the other night, then the last night we had spoken before that. I start to scroll back and then stop. All those nights. I press call.

Only when it starts to ring do I think about what to say about the other night. I could say what I already said, about my phone being out of battery. It sounds like a lie, but I did already say it. What will I say we were doing, anyway? Who were we with? Or I could say it was a fun night, don't remember too much . . .

The ringing stops.

Well, hi! I shriek down the phone.

Hello there, he says, in a normal voice. I can feel my face going red. He asks how it went earlier today and I don't know what he means and then I remember he means my errand; I did tell him about my mum.

I tell him fine. *I meant to call after but it took longer and then. You know, I had things to sort out here*, I say.

He says those things always do take longer. Not to worry. *Anyway, what's on tomorrow?*

I tell him, honestly, not a lot. He is also free. He says we should go for a drink. *Or something else? I'm easy*, he says.

Sure, yes. Let's do that. Let's do a drink, I say. He suggests somewhere in town, meeting late afternoon. We agree to meet at four.

When we say goodbye and hang up I think that was easy, and then I think, too easy. And then I wonder if there is another meaning to the ease of it, the time, meeting in town instead of around Botanic, where we would be more likely to bump into people we know. What is he up to? Because he is always up to something, as long as I have known him, since we were teenagers.

I look once again at the computer, at the photo of the little swimming pool and the tans and the wine glasses, before I close the tab and fold the laptop shut.

After eight I walk down to Declan's bar. My local now. It's dark out. Fog blurs the light from the street lamps and cars. I wrap my scarf around the bottom of my face to keep the cold out; occasional gusts of wind sting the top of my cheeks and my eyes. I cut through Queen's University. The big red castle-like building is lit up with spotlights at night, which make it stand out against the mist like it's been framed.

Students walk in the opposite direction wearing square, stiff backpacks and sometimes even clutching books or laptops protectively to their chests. Leaving the library far too late, having put in a long shift of last-minute cramming, probably. Nervous for their first exams.

When I open the door to Madame George's, the heat makes it feel cave-like, after the cold walk. I see Declan at the bar and start to walk over. Then I see he is talking to the American. I look at him for a few seconds. Did we arrange this? No, we didn't. This seems to be something he just does now, every evening. I notice his feet are unmoored from the wooden ledge near the bottom of the stool and he is swinging his legs back and forward. Happily, it looks like.

He doesn't notice me approaching. I touch his shoulder as I sit down to say hello. *Good to see you again, man*, I say. He smiles nervously. The slightly apologetic smile of someone who's been caught out. He says it's good to see me again. He kind of slaps my back with one hand like we play sports together or I'm his son and then laughs and says he doesn't know why he did that. *That was very awkward of me, sorry.*

I laugh, a laugh that is obviously not real but still polite, and say it's fine, of course. *I took you by surprise there, coming up behind you*, I say. I smile awkwardly; he smiles awkwardly. Yes, it is awkward, but then this situation is always awkward. When you go back with someone, see the way they live, the way they wake up. It's that more than sleeping with them; you know too much. And that's before the extra context gleaned from the internet.

But then he decided to come down tonight, which has created this situation. Maybe he wanted to get it out of the way.

I see his glass is almost empty. A half-pint glass with two fingers or one sip's-worth of liquid. I say I'm going to get a drink. I ask what he's drinking. I definitely owe him a drink.

He smiles and says thank you, but he isn't staying. I'm surprised by my disappointment at this; I can feel my face reddening. He is meeting someone from Dublin, a friend of a friend, who is up for the evening. He thought he would stop in for a drink on his way into town. *I was around here anyway, in the area. I had time to kill. It didn't make sense to go back and come out again*, he says. I think he's trying to tell me it was convenient for him to come here, rather than him having gone out of his way to see me. I think of the holiday photo with the wine glasses and the little swimming pool again.

I say it's good to see him. Thanks for stopping in, as if it's my house. He smiles. I ask where he is going in town. He shows me the name on his phone; he can't pronounce it. An Irish word; I can pronounce it but only because it's just one of those words you know. It's not like I speak the language either. In the photo on his phone the outside is painted green. It's a new place, for tourists. I've never been. I tell him it's supposed to be nice. I say the name for him and he repeats it back, not quite right. His accent isn't hard enough. Like how English people can't say Paddy; they always say Patty, like a burger. That's not even an Irish word, but it shows the problem. The same way when someone's called Matthew I can't say Matty; I always say Maddy.

He slides his half-pint glass across the bar. *Right, I'm going to make a move*, he says. But when he gets up he says, actually, since he has me here. He was going to go see a film, later this week, at the QFT, and would I want to join him? *It's an independent theatre; it's part funded by the university*, he says. I say I know what it is, I live here. He laughs.

Sorry, of course, yes, he says. I tell him sure, let's do it. Why not? What else have I on? And when someone's sitting there, asking you in person, you don't want to say no. He waves goodbye to Declan, who is serving a customer, and leaves.

When I tell Declan, he finds it hilarious. He cackles, throws his head back and really screeches. He has a tea towel tossed over his shoulder and it's thrown to the floor by the great force of the laughter. He says I am going on a date to the cinema. *Is that why he came in tonight? God, what age is he? I feel like we're at school*, he says. *What flick will you see on your date?* I laugh and tell him to fuck off.

I tell Declan about my social media findings, that he looks to have had a break-up recently. He asks what she looks like. *Show us a picture?* He says. I can't; I blocked the account in case my creeping made me come up as a suggested connection. I should have screenshotted it, but she looks like you'd expect. *Pretty, brown hair?* he asks. I laugh. *Exactly, exactly.*

Later in the night a guy who Declan used to sleep with, maybe still does the odd time, but not seriously if he does, comes in with some of his friends. Fintan, he's called. He has light blue eyes and black eyelashes. He is very funny and he laughs at your jokes and says noooo and my god a lot, and he slaps his knee when you tell a story and you feel like you're as funny as he is, or funnier even.

They sit with us, with me, really, and none of them ask if I've come down by myself. One of the girls tells a story about someone she knows who works for an MP, who knows from someone else who works for a different MP, that one of the unionist politicians, a real fire-and-brimstone type, is secretly gay and has real boyfriends, not even one-night stands, and even his wife knows and they have three kids. The kind of story you hear every now and again, and you know it's true and that probably hundreds, thousands of people have heard this secret. The dogs in the street know. You're almost surprised you never heard it before.

One of them has terrible coke which even he describes as terrible as he offers it. *It's been in my room for ages*, he says. *I need to get rid of it*. Making excuses for it. I do keys in the bathroom with the girl, and it doesn't seem to do anything except make my nostrils sting and feel raw, and then fuzzy. We all keep doing keys of it anyway, because it might do something, because it's free, because it's there, because you might as well, because half the point is bonding over doing the bad coke.

Everyone keeps saying different things are wrong with it. *It's cut with speed. It's not really coke, it's MD. It was got from a dealer nobody had tried before. It cost thirty pounds in an introductory offer. It's ancient. It got left out in the sun.*

It smells strongly of washing powder. But I don't mention it. The guy who brought it also smells strongly of washing powder; it probably smells exactly like his pocket. He is the kind of man who always uses too much washing powder, out of not under-standing how the machine works properly.

Someone else tells a story about their family cat, who ran away five years ago and this week their mum found out he'd been living with a woman down the street the whole time. Five doors down. She only found out because some of the women on the street started a book club. This neighbour hosted one evening and there he was, with a new collar and a new name but unmistakably the same cat, white with a black streak over one eye and the centre of his nose. Sitting in the living room. The mum couldn't tell if he recognised her; he was friendly but not especially so. The new owner agreed to let him be taken back to see his old house, after she was shown pictures of him in his old life, and that's happening tomorrow but they aren't sure what to do, moving forward. *Leave him where he is, surely?* shouts the girl. *He's happy or he would have gone back down the road. He could have gone any time.* Fintan slaps his knee.

It's not a scandal like the other story, but it's the one I keep thinking of, as I get drunker and drunker and the night starts to get away from me. Did he just get up and leave one day? Where was he trying to go?

When Declan closes the bar, they go back to the house of someone who someone else knows and I call it a night. I might have done the washing-powder coke but you have to draw a line somewhere.

I walk up the streets full of old terraced houses with big windows and big doors and feel proud of myself. I feel like it was the most normal night I have had in a long time, just like before. I think about the cat with his black streak and his new house.

13

I WAKE UP BEFORE TEN AND get a pint glass of water from the kitchen and take it out to the garden to drink. It's a horrible day. There's drizzle. The sky is a great, unbroken stretch of grey, as far as I can see. One endless cloud, fractured by white veins of sunlight which don't quite break through but make it look white in some places and bruised purple in others. I feel worse than I think I should, worse than I deserve to, considering I left early.

On my phone I see Declan posted a video from the afters two hours ago. A few seconds of people laughing and someone singing.

You can't tell who's there, but it seems like a huge crowd, with everyone having the absolute best time of their lives. I watch it again and then twice more. I can't make anything else out. I know it looks better than it is; everything does when you see it like this. But still. There is the chance that maybe it was the way it looks. I watch it again. There is the chance. Even if you were invited and you didn't go on purpose. Even if you decided to walk home by yourself so you could have an early night and be in a better state today because you have planned to go for a drink with Mikey, and you didn't want to look and feel like crap. Even though you now do anyway. It still does look like everyone had a great time. Fuck.

I sip my water and look out at the garden. It's tacky and plastic in this light. A bird with short orange legs is stalking the fake grass, pausing every few steps to bend down and inspect it, like one patch might be real. Depressing. It makes me think of the videos of ocean animals trying to free themselves from plastic containers they have become entangled in. *Kaw, kaw.* I shout and wave my hands to chase it away. Fly away, bird, go find the real thing. Mornings like these I wish I smoked, properly smoked. I go inside to get another pint of water to drink while I get dressed.

I try on a few outfits, weighing up the balance between something which is flattering but also conveys insouciance. I try three skirts but they all look too ritzy . . . too much like skirts. In the end I settle on the first pair of jeans I tried. Simple, understated, classic, I tell myself. There is a silk top in the bin bags which would be perfect but it smells too much like it has spent a long time in storage. Everything else I try has the ritzy problem. I go with a red jumper.

I choose a new pair of boots, to dress the ensemble up slightly. I take a few laps around the garden to check I can walk a reasonable distance in them comfortably.

I get to the bar we agreed to meet at more than half an hour early; I do it on purpose. I don't know what today is supposed to be, and I wanted to get a drink before, to loosen up, and be sitting with my drink and my book when he gets here. To not arrive looking flustered, with windswept hair or smudged mascara.

The bar is tiny. Just a bar really, with a few stools and three little tables lined up against the wall facing it, with two chairs at each and a bench running the whole length of the wall, providing a few potential extra seats for each table. If the place was full it would be about thirty people. No more than forty. There aren't many here now. A few old men. Maybe it's the emptiness, but the place has a slightly desolate feel, and there's too much sunlight. I feel too aware I'm drinking during the day.

I order a coconut-flavoured cocktail and immediately regret it when it comes with a wedge of pineapple and a multicoloured straw: the flamboyancy of it. The barman doesn't look much older than eighteen and is dressed as an emo, a style that never seems to truly die here. I watch his eyes, fixed nervously on the cocktail as he ushers it across the counter to me.

He smiles without looking at me when I thank him.

Or is he nervous? Am I projecting my own nerves onto him? I realise I have been biting my nails without realising it. My hands are clammy too. This nervousness, it's mortifying. I want to throw cold water over myself.

One of the old men by the bar whistles at the drink and says it looks beautiful and he'll copy me and have one next. I laugh. I leave my book and the drink at the table in the corner and ask if he will keep an eye on them while I go to the bathroom.

We will, aye. I can't promise the drink will still be here. He laughs.

If it's not, you'll be my first suspect, I say. He laughs again. In the cramped, dark bathroom I fix my makeup. My mascara is smudged: a blurred grey line under my left eye. I'm glad I did come early.

I smile at myself in the mirror. *Calm down,* I say. *Calm down. Have a drink and calm down.* I check my nails and they look like crap. Is this what it means to care about someone? How bleak, to ask myself this. How, over the years, have I let this relationship

119

become so meaningful? He is a year older, and that counted for something back when we started sleeping together. And he played sport, and looked like he did, which he still does. And I considered myself too cool for all that, but clearly I wasn't. I was flattered by the attention. And then, when we both moved away, it was something to revisit, old ground to re-tread when we were home. The same sense of being flattered, but now with nostalgia too. Well, that's what I would tell myself it was. Because, really, I don't understand how it's kept going on for as long as it has. I mean, what's my excuse now? I'm not a teenage girl, needing the validation. Or maybe that need was never just because I was a teenager. You don't get to choose which parts of yourself you outgrow, I suppose.

The thing with Mikey has run away with itself. But maybe that's how it works.

When Mikey arrives he finds the drink very funny. *What is it, like a cocktail?* he says, poking the straw and laughing. It bobs up and down in what is left of the white liquid. *Are we getting on it then?* he says.

Yes, I think so, I say, also laughing. *I'm very hungover. I've nothing on tomorrow.*

He laughs. *OK, great, snap*, he says. He is hungover too. He doesn't look it; he never does. His hair, which is too dark to be blonde, but has some blonde through the front, or suggestions of blonde, hints of sunniness, is slightly messy maybe. But maybe it always looks like that. There is a little bit of grey under his eyes but he doesn't look tired; his face looks lived in. His slightly crooked nose and crooked teeth look relatable, open, like they always do. I glance at his nails. Short and neat. Was he nervous before this meeting? Does he even get nervous?

He goes up to the bar to get us both one of the coconut drinks. I drain what's left of mine while he is at the bar. When he sits down I ask what he got up to last night.

Nothing special, he says. *Just Keenan's*. They watched the match, he says. Does this mean no girls? Or is it meant to imply that? I don't know enough about matches to know if there really was one on.

He tells me he is enjoying being back. Of course he is. Everything is going well, which it always is for Mikey. His placement at the hospital has worked out great, so far. He likes the people he works with. But of course he would, or if he didn't, he would make himself like them. There have been some interesting cases. It is still early days, but if it works out well, he will stay here and move back permanently. Something he had planned to do, as long as I've known him. Everything is going to plan. I sip the coconut drink through my stripy straw and smile and nod. This way of being, where things work out or if they don't, you make them, and there's a plan and you stick to it.

Living with his parents is fine. It's an adjustment but he can't complain. It doesn't make sense to rent, since the placement is temporary until his review. His younger brother Matt is often having arguments, with his dad especially. There's not even two years between Mikey and Matt; not quite Irish twins, but not far off, but the distance between them has grown over the years, as Matt has settled into a somewhat chaotic lifestyle. Getting caught doing things he isn't supposed to be doing, going out too much. But Matt has always been like that. Mikey is used to it. Matt is a notorious taker of gap years, failer of exams, resitter of years and lover of late nights and substances. Everybody's used to it. Matt and I knew each other fairly well at school; he was the year below. We'd never have hung out just the two of us, but we were friendly enough. We'd have gone to some of the same birthdays and pre-drinks. I haven't seen loads of him since school, the odd night here and there, but he was always good craic.

Everything's going well then. I laugh. *But you've always had this, haven't you? This clear idea of what you're going to do and how the options available fit with that. And you just do it?*

Do I? He laughs. *I don't know about that. Maybe. Well. I know my limits, definitely. If that's what you mean.*

My turn to laugh. *I wasn't insulting you.* I shake my head and sip my drink. *It was a compliment. I meant it as a good thing. I promise.*

He laughs and says sure. He asks if I want another drink; I say it's my round and he stands up and says he'll get them. *I'm not paying rent, sure. And I'm on decent money at the minute*, he says.

Technically I'm not paying rent either, but my job is essentially a fake job. I'm not exactly on decent money. I've never been proud about money the way some people are. I let him. He probably doesn't even have an overdraft any more. He maybe even has a savings account.

When he comes back it is my turn to say how everything is going. I realise I have crossed my arms in front of me, elbows on the table. I uncross them and then don't know what to do with them so I cross them again. I tell him everything is great. The work arrangement with Anne Marie suits us both very well, the boys aren't there all the time because the dad has them most weekends, or there are weeks like this when she is away with them, so I get some time to myself. She is easy to live with and I am getting to cook a lot, and it's great to have time to do that. We haven't decided how long I should stay for so I am half looking at other jobs but I don't need one urgently, and so far there isn't any reason to think I'll need one at all. It's good to be prepared; I'm being sensible.

I maybe said the other night, but I'm on a break from my course until next September, I say. *Like the way it worked with the years. Kind of filling time till then, if I go back.*

Right, no, no, he says. *That all makes sense. Yes, you said. You did say.* He scratches his nose. *Well, you've done very well to sort things out after everything that happened*, he says.

I think of his friend from the other night. *God, you're that person.* I want to say: Do you really think that? I feel like my life is in this terrible place and I don't know how to go forward, or if I want to. I'd do anything to go back but I can't. And all I really can do is try to hide from it, distract myself. And I can't talk to anyone about it. Nobody knew her.

But I can't. I don't know what it would do. It could unleash a tide and start me howling in the bar, into the coconut drink. I might never stop. And to say something like that to Mikey. To test our closeness. He would say the right thing, probably. But that might be it. If you try to get closer to someone and they pull away, they'll end up further out than they were before.

He is saying it's a good idea to get a break, and talking about how when I go back in September I'll have a fresh head. We have another drink. I get this one. I insist. I don't know why. To prove a point. What point? Maybe I'm drunk enough, by this stage, to have forgotten I'm not one of those people who is proud about money.

When I sit back down we cheers our glasses, even though it's not the first drink and I don't think we cheersed the first one. *So you're here till September then?* he says. *Right, that's what the cheers is for then.*

Or maybe not. Maybe I won't even go back then, I say, laughing. *I don't know. The world is burning.* He asks what I mean and I say I don't know. I think about going back to the lab, in the weeks after Kate died. About how it never felt normal. But how to say that?

I don't know. I don't know if it feels important, in the same way it did, I say.

Research into cancer mutation isn't important, is it? He laughs. He takes a sip of his drink.

I don't know. I mean it obviously is, yes, I say, also laughing. Is it real laughter? Was his? *But.* I tell him a lot of research sounds more important than it is. Extending the lifespan of someone in a rich part of a rich country by five years. Keeping a ninety-year-old alive. There's so much money funnelled into it, it's depressing. And still the world is burning.

You could say that about anything, he says.

You're right, you could, I say. I sip my drink and shrug.

You're right, you're right too. He sits back in his chair. *So what would you do instead? What is important?*

Don't ask me. I laugh, a real laugh this time. *Do I look like I know?*

He laughs too.

By the end of my drink I'm drunk enough to think I could try to explain the way it didn't feel normal, going back, that I'd be able to. The drinks I've had seem to have reactivated some of the residual drunkenness from last night. But I'm sober enough to know I only think that because I'm drunk, which is sober enough to know I shouldn't get much more drunk. Mikey suggests getting food. It's early, just after five, but we can't keep drinking without eating.

When we leave the bar it's a beautiful day, all of a sudden. The sky is light grey, marbled with streaks of dark grey and pink. Dark pink with some yellow in it. Not enough to make it orange. Warped streaks that look like the satellite pictures you see of stars forming a galaxy; stretched-out spirals with mashed edges and stray wisps. Clouds that don't look like clouds. Somewhere, the sun is setting. That's what it means when the sky is like this.

Man, look at the sky, he says. He's rolling a cigarette to smoke while we walk.

Where else could anyone look? A sky like this is unbelievable no matter how many times you see it.

I know, it's crazy, I say. *The sun is going down.*

We walk down the cobbled streets in the Cathedral Quarter to a burger chain. I order one of the fake meat options called Just Like the Real Thing. He has something called The Lardo that comes with an onion ring with bacon inside it instead of an onion. I can't stop looking at it but I don't say it's disgusting.

He asks how it went with my mum. *Oh, terrible, of course*, I say. *Absolutely terrible. I had to go and say a prayer after.*

What, did you really? He laughs. There is tomato sauce on the side of his mouth. I nod at it and he wipes it with a napkin. *So. What did you pray for?* He asks.

No. Obviously I'm joking. I laugh. *What do you think I am?*

A good God-fearing Catholic girl. He laughs.

I laugh. *Of course. Sure.*

I order us more drinks. I suddenly feel too sober. He tells me what other people from the school we both went to are doing for work, or where they are travelling, or living. *And they're doing very well*, he seems to say, about everyone, no matter what they're doing. Teachers, the other doctors, someone who is a nanny for a rich family in Hong Kong. Everyone is doing very well. I don't know why the idea of everyone doing well makes me feel uncomfortable but it does. I say it all sounds brilliant, great and amazing.

We keep drinking, talking about nothing much. Then we are in another bar and I get us waters but don't drink any. Then I am asking why he wanted to meet in town instead of, say, Keenan's, where we'd more naturally go, where people we know from school would tend to go, and he is saying it's a nice change and privacy, and I am saying privacy in what way, from what, he says people we know and I say who.

What do you mean? he says.

Like from who? People or a specific person? I go to sip my drink but I tilt the glass slightly before it gets to my mouth and pour some of it onto my legs. I pretend it didn't happen.

He laughs. *You mean your woman from the other night? Sure, OK. There's nothing going on there, no. If that's what you're asking*, he says. They aren't seeing each other, they genuinely aren't. He keeps talking because I don't say anything. He has slept with her before, but ages ago. He didn't arrange to meet her the other night; they bumped into each other. He was flirting, but it was nothing more than that. Maybe he was leading her on a bit, maybe she did think something was going to happen, but it won't again, it's all in the past.

I didn't ask. I didn't ask, I say. I focus so much on my voice not sounding brittle I come off as sort of corky and jovial instead. *I don't need the whole backstory. I don't need to see her birth certificate.*

Yes, you did! he says. *Don't try to make a joke out of it! Or you were getting at it. But right. It was a bit of attention, that's all there was to it. You know as well, like, I never really go back over old ground. I'm not a one for that.*

That's a lie. That just isn't true. I mean.

His eyes meet mine. *Or, right, well, obviously. But usually.*

I wonder if this is a lie. Probably. But which bit? I don't push it. I let it go.

Then he is telling me about the most dramatic argument with Matt and his mum recently. She found coke in his room, went mad over it and staged a mini intervention. Matt's girlfriend had to come, a priest had to come. *Well, his girlfriend at the time, I think that's off the cards now,* he says. I say his mum is spiritually Presbyterian. I am watching my drink every time I pick it up so I don't pour it over myself again. I can't stop laughing at the image of the priest and the girlfriend sat in their living room. Matt pretending to take it seriously.

I'm too drunk already. But it's not even eight o' clock. The night is young. I ask if he wants another drink. He says he was actually going to suggest going back to his. He has some nice rum. His parents are at some fundraising GAA thing. Convenient. But I suppose it is a Friday night.

14

AT MIKEY'S PARENTS' HOUSE HE stumbles around the kitchen, opening cupboards and closing them, taking out glasses and a bottle of rum. He opens the fridge and takes out a bottle of coke. *Oh, we don't have diet,* he says. *I think we only have this.* I tell him it's fine, whatever, it doesn't matter. In the white light of his parents' cream kitchen I can see how drunk we are. Too drunk. The white light has too much blue in it. It's too cold. I don't even know if I usually drink diet coke but I guess I'm supposed to. Girls are supposed to. There is a wooden ornament hanging up on one of the walls, above a counter with a bread bin and a kettle on it. It is shaped like a heart and it says *Home Is Where the Heart Is* in black swirly writing. I keep glancing over at it as I sip my rum and full-fat coke.

In the blue light I think Mikey looks older. Different at least. Still good. But not too good-looking. He is right on that line; that's his trick. With his fair hair that isn't quite blonde, not properly blonde, and his slightly crooked nose. The kind of nose which might make a woman ugly but makes a man look approachable. I think of the American and his very white teeth, smiling beside the little swimming pool. Mikey's teeth aren't noticeably anything. They're just teeth.

He is talking about where the rum came from: brought back from a holiday, duty free at the airport. I am thinking about what I look like in the harsh, clean light. Old too? I want to check in a mirror, but don't really want to see, at the same time. I am sipping my drink, although I am drunk enough already. I want to make a joke about the wooden Home ornament, but what joke? It's his home.

Then we are in the living room. He is walking around turning on lamps dotted all around the room, on circular side tables and shelves and the mantelpiece. They seem to be everywhere. I'm grateful the big light stays off. I glance up at it and smile. He is talking to the living room's speaker system, trying to get it to connect. *Hello, connect,* he is saying. *Hi. Connect. Connect. Connect, connect.* He claps once. *Fucking connect.* Only then, when he swears at it, does it answer in its robot voice. *Good evening. Device connected.* It says. *Happy listening.* Then it makes a robot noise, like the sound equivalent of drawing a squiggle, to say it is ready.

He asks for music requests, and I say I don't have any, play whatever. He chooses a new, generic pop song, full of samples and sound effects. I think it was playing in the cafe during my trial shift. If it wasn't, it sounds exactly like the ones that were.

Oh Jesus, not this. I laugh. *I forgot about this. Your terrible taste in music.* He laughs and says what's wrong with it, and that I said whatever. I did, it's true. Nobody ever means that though. I say nobody actually listens to this stuff and he laughs.

Well, they obviously do or why would they make it? he says. He looks at me and sips his drink. *Actually, it is bad, isn't it?* He laughs.

He tells the speaker system to put an old song by The Strokes on. *OK, better,* I say. *Much better.* This is the safe music to put on, the music everyone our age likes and agrees is good, and kind of cool even though it's old and everyone likes it. I am sober enough to wonder why there isn't any new music like this. And sober or drunk enough to wonder why neither of us would, after all this time, so many nights like this, put something else, something less safe on.

What are you thinking about? he asks.

Nothing. Just that this was old even when we were young, I say. He says we're still young in a voice that has an exclamation mark, a laugh, a joke, a question, a suggestion, and years of history in it. Too many years. But we are still young.

Then we are kissing, and I don't know who started it. Who ever starts it? And with the old music, which was always old music, in the background, and his parents' living room and the rum from the airport, it is like no time has passed. Like we are sixteen or seventeen, young, when everything was always easy and anything was possible.

When we go upstairs to his room it is meticulously tidy. The bed is made, the four pillows arranged in sets of two. He has always had a double bed and four pillows. We take each other's clothes off. I barely even realise we are doing it until his jeans, with the belt still in them, fall off the side of the bed with a slight thud. I think of the American stumbling out of his jeans, only for a second.

Mikey pulls the side string of the red underwear I am wearing. *Did you want me to fuck you tonight?* he says. *Is that why you wore this?* The same porn talk as the other night; everyone does it. I could ask if he tidied his room for the same reason. But I don't.

I remember it was always tidy. But maybe always for the same reason.

He fucks me from behind, standing up with me bending over the end of the bed. So deep I feel myself trying to crawl away from him. So deep that for a few seconds, minutes, whatever, I don't think about anything else, which is why I always do this. Every time.

He comes just after I do. *Fuck, Erin*, he groans. *Fuck.* When he pulls out I notice he didn't wear a condom. I didn't ask; I was too drunk to think about it. Or too turned on? Whatever, I'm on the pill. I'm due an STD test anyway; I'll sort it out tomorrow.

I wipe the cum from between my legs with his t-shirt. He lies back on the bed, propped up against one of the sets of pillows. *Fuck.* He laughs. *So we're here again. What happens now?*

I laugh. *What do you want to happen now?*

He laughs. *I asked first?*

I tell him I'm tired, I want to sleep more than anything else. He says he is too, I might as well stay here. I throw my extra pillows on the floor as I lie down to sleep.

I wake up and it is the middle of the night and I need to use the bathroom. I use the light on my phone to find clothes to wear in case I bump into anyone on the way – my jeans and his t-shirt, crusted with cum from earlier. The bathroom is at the end of the hall. When I open Mikey's door I can see someone has left the bathroom light on and the door is slightly open. There is enough light that I don't need to turn on the hall light. I try to be quiet, lifting one foot at a time and setting it down on the carpet carefully.

When I push the door open there is someone sitting on the toilet, with the lid down. There are drops of blood scattered across the tiled white floor and in the sink, and I almost scream. Then I realise it's Matt.

He is holding a towel, thick with blood, up to his face. He's gripping it limply; it isn't pressed to his face. He's sort of just holding it up in the air. The top of his left cheek, just below his eye, is shiny and red with patches of gravelly black in it. He looks up but doesn't seem to notice me. He turns his face to the ceiling and sighs.

I speak to let him know there is someone else in the room. *Hi, Matt, sorry to interrupt*, I say. He looks at me for a few seconds, probably trying to remember where he is as much as who I am.

Oh Jesus. God, sorry. He starts laughing, a barking hysterical laugh. I can see he is very drunk. He has done coke or pills or both. His mouth hangs open, slightly, when he isn't speaking. *Oh god, I must have scared you.* He laughs again. He lets the towel fall into his lap and I can see the left eyelid is swollen and pressing down on his eye. I can see the yellow and green beginning of a bruise.

No, you're all right. I smile. *I was coming to use the bathroom. I didn't want to shock you.*

Yeah, of course. This is the bathroom. He laughs again. He is talking loudly, but I know if I tell him to try and be quiet he will revert to the shouting drunk person whisper. *It was a bit of a mad one*, he says.

It looks like it, I say. *Do you mind if I use the bathroom and then I can help you clean up after? If you want?*

Certainly. I hear him laughing to himself in the hall while I use the toilet. I use his bloody towel to wipe away the drops of blood he has left on the floor before I let him back in, so he won't try to help and make even more of a mess or fall. I could ask what happened. I might not get a straight answer. I might get a long, winding story about who started what. I might get the truth, but I don't know if it matters.

Thank you, thank you, thank you, he says, when I let him back in. *I know it's annoying. I know I'm being annoying. I didn't mean to make a mess.* Contrition has set in in the interval, out there in the hallway.

He sits on the toilet lid again with his hands clasped together on his knees. I hold the cleanest area of the towel under the hot tap until it is soaked through. He looks at the ceiling, blinking occasionally as I dab the wet towel to his cheek. The crusts of red and black blood soften on contact with the towel and become an orange stain on the fabric. I rinse the towel and dab again, a few times. It must sting, but he barely flinches. He mutters apologies whenever he blinks or glances at me.

When the cheek is clean I can see it is red and swollen. The break in the skin is bigger than I expected. I tell him that's most of it. He gets up to look in the mirror. *Beautiful,* he says. *Good as new.* That makes me smile, not a forced smile either. He touches his eyelid gently, with one finger, and winces. *Not going to look good tomorrow, is it?*

He turns around and smiles at me. *Thank you. Stick that in the bath, I'll sort it out tomorrow,* he says, pointing to the towel. *So, enough about me,* he nods. *You're back?* He points out into the hall and I don't know if he means back in the country or in his house.

For now, I smile.

Well, it's good to have you back, he says, nodding again. He sways forward slightly and then sits down on the edge of the bath to steady himself. *Also, I meant to say I heard about everything that happened. I hope you're OK as well. It's good to have you back, really.* He meets my eyes while he says it; he doesn't look down.

Thanks for that, I say. *Thank you.* I hear my voice slip, as if I might cry. He doesn't look away.

He stands up. *Come here for a hug*, he says. *I need it after my night.* I wrap my arms around his back. His hair smells slightly sweet. His clothes smell clean. His heart is beating fast. Adrenaline and drugs.

Thank you, I whisper into his neck. *Thank you.* I can feel my throat tighten. I breathe in the sweet, clean smell and count backwards from ten. I try to think about whether the yellow eyelid will be purple or blue tomorrow.

When we separate I tell him I'm going to bed.

Of course, of course. I have kept you long enough, he says. *Thank you again for your assistance.* He half bows. *Assistance with my situation.* He laughs. *Seriously though. Thank you.*

I walk him to the door of his room and watch him trip over a pile of clothes on his way to the bed. When he reaches it he lies, face down, with all his clothes on.

When I creep back into Mikey's room he doesn't wake up. I get back into the bed; he is facing the wall. His hair smells like mint. *Mikey*, I whisper. He doesn't stir. I kiss his neck. He doesn't wake up. I wait a few seconds. He still seems to be asleep. *I'm in so much pain*, I whisper. *I wish I could tell you.*

15

IN THE MORNING, I FEEL terrible; feeling terrible in the
morning is becoming a habit. Still, I'm better than Matt. If
he is awake. With his split face and no adrenaline to numb the
feeling. He'll be on a comedown too, as well as a hangover.

Mikey is awake already, sitting up with his back against both
his pillows, as if he's in a hotel. He is holding his phone up in
front in both hands, smiling at the screen but not typing. Watching
something, maybe. I watch him for a few seconds. The light
from the screen is reflected in each of his eyes as a grey panel.

Good morning, I say. *I feel terrible.* He puts his phone down on
the table beside his bed. There is a pint glass with a few centi-
metres of water in it, a book I can't see the cover of and a lamp.
It looks like a cartoon of a neat bedside table. He says he feels
all right. I say good for you. He laughs. The light in the room
is grey. The curtains are open and I can see the sky is white.
The window pane is studded with drops of rain.

I want a glass of water but not enough to walk around the
room naked in this light. This unflattering grey morning light.

Do you want a smoke? he asks. I don't want to go outside. He
meant inside.

Are you allowed to smoke in your room? I say. *I feel like you aren't.* He says he'll open a window. He does it all the time. I feel old. I don't even smoke, not properly. I say I'm thirsty and he gets up to get a glass of water.

When I hear him starting down the stairs I get up to look around the room. For what? I don't know. Just to see. There are papers beside his laptop on his desk. Work things, they look like. I don't touch them in case he can tell. The top drawer of the bedside table is immaculate. A neat stack of condoms, which I note he didn't mention last night, in one corner. An old-fashioned camera with its strap folded around it in the other. Has he ever mentioned even a passing interest in photography? If so, I don't remember. A passport. A photo of Matt and Mikey on holiday as children, wearing matching cartoon crocodile t-shirts. A bag of either coke or MD. I don't examine it. There is a little tin at the back of the drawer. I look at it for a few seconds and then pick it up and open it. Weed. Nothing really. I close the drawer and put my t-shirt from yesterday on.

He comes back with a glass of water and ice, a can of coke and painkillers. He noticed blood on the hallway carpet. I really didn't think we'd left any. *Matt must have been on one last night*, he says, shaking his head.

I think about Matt sleeping with his face down on his bed with his clothes on. His heart beating so fast. *Oh god, is he all right?* I say.

He is, yeah. Or, well, I didn't see him. But it wasn't a lot of blood, like. A few drops, he says. *I heard him snoring when I went past his room there. I could hear him, like. So it can't be too serious.* He opens the window and rolls a cigarette and sits on the window seat smoking it, holding it outside between drags.

I take two painkillers with my water. He asks what I have on today. I tell him I have errands and work because you can't say I might lie in bed all day with my laptop feeling sorry for myself. I don't know if I'm supposed to leave, but I decide to anyway. I feel awkward. I shouldn't, but I do, and I want to shower and eat and not see Matt when he wakes up. I watch Mikey, smoking on the windowsill, looking out the window, for a few seconds longer.

I should head on soon, actually, I say.

Oh right? he says, turning back to face the room.

Anne Marie will be back soon. I have a checklist I have to work through before.

He raises his eyebrows. *A checklist? Goodness, very serious business.*

Oh, you better believe it, I say.

I can see my jeans at the side of the bed. I hold the duvet to my chest as I lean down to get them. It seems ridiculous to put them on under the covers, but I have that image of the American stumbling out of his jeans, the ungainliness of it.

Here, I'll have a look for your jumper, Mikey says, climbing down from the windowsill, as if he can sense my predicament. He busies himself in the corner of the room as I pull the jeans on, and then walks across the room and passes me the jumper as he sits down on the bed beside me.

Before you go, he says. He pulls me onto his knee and we kiss goodbye, a gesture he executes with impressive grace. I pull away after a few seconds and look at his face. I want to say: Thank you for being so smooth, it's one of the things I've always liked most about you. Instead I find myself saying: *Well, yes. Thank you. Good to see you, and goodbye then.*

Till next time, he says, smiling.

★

Outside the weather is even bleaker than it looked. The air is cold and wet. Colder than yesterday. The black suede jacket I am wearing was fine then but doesn't feel anywhere near heavy enough now. It doesn't have any pockets; I don't have anywhere to put my hands as they turn pink in the cold. Twice my boots slide across the wet pavement and I almost fall. Gusts of wind make my hair fly around my head and my left eye starts weeping. What a day.

At Anne Marie's I shower and sit in bed to read the environment section of the news on my laptop. A widely used pesticide which was thought to be relatively less toxic to soil has been found to disorientate bees and disrupt pollination. Global food waste was estimated at five billion tonnes last year. The average size of certain species of fish has shrunk by up to a third in five years, which might be because of plastic particles in the water. Steps have been made in the effort to produce artificial dairy milk. A new version has passed taste tests and has a shelf life twice that of normal dairy milk. They are hoping it can be successfully used to make cheese.

I close the environment section and search Kate's name. Nothing new. I open our chat and search Mikey's name. There is one conversation where she is saying I am right, that he does look better in person than in photos. *Bad clothes though*, she said. I smile. It's true. She is right; she was right. Always bad clothes.

That was the first of a handful of times they met, when he came down to visit. We went to a party. The three of us got pretty fucked up. They got on well, actually. That party: a memory I haven't thought about in a long time, since before I moved back, before she died. I don't know if I can think about it now,

138

either. I take a long breath in and then out. In and then out. My room seems very quiet. I realise I'm sitting in the dark. I turn the lamp beside my bed on.

I click to the next instance of his name in the chat. A debrief from a time when we slept together during a university break. *Again lol!* she said. *Were you really drunk?* A polite way of saying: what were you thinking? A good question.

I replied:

Lol no.

Well, yes.

It was a night out.

But it's not like I was plastered. Just regular drunk.

Shut up lol. What was I thinking though? And what was I thinking last night?

What would she say about last night? *That was a bad idea, wasn't it?* Something like that. A polite version of that.

How could I explain it to her? I don't know. To prove something to myself. It makes me feel young. Younger. We grew up the same way, almost, well, not quite, in the same place at least. He knows about things that are hard to explain to people who didn't. We have the same sense of humour. The sex is good. Part of the appeal is that he is a bit basic; he interacts with the world in a different way to me. I find that interesting. Because I don't really know what he's thinking, what he wants. I feel like I need to find out. To see where it goes. I don't know.

I set an alarm on my phone for four and go back to sleep.

When I wake up and check my phone there is a message from the American. *Hi, still good for tonight?* it says. *I checked and there are screenings at 7 or one at 9. Maybe 9 is better? And we can get a drink before :-) ?*

A smiley face. A smiley face with bright white teeth. Good manners. Christ. It is Saturday. We did agree to do that today. I did agree to it. A drink before, when I have spent the whole week drinking. Fuck. The message is from half an hour ago.

I close the chat and open it again. *Hi man*, I say. *Yes! Let's do the later one.*

I don't know if you know this already but they have a bar in the cinema, so we can meet there.

16

AT THE CINEMA BAR I order a bottled beer and olives. I get there early, like last night. This time wearing a black leather blazer instead of yesterday's black suede jacket; flared jeans, which have gone out and come back in again so many times they are now always in, with a black leather belt; a top with thin straps over a grey t-shirt; and the same black boots as yesterday.

I smile at myself in the mirror behind the bar and fix my hair while the barman uses a teaspoon to usher my olives into a bowl. It is a slightly different kind of look to yesterday's. Only slightly, but suggestive of a different girl. I can see that. Not on purpose though; subconsciously a different kind of girl.

There's your wee olives there, the barman says, pushing the bowl towards me. He extends the card machine and I see I have to pay eight pounds. I smile, thinking of my few-hundred-pound bank balance. It would cover less than fifty rounds of this order. Less than forty, maybe. A good balance in the grand scheme of things, in the history of my bank balance. In the black at least. But still less than forty bottled beers with olives.

Brilliant, thank you, I say, smiling.

There are students – well, they look like students – standing in clusters in the foyer. Every group has at least one boy wearing a brown or mauve corduroy jacket or trousers. Sometimes both. This is a look for a sizable minority of the boys who go to Queen's. I remember meeting them in clubs and bars as a teenager. They were always studying English or History; sometimes they came from the country, sometimes from England or Glasgow. Sometimes they would be holding a tattered book but you would know better than to comment on it. It would just be giving them what they wanted. If you spoke to them they would say things like: I'm a cultured culchie. Or they would quote lines of poetry and then act apologetic for doing it, like it was a big accident. *That just came into my head*, they would say. They were all the same. It was that thing where someone tries to do their own thing, to be an individual, and ends up as such a clear type they're conforming more than any of the rest of us. I can see one is holding the tattered book under his arm. I can't see what it is without being obvious. I smile and sip my beer.

There is one boy on his own, holding a programme, wearing a full Gaelic kit. A Gaelic man who likes arthouse cinema. There's someone doing his own thing. Or on a date, maybe. Trying to impress someone. But would you wear the kit on a date? He looks up and sees me looking at him and I smile and go back to my drink.

I see one family outing. A dad and a teenage daughter. She is wearing a lot of makeup and she looks mortified to be out with her dad in a cinema foyer where lots of students are. She is examining the ends of a section of hair, trying to look busy. Everything is mortifying at that age. She could be thirteen, fourteen or sixteen.

I remember I was tall for my age at thirteen so people always said I looked older. But then everybody always seems to say teenage girls look older than boys the same age. Her dad points at a poster hanging on one of the walls and I look away.

I sip my beer and take the book I have brought with me out of my bag and check my phone. I have a message from the other Matt. Matt from last night, with his bloody cheek and eye which might be blue or purple today. I don't know if I want to open it. I don't want it to be something sad or serious. I don't want him to see that I have read it. I put the phone down. I pick it up again and slide the message open; it's like a reflex.

Hi I think I saw you last night?

Sorry if I was talking shite and thank you for cleaning me up I must have looked an absolute mess lol

The first message is from twenty-four minutes ago. There is a seven-minute gap between the first and second message. Was he sitting, looking at the phone, deciding what to say? Typing and deleting messages, trying to think of something to say that was casual but not too casual? He is online now. I type a response.

Hi man

No worries

I can see he is reading the messages as soon as I send them. I continue typing.

It was totally fine. You didn't say a lot at all. I was pretty drunk too!!

You only had trouble with the blood because your eye was swollen so it was hard to see

143

I want to ask about the colour of the bruise. I don't want to seem like I'm making light of the injuries. I want to make light of the situation but not the injuries. Maybe next message? I can see he is typing. I wish we weren't online together. Talking at the same time.

Yeah I half remembered seeing you and then Mikey said you were here

I was thinking I might have been carrying on

But anyway thank you

OK, good. He seems OK. The conversation is normal. I type again.

No problem man, any time. It was nice to see you

One question but?

Sure, what's up?

What colour is the eye today?

Hahaha. Blue, purple at the edges. Not too dark tho

Actually heading into town to buy concealer now lol

Good. We seem good. The conversation is normal.

Remember to try the tester on the back of your hand instead of the inside of your wrist

Your wrist is paler than your face

Lol thank you. I will

It's a common mistake

Hahaha I'll buy you a drink sometime soon to say thank you for last night btw

Good, I'll hold you to that

See you soon

I put my phone back in my bag and lean across the table to put the bag on the chair opposite me. I don't want to check it again. I can't think of any more light-hearted, casual-seeming responses to surprise messages.

I pick up the book and open it. I read a page and then, when I start on the next one, I realise I have no idea what happened on the one I have just read. I go back and read it again. The same thing happens again.

Reading has been like this for months.

I start on the first sentence of a page, focusing on the words and what they say, and then I continue on and my thoughts go somewhere else. I don't even notice they've gone. But then I get to the end of the page and I have read all the words without knowing what they said. I don't see the American approach; he comes up behind me while I am trying the page again, for the third or fourth time.

I look like the sort of person who arrives early to things and enjoys spending almost ten pounds on olives and one bottle of beer and is so engrossed in a good book she doesn't even notice the boys wearing the mauve corduroy jackets or the family outing.

What do you think of it? he nods at the book, smiling. *I read it last month.* He looks up, as if he is doing a calculation in his head. *Actually, the month before that, maybe. But recently.*

I look at the book. I don't know what to say. I don't know anything about it. *I can't read,* I say. *I'm trying to learn.*

He doesn't say anything. His eyebrows turn down towards his eyes.

I'm joking, I say. *I like it so far. I haven't finished it, so no spoilers.*
Oh god. Right. Yes. He laughs. *We can discuss it when you finish.*

He is going to get a glass of wine. He asks what I want and I swap to wine too. When he comes back with the glasses he asks what I did last night. *Not a lot,* I say. I tell him I went to the pub for a few drinks, early in the evening. *You know I saw this friend I have who is also called Matt,* I say.

Well, it's not exactly the most exotic name. He laughs in a self-deprecating way, as if having a common name is a personality defect.

I ask how it went the other night with the friend he was meeting. The friend of a friend. It went well. He's a nice guy. He will be working up here fairly regularly for a project so they will likely meet up every few weeks.

But wow, he says. *People here love to drink, let me tell you.*

He's from Dublin, did you say? I say. He says yes. I could say I think people from the North love to drink for a different reason to people from the South. But then he might ask questions about the Troubles, or reel off facts about that, and about Irish history generally. Or explain that he read in a book about how Sinn Féin started. Or go off about Gerry Adams. Every American I have met loves talking about Gerry Adams. There was a book a while back that put them onto him. But then, he might not. He might say nothing. Nod and say of course. And I could be wrong. Maybe we all love to drink for the same reason.

I paid for that night with the entire next day, he says. *The next several days, even. Still now.* He laughs.

You're not wrong about that, the drinking. I laugh. *We love to drink. Everyone says it. It's true. Cheers to that, I suppose.*

The film is about gangsters in New York in the 1970s. It is new but made to look like it was shot on old film using an effect. Old buildings which don't exist any more have been meticulously recreated in certain scenes so the skyline looks just like it did at that time. I wouldn't have noticed but the American keeps pointing at the screen and whispering extra information. The effect is convincing, but I keep thinking if I wanted to watch a film that looked like this, I would just watch an old film. Two rival gangs are at war over a specific area, just a few blocks, and different members of each keep being kidnapped and murdered.

After the film we get a drink. The cinema is closing so we walk to a bar around the corner. He loved the film. He has a lot of thoughts on the meaning, the symbolism, the themes. He says things like setting it in the 1970s is to explore the limits of utopian potential. The grainy old film effect references futurism. The gang members' competition over their little area, their couple of blocks, is a comment on the scarcity of prospects in our era. He says the word technocapitalism. He says survival under technocapitalism.

I don't really know what he's talking about. I have the feeling he doesn't either.

Wait, what is technocapitalism? I say.

He laughs. *You know, everyone uses that word,* he says. *Like the link between technology and new forms of technology and capitalism.*

In a way it's easier to talk about capitalism all the time. Because what if what's wrong with everything goes much deeper than capitalism? If the problem is human nature, what do we do then?

Right, I say. *There wasn't any technology in the film though? They didn't have phones, even? How does it link to the film? And to survival?*

Yes. As in young people now, with the scarcity of good jobs. The scarcity of housing, he says. *And the gangsters shooting each other. It's analogous to what we're all doing, trying to survive in this world where there's just not enough.*

Sure, I nod. *Have you ever been shot at?*

He laughs. *No.*

Me neither, I say.

But you know what I mean, metaphorically. As in that's what it symbolises.

Who did you shoot to get your academic job? I say. I feel my forehead tighten as my eyebrows instinctively raise. I relax my face. I'll drop it in a second. *Or did you kidnap and murder somebody?*

He laughs. *Nobody, of course not. No, I've never shot or kidnapped anybody.* He holds his hands up. Like he's being questioned by the police.

No, me neither, I smile. *But it does happen.*

Oh no, of course. His eyes open wider. The whites look very bright. *Oh no. Right. No, I hope that didn't sound insensitive,* he says. *You know, about the Troubles, and the history. That's not what I meant.*

He thinks he has said something culturally insensitive. Maybe he has. I could make a big thing out of this. Everyone knows that saying something culturally insensitive is one of the worst things you can do. Where would I start? I could say it's not history here, yet, not everywhere. Even though it is for me, kind of. I could allude to my personal connection. I could do that and then say he had forced me to divulge it. He left me no choice. I could say he doesn't understand what it's like to grow up in a post-conflict place. But do I really? It's not like I can compare it with growing up anywhere else. I never even heard the word post-conflict until I left. I could say that.

I could say nobody talks about it. That people who have lived with shootings and kidnappings don't talk about it. That they barely talk about anything else either. But you can feel the sadness in their silence anyway. You feel haunted by the rupture. By the fact that that was survival and your life is comfortable. By the fact you left. I could ask if he came here because he thinks it's a crazy place, or weird, or interesting. Or because he thinks it's a way to get away from something. Or back to an earlier, purer version of life. But I could ask myself that question too. He might not have thought about it all. Do I even think he said something insensitive? Do I care? Do I want to have a conversation about it?

Ah no, don't worry, I say. *That isn't what I meant. I wasn't talking about the Troubles.* What I mean is I did mean to say the Troubles but I didn't mean it as an admonishment. I just meant to say they happened, that we have more than they had. Even that sounds like an admonishment. I want there to be a way of saying the Troubles happened without the whites of his eyes becoming huge because he might have said something culturally insensitive. But everybody's scared of doing that because it's one of the worst things you can do so it's easier not to talk about it.

He laughs. *You're allowed to.*

I didn't mean it that way, I say. I laugh too. *I suppose I mean do you feel like you're trying to survive?*

He laughs. *No, OK. Yes, right. No, I see what you mean. I don't, literally. But just metaphorically.*

I guess I'm saying it's heavy-handed, I think, I say. *As in, that's what I think. That it's heavy-handed. Not that I think that might be the word to describe what I think.*

He smiles and sips his drink. *Sure. That's a fair point.*

Then he is talking about what different reviews of the film in different publications said. He read them before watching. He refers to specific reviewers by their surname, as if I follow them. Or maybe because he knows I don't. I am starting to resent not making a thing about the Troubles comment. He says technocapitalism again. I laugh and ask if he can use literally any other word. He laughs and says why.

It's ugly, I say. *It just sounds bad.*

Right. Sure. He laughs.

I finish my pint and set the glass down on the table. It clinks against the wood. The foam has made a white web form around the inside of the glass. His glass is almost empty too. *Another drink?* I say, nodding at his glass. He offers to get them but I insist. I really make a point of insisting, as if I'm suddenly proud about money.

Are you sure? he says. *I'm still getting used to not paying New York prices. I feel the richest I've ever felt in my life. I feel like a Trump.* He laughs.

Was he not bankrupt? I ask before getting up. He laughs again.

There are a few people waiting to get served at the bar. The barman is standing with his hands gripping his lower back, one on each side, and his head tilted back slightly as a woman with white blonde cropped hair leans over the bar top to order. She has one hand extended in the air, pointing as if checking off items on a list.

I watch her for a few seconds, ticking off her invisible list. I think about the Trump comment. A tired reference. But Americans love talking about Trump. I suppose he felt like an inflection point. Like the moment when a firework, moving through the sky as a single string of light, stops and becomes a point. You know it is about to explode and, just before, there is that intake of breath in the darkness. America felt urgent again, corrupted and dangerous, but urgent. And then it didn't come to anything. He went away again. Everything went back to normal – or not quite, a little worse. But they had that moment.

I think of the holiday photo in the garden with the little swimming pool. The wine glasses. What would you talk about in the garden while you drank your wine? Technocapitalism? Reviews? Trump and that moment in the darkness?

The woman at the bar has been given her drinks. One red wine and three glasses of clear fizzy liquid. The barman hands her a bag of nuts and she picks them up and holds them between her teeth. She nods and manages to pick up all four glasses at once; she walks to her table slowly in what seems like a more complicated operation than two trips would have been.

The next person at the bar is a middle-aged man with light orange wisps of hair. Almost yellow. He is wearing a navy short-sleeved polo neck and shapeless jeans. He sets his elbows on the bar and I can see his chubby white arms are covered in grey freckles and orange clouds of hair. He asks for a kind of beer and the barman says he would need to change the barrel and the man says no problem, he'll wait.

I roll my eyes and put my hand in my bag to check my phone without thinking about it, as a reflex. I pick it up and then remember Matt's messages and drop it back into the bag without checking it. I think of his cheek, shiny with blood, and the blood on the towel and the floor. His swollen purple eyelid pressing down on his eye. I wonder what he's doing tonight. Taking it easy, nursing his eye? Sitting in a bar explaining how it happened, telling the story of it for the fourth or fifth time? I wonder, would he include the bit where I appear in the bathroom, like a ghost? I wonder if he found the right colour of concealer. I wonder what Mikey's doing tonight too.

At the bar I order two beers. I bring them back to the table. We talk about the work I do with Anne Marie, which I describe as sort of being around the house. Doing odd jobs. Cooking. He says I'm an au pair, which I remember him saying the other night. I shake my head. It's not quite right. It's true that I can help with some homework but I'm not really a dedicated tutor, I don't speak a language, I'm not French. It oversells me. I tell him I can't speak another language. He says au pairs don't have to. I laugh. I think they do. I think if she wanted an au pair she would advertise for a proper one. He asks what I would call it. Again I tell him I'd describe it as being around the house. He laughs and shakes his head. I laugh and say he's making it sound stranger than it is. He asks how I know Anne Marie. I tell him I suppose she's a friend. He asks what kind of friend. I ask what kinds are there. He laughs and holds his hands up and then says OK, OK, let's talk about something else.

I say I'm not trying to be evasive. He's making it sound stranger than it is. *Fine, fine. I'm an au pair*, I say, laughing. *If you want me to be an au pair, I'm an au pair.*

He takes a sip of his beer. *OK, let's talk about the course you were doing*, he says. I tell him about the last research project I worked on. MRI scans of rats. Using radiation to instigate cancer in a patch of cells. More MRI scans. Different treatments for different rats. More MRI scans. Then more. Put MRI scans into the computer. Graphs. Models of the different treatment outcomes. More rats. Click click click.

Well, wow, he says. An elongated wow. *That sounds very interesting. Wow, very interesting.*

There is a hint of disbelief in his voice. And too much congratulations, as if I might be lying but I have to be humoured anyway. Like I am an eleven-year-old who has just said I can drive and my convertible is parked outside. I'm being patronised. Why don't I feel more annoyed? I realise because it's not personal. This is the way men respond, used to respond, when I explain about the research work. Almost every man. On dates, at parties, friends of friends. I had forgotten that. I smile. How had I forgotten that?

And I never knew if it was because I was a woman or a woman with a voice from somewhere where they think everyone is stupid or a woman they think is hot. I remember when it happened I used to think: Talk down to me all you want, you patronising fuck. It doesn't change who you are and who I am. That memory makes me smile again. So much I almost break into laughter. What a fighting spirit. It feels like it was about a hundred years ago. I was right though.

Then I do laugh. I burst out laughing. It sounds fake at first. A cartoon ha ha ha. But it is real. That was my life. That was a normal interaction. That is the way people speak to each other.

He sets his drink down on the table. He is smiling but his

eyes are confused. He turns to look over one shoulder, like the reason for the laughter might be standing right behind him. That makes me laugh even more.

What's funny? he says, still smiling. I have to breathe and count to ten to stop, as he sits, smiling with the confused eyes. I tell him what he said reminded me of something someone else said. It would be too hard to explain. It wouldn't be funny. It's only funny to me. Anyway, he said it was interesting. It does sound interesting, but it sounds more interesting than it is. It's just fiddling around on the computer, it's quite depressing really. I didn't feel interested in it any more so I decided to take a break.

He nods and leans back in his chair. *OK, right, can I say something which might be off the mark?* I nod. *I kind of get the sense that that isn't the whole story.*

I smile and ask what he thinks the whole story is. He says he doesn't know.

But if you had to guess? I say.

Bad breakup? Like, and you were living together? he says.

No, I say.

OK, maybe rehab? he says. He doesn't seem to be joking.

What? No. We're in a pub?

He laughs and holds his hands up. He says that wasn't a serious guess. I think it was. I say I don't think his story is the whole story either. He says maybe not. He points at my glass, almost empty, and I say sure and he goes to the bar.

I don't even drink much of the new drink and I am already drunk enough to be standing in the bathroom, looking at myself in the mirror, asking why I am going to have sex with this man tonight. The loneliness in him means something to the loneliness in me. I feel less strange around this other obviously lonely person. Is there something else too? The sense that his vulnerability makes mine less obvious? That I have the upper hand?

I look pale. I dust powder over my face and then bronzer over my cheeks. I smile at myself. Much better.

He is someone I get to be a normal person to. I think of the rehab comment. Well, normal enough. I can say whatever I want. I can lie and it's fine because he's lying too. And he is attractive. Declan thinks he's hot. He is objectively hot. He is the kind of man who people would consider attractive. Do I? I don't know. People would, and that's attractive. I feel more attractive by our association. It's hard to separate what I think from that. I think about the little swimming pool and the pretty girl with the shiny brown hair. The matching white teeth. I smile at myself in the mirror.

We stay in the bar until it closes. Then we stand in the street outside making small talk, talking around how the night should end. It's cold but not too cold. If we were drunker, or if it was raining, one of us would have ordered a taxi already and then we would suddenly be in one of our rooms. We wouldn't even have had a conversation about it.

Instead we are standing in the street, talking about what we have on tomorrow, for the rest of the week, the film again, the weather, how it's not as cold at night as you would have thought, how the bar closed earlier than you would expect and how Madame George's is a great spot. Talking about nothing. Every so often one of us glances away from the other and looks down the street for a few seconds. Big grey seagulls fly over our heads occasionally, looking for chips and kebabs abandoned by students on their way home.

A few times I go to ask how he is going to get back to his flat, to move the conversation that way. And then I stop. Why should I ask? He should be the one who asks. And what if he says no? That he's tired, or it's late. Or just that he's walking, and he should be heading now. Goodbye, goodnight.

He gets out his phone to check the time. *Right. So,* he says, finally. *It's just after one. Do you want to get a taxi back to mine?*

I pretend to think about it, say I have some things I need to do tomorrow. He smiles and nods. *I suppose I can get up early though,* I say. *And head back then.*

You sure? he says. He doesn't seem to mind either way. I realise I expected him to jump at the chance. It crosses my mind that we might both think we're the one doing the other person a favour. Maybe at some point this evening he has stood, looking at himself in the mirror, thinking: why am I going to have sex with this girl later?

Somehow this makes me more sure, not less. *Yeah, it's not a big deal,* I say. *Let's get a taxi.*

The taxi leaves us a few doors down from the house. I look up at the windows as we crunch over the gravel, but no lights come on. In the basement flat the suitcase is still open on the floor. Some of its contents now occupy one side of the sofa and some are spread across the floor between the sofa and the suitcase, as if they got up and tried to make the journey by themselves.

I am aware of what this looks like by the way, he says. *I'm still in the middle of sorting everything out.* He raises his voice as he goes into the kitchen to make drinks. A pair of gin and tonics, with ice and a lime this time. Touches I didn't expect. We sit on the empty side of the sofa, slightly too close. We finish the gin and tonics with more small talk and then we kiss. He kisses me this time, not the other way around.

I'm drunk enough to start taking his t-shirt off. It smells clean, but not like detergent, like it's new. I kiss his neck. He smells slightly of sweat. *We should go to the bedroom*, he says. He takes off his jeans and boxers before lying on the bed and I do the same and kneel beside him. He touches me while we kiss. I still have my t-shirt on. I kneel on top of him and we start to have sex.

It hurts at first, maybe because I had sex last night too, but then it starts to feel good. God, he actually feels good, I think.

Fuck, that's so good, I say.

Do you like that? he says. *Yes, you fucking like that.*

I am holding on to the headboard of the bed when he cums, just as I feel like I'm getting close.

Fuck, he says, as I climb off him. *Sorry I came so quickly. Just the drinking, you know. I'm surprised I could even get hard.*

Did he say almost that exact thing the other night? One thing you can say for Mikey is he never says that. I tell him not to worry about it; it's not a big deal. It's really not. He touches me until I cum and then we fall asleep.

17

I N THE MORNING I WAKE up before he does. I turn over and
see his eyes are still closed and his mouth is open. A thin
white line has formed on the inside of his lower lip. Saliva or
dry skin. My own mouth is as dry as unvarnished wood.

I watch his face for a few minutes. His dark eyelashes pulse,
but his eyes don't open. I think of Matt's purple swollen eye
and imagine the dull pain whenever his eyelashes flutter over
the bruise. I go to the kitchen for a glass of water and when I
come back to the room he still isn't awake. He has rolled over
in his sleep and is now lying face down. The room smells like
stale alcohol and fresh sweat.

I start to get dressed, trying to be as quiet as possible. It's only
when I start to look for my bag and phone that I realise he has
woken up. He is sitting up, watching me. He smiles and says
good morning. I say I'm sorry if I woke him up, I need to go
and sort out the thing I mentioned last night.

Oh yes, I remember, he says. He wipes his left eye with one
finger. *Actually wait, what was it again? Did you say? I remember
you had something to do.*

I didn't tell him last night. I didn't intend to tell him. But it is too early and I am too hungover to think of a good excuse, a believable lie. What's the point in lying anyway? I say I collected some things I had left at my mum's house. I need to work out what to do with them, maybe figure out a way to put them into storage today. He nods and asks if I have a storage locker. I laugh and say that's part of what I need to figure out. He nods and wipes the other eye.

I spot my bag, on the floor at the bottom of the bed, partly hidden by the overhanging duvet. I pick it up and check nothing has fallen out. Makeup bag. Phone. Book. Bank cards. Keys. All there.

He clears his throat. *You know, I don't know if it's helpful*, he says. *I have that closet. In the main room. I don't need that space really, I don't think. I mean you could leave some things there if you wanted?*

It takes me a few seconds to realise what he is offering. I can leave my things here, in the closet. Why is he offering this? What does he get out of it? He could go through my things. Would he bother? I could keep anything personal at Anne Marie's. Is there even anything personal in there? Where else would I leave it? It would be an easy solution to my problem. It would buy me time, at least. I could move it whenever I wanted, if there was an issue.

Will you not need the closet when you unpack? I say, as if I haven't already decided to take him up on it. He laughs and says it's not as if he has lots more to unpack, and he has the wardrobe and the drawers. He has enough storage space. We go into the living room and he opens the door beside the kitchen. The cupboard is small, slightly wider and taller than the door and about as deep as the door is wide, spotlessly clean. It is divided into three shelves, all around the same distance apart. A natural place to store a hoover and a mop, except the shelves mean there isn't a space tall enough. Besides, will he get around to buying a hoover or a mop?

I say it looks great, I'll go and sort everything out. I'll bring it later. I'll text him when I'm coming back. It all seems so easy. I say goodbye and leave his flat early anyway. I'm dressed, I might as well.

Outside the sun is bright. Puddles have formed in indents in the drive. It must have rained last night in the end, some time. When I get into the street I don't want to go back to Anne Marie's yet. I need to walk and think. I start off aimlessly and when I notice I'm near a train station I get on the train to Lanyon Place. I don't buy a ticket and the man never comes to check.

When the train stops I walk out to the front of the station and look out over the city. I'm on a slope, not really very high up, but high enough to work as a vantage point. I can see blocks of offices for big companies, with signs bearing the corporate logos and slogans that are always so generic you couldn't write them; the area around the Lagan that was regenerated when I was a child, so that we could have the same shops they have everywhere, or slightly outdated versions; a derelict patch of land beside a housing estate with ancient Union Jack bunting, feathered by god knows how many years of weather, drawn between the lampposts all down the entire street like a washing line, with the odd lamppost flying a white flag with a red cross and a red Hand of Ulster too, for good measure; and the new tall glass buildings, so much taller than they need to be.

Behind everything, the mountains. Lumps of dark and light

grey, and blue. A mix of two distinct blues, mainly: one so light and yellow it is almost pistachio green and one so navy it is almost purple. But the beauty of it is that it is only almost; they are both blue. And that blue behind everything brings out every colour other than blue in everything else you see. Red and yellow buildings that look so red and yellow it's as if you've never seen buildings in those colours before, as if every other building has been grey. Silver with all the white showing, so it sparkles. Yellow-black which isn't brown, somehow.

I look out at it all. This is a place which shows all its history, all its personality, all the time. It can't help it, the way some fucked-up people are, where they can't hold anything of them-selves back, even as it leaves them exposed. And it's not just the recent history, the flags and religion and borders. It's the mountains everywhere too. The coast, never so far away you can't drive there in an hour, usually less, always devastating. A landscape that won't let you forget that there was a time when all the earth would do was pull itself apart and smash itself back together, splintering one land mass into fragments and folding another back on top of itself, crushing it into ridges and valleys. It still does that, I suppose. But you only see it in hindsight.

Thinking about that ancientness always makes me feel strange. The species which lived and died; which looked monstrous, with enormous teeth and grotesque eyes in the wrong places and scales and slime instead of skin, or coarse fur; and are buried now, in the ice or the ocean or under layers of rock. Tropical climates and mutant plants. An alien environment on earth. Nothing lasts.

I think about asking the American what he thinks this place

looks like. Does it look like he thought it would? Can he see the history? Does it look run-down or strange or beautiful?

I wouldn't ask though; I won't. Whatever he says would be the wrong thing to say. He could say it was beautiful and I would think: You just think that in a touristy way. If he said it was run-down I would think: What the fuck do you know? I don't think he would mention the mountains. But really, if he did, whatever he said, I would think: What the fuck do you know?

I smile thinking about that. It's unfair of me. But it's not just me. He's the same way. Thinking I might have been in rehab. Being surprised if I do or say something he thinks is impressive or interesting. Needing to know what book everything is from, or which famous person said it, or where you can find it on the internet. It's a different thing, but it's the same thing.

I check the time on my phone and look up the mass timetable for the big cathedral in town. On Sundays they have one at six, one at eight thirty, one at nine thirty, one at ten thirty, and one at one fifteen. It is eleven now. The ten thirty will be ending by the time I walk over there. I never go there normally, but why not?

When I arrive, there are groups of people standing talking in the courtyard outside. Middle-aged men wearing shirts tucked into jeans and grey jackets, and women wearing long skirts or dresses printed with flowers. More people than I expected, maybe planning to do their shopping in town after.

I sit on the bench in the park opposite the church until I can't see any more people leaving the building. I walk past the groups still lingering outside and enter through the big wooden door. The place seems empty. I dip my right hand in the gold tray of Holy water by the door and let the coldness coat the tips of my fingers. I touch my hand to my forehead, my chest, then my left and right shoulder. I walk down the aisle and sit in the middle of the third pew on the front right. I don't see anybody on the way. The place is empty.

The altar is a rectangular block of white stone, stationed on top of a raised white stone plinth. A green cloth with a gold border runs down the middle of the altar. There are long, thin stained-glass windows in the wall behind it. It's backlit with a dark red light.

A sculptural, abstract cross is suspended above the altar. Strands of metal wire twisted together like branches into thick bunches form the arms of the cross. A slick metal abstract Jesus is pinned on top of it. The body is a squiggle shape with a flat line at its base and stumps for arms, like a dolphin standing up and spreading its flippers. The head looks like a little metal spoon. Who prays to this? It looks like something you'd see in a gallery.

I can't see any other Jesuses around the altar. I glance around and spot one nailed to the wall by some stairs, probably leading to the basement where the priest gets ready before mass. A small varnished wood cross with a ceramic Jesus affixed to it. Dark, almost red wood with a glint of shine. So small I can't see him in detail, but better than the dolphin.

I turn towards it. What would the American think I was doing if he knew I was here? Sitting with my rosary beads, saying Our Fathers and Hail Marys? Saying, *Forgive me, Father, for I have sinned. For drinking too much last night, having sex outside marriage, twice in two days. Lying.* What else would he think? I would go to mass with everyone else and we would all wear our Sunday best and hats. The priest would admonish us, call us sinners.

It would be fire and brimstone. That's Presbyterians, but he'd think it was Catholics.

I smile at the little ceramic figure on the wooden cross. That's what he would think. *So why am I here, Father? It's not what he would think. But what is it?*

The dark red wood of the cross shines. An unnatural shine, layered with too much varnish and endlessly polished, like Matt's cheek, glazed and sticky with blood.

I bow my head. I think of our hug in the bathroom. Counting down from ten as my throat tightened. As I had that feeling, like something was trying to jump up into my mouth but had got stuck in my throat. He never said what happened. I didn't ask. I can guess. A fight or a scuffle. A misunderstanding. Just guys being drunk.

Father, what does it feel like? To get your face mashed up like that? To mash someone else's up? Blood all over your nose, your whole face. Both of your faces. I don't think it would feel like anything. You wouldn't think about anything. You'd forget everything else, like there is nothing in the past. No future.

You don't exist and your friend didn't die. There are no forest fires. No bleached coral or extinctions or ravaged pollination cycles. No chain restaurants or second offices of companies based in London. No news. You are just a body, punching a wall or another body or a face. Until maybe someone would pull you back. Or how else does it end?

I look up at the cross. Black-red with its peach ceramic figurine. I can't see the face, really. But I can make out the fingers on each delicately sculpted hand. The ridges on its torso, to show straining muscles or hunger.

Look after Matt, Father. I know everyone thinks he needs to get his act together. He's trouble and chaos. Dysfunctional. But he's kind. He feels things. I think he feels the same way I do. I could have said that in the bathroom. *I think I know how you feel. I think I feel it too.* But maybe he knows already, maybe that's why he hugged me.

Father, does Matt feel the same way as I do? The cross stays as it is. Nailed to the wall. Shiny and black and red. The tiny fingers on the tiny hands of the ceramic figure stay as they are. I glance up at the dolphin Jesus and shake my head at it. I look back to the cross before bowing my head.

I remember a story a girl I knew told me, years ago, when we were both drunk, about when she was a child, in primary school. She woke up in the middle of the night to all these sounds of banging and crashing. It was her dad. Her mum ran into her bedroom and took her and her duvet to the bathroom and closed the door. Locked the pair of them in the bathroom. She told me she probably went to sleep on the bathroom floor. If she didn't, she doesn't remember the rest of the night anyway. In the morning there was blood all over their kitchen and the bannister and stairs. Dried on in thick clumps. So thick it looked like brown candle wax, I remember her saying that. I never forgot that image. Brown candle wax.

She told me she touched it. She wanted to peel it off like you would with real candle wax. Her mum snatched her hand away and said it was dirty. Not to go near it. They went out for the day and when they came back it was gone. He must have cleaned it up, even though he never normally cleaned up. They never talked about it again. Nobody did. Neither did we. She only told me because we were drunk, I knew that even while she was telling me it.

She was so angry. Her breathing was faster and harder, just telling the story. And that was just one story. He was just that kind of man. Always going off about something. Impossible to live with. But, of course, she had to. My legs have gone stiff. I stretch them out in front of me. Jesus, she was so angry.

There were always stories like that. Boys fighting on nights out. Dads fighting at home. Letting their anger out.

I look up at the cross. The shine has gone; the sun must have moved. I can make out the face of the ceramic Jesus better. It's smiling, as if you'd smile while you were crucified. I look back to the dolphin Jesus.

What am I supposed to do with my anger, Father?

OK, one more question. Is this a terrible idea? Leaving this stuff with Matt? The American Matt.

The dolphin doesn't change. The flipper feet and fin arms stay as they are. I smile and nod at it again and slide to the end of the bench. I nod at the cross as I stand up.

I walk over to the candles and light one for Matt.

When I push the door open the sun seems very bright. The courtyard is empty now and I walk across it, squinting as my eyes adjust to the light.

Back at Anne Marie's I pack everything I need to keep, anything that has more than sentimental value. Clothes and shoes. Dresses and skirts for summer I'd half forgotten I own; a grey jumper I started to hate because I wore it too much but now think I like again; one pair of jeans that I reason is only half a size too small. I will wear them again. Really, not much else. It fills the suitcase and one bin bag. I drag them over to the wardrobe, so I can see all my belongings together. This is everything I own, everything to do with me, all collected in one compact place.

I need to get rid of the baby clothes and toys and everything else to do with being a baby. My old school books, everything like that. I flick through some of the pages to see if there is anything I want to take a photo of. What am I looking for? Drawings or notes that would explain myself to me? I don't find it, whatever it is; I don't take any photos.

Everything I need to get rid of is paper and fabric. There is a recycling depository in the car park of the big shop nearby. I can take it all there in a couple of trips walking. I take the clothes, toys and shoes first. The recycling box has a chute designed to take only a certain weight at a time so I have to stand and wait between each deposit. It has started to drizzle and a cold, persistent wind blows; the day seems much bleaker than earlier. There are signs saying no toys and no shoes. I squash them into the chute anyway. It seems like a stupid rule. Where else would I put them?

When I arrive at the American's with the suitcase I knock on his door and he shouts that it's open. He is sitting on the sofa, typing on his laptop.

Hi! he says, looking up at me over the top of the screen. *Just finishing something here, sending an email. Then I can help.* I notice he's not wearing trousers, just boxers. It doesn't seem like the most comfortable way to work.

I get the sense the offer to help might only be politeness. I say it's fine. *It's just this case. It won't take long.*

It doesn't. It's all sorted, painlessly. I don't even need to unpack the suitcase; it fits lying down on the bottom shelf. He taps on his laptop while I manoeuvre it into the cupboard. I thank him again before I head back to Anne Marie's.

I say it from across the room, as I walk towards the door. I could go over to him and hug him, or kiss his cheek. But the way he's sitting with the laptop, he seems engrossed. He waves and smiles at me but he doesn't get up.

18

ANNE MARIE'S HOLIDAY WITH THE boys was a great success. In the evening when they get back they all bring their suitcases in from the car. Rory carries his even though it has wheels. Proving to Calum that he's a big enough boy not to need them. He holds it across his body, with one hand gripping the side handle and one hand gripping the extendable top one, and almost runs into the house where he drops it in the hall and stands, gasping from the exertion of it. I try not to laugh. *Brilliant boy*, I say.

When the bags are gathered at the bottom of the stairs we all sit in the living room together. Me on the decorative wooden chair that faces out into the room from beside the TV, the three of them on the stiff, formal sofa with its rigid cushions. Anne Marie sits in the middle with a boy on either side, both holding their phones up in front of their faces. She talks about their dinners and the pool and what temperature it was in the sun and the shade on the hottest and coldest days, using the words brilliant and fantastic a lot.

They all have tans. Golden skin and flashes of light, almost white, blonde in their dark blonde hair. Their arm hair is bleached white too. The boys are wearing pastel-coloured t-shirts. Yellow and green. Their necks are a deep, regal gold against the t-shirts.

I tell them, honestly, that they all look great. *Really, great,* I say. *You all got the sun.*

Well, thank you, says Anne Marie, smiling. She tucks a section of hair behind her ear. *You know what, it was relaxing. I think it was the break we needed. Wasn't it, boys?*

Rory says yes and Calum hums. They don't look up; they keep looking at their screens.

And they were brilliant. Weren't you, boys? she says. Calum says yes this time. As the older brother, the responsibility to reply ultimately lies with him. *Tell Erin about the day we rented a pedalo,* she says. Neither speaks. Anne Marie squeezes Rory's shoulder.

We rented a pedalo on one of the days, he says. He doesn't look up. Anne Marie smiles encouragingly at me, as if I'm the person who should be speaking. What am I supposed to say? Is it helpful to ask Rory another question or not? I smile back at her – I hope my smile seems bright and encouraging – and say that sounds brilliant. A brilliant day. Calum's phone makes a crashing noise, like a sound effect from an action film or game.

Pow pow pow, he shouts. He punches the air, jumps off the sofa and runs out of the room. Rory screams and runs after him. We can hear them both crashing up the stairs, like a herd of animals. Doors bang, out of sync, and then silence.

Anne Marie raises her eyes to the ceiling and laughs.

God, never have kids, she says, laughing still.

I want to ask if she thinks the phone vibration was real. Obviously it was real, but real in the sense that it happened by itself and provoked that reaction from the pair of them spontaneously, or if Calum made his phone do it so they could exit the conversation by pretending they were both playing a game. Like someone in a spy film throwing a smoke bomb. But I don't; I can't really tell how she would take it, if it would seem funny or rude.

Oh god, no. You don't have to worry about that, I say, laughing too, thinking for a second about the other night. Thank god for the pill.

Oh no, of course. I was joking. She laughs. *I was joking. They're very good.*

I agree they are, absolutely. She compliments me on keeping the house so tidy. She's impressed. She asks what I've been up to and I say not a lot. Hanging around Declan's work some nights. Drinks with friends, but no late nights, no parties. I went to the cinema. Didn't think the film was up to much. Really not a lot. Nothing strange or startling.

In the days after the holiday we settle back into our routine quickly. I get back from my runs in time to make the boys breakfast. Toast, fruit or porridge. They ask for things like English muffins, bagels because they saw them on TV, and sausages. Once, spaghetti. I say they know the rules. They argue, but it's half-hearted. Days when it's not raining I walk them to school and they kick leaves or walk with their phones held up in front of their faces. Anne Marie is at work during the day or running errands or going to see something with her sister or a friend. I iron uniforms, hang out laundry, clear the fridge out, hoover, mop, clean bathrooms.

After school there is sometimes sports or music. I help with homework before dinner and check it has been uploaded to the system or packed away in the right school bag. If I go out in the evening for drinks, or to meet Mikey or the American, I come back quietly and don't turn any lights on in the hall, try not to wake anyone up. We don't discuss it but that seems to be the agreement. I always get up to make the breakfast and if I'm really hungover I go back to sleep when everyone is out. Days turn to weeks.

In a lot of ways it's a good job. An easy job. An easy way to live. I have my own life, privacy, time to myself. Absorbed in the day-to-day. I don't think: What about my course? My career? My friend? What next? It feels that maybe I could just go on like this forever.

Then one evening I come back from leaving the boys at their Wednesday Mandarin class. Early evening. The sky is black, but only because it's winter, or the very end of autumn. I go up to my room to find all the furniture has been moved into the middle of the floor. The wardrobe, the bed, the desk. All of it. The mattress is standing up against the wall. There is a smell of lemon and pine but it doesn't cover the chemical tang of cleaning sprays and polishes.

Anne Marie appears. She comes out from behind the mattress smiling.

Oh goodness, sorry about all this, she says. It doesn't sound like she is apologising, more like she is giving me exciting news. *I wasn't meaning to invade your privacy, I just wanted to air this room out.*

She walks over to the box of cleaning materials, picks up a bottle full of blue liquid and strides over to the window and sprays, twice, purposefully. She rubs the glass vigorously with a yellow cloth and I tell her not to worry about it.

I didn't go through your drawers or anything like that, she says, without turning around, as the cloth squeaks across the window pane. *But they all look tidy. Thanks for keeping your things in good order.*

I think this means she did go through my drawers. But at least she's telling me. And then, they aren't really my drawers. This isn't my room. It's a temporary arrangement. How much privacy can I expect? I look around at the mattress, standing up against the wall, and the box of cleaning equipment and Anne Marie, squeaking the cloth up and down the windows. I remember that this isn't really my life. Or it's as if I've remembered. I must have known it all along.

Brilliant, thank you for that. For tidying, I say. I hold the skin on the inside of my cheeks between my back teeth, biting without applying pressure. I ask if she needs a hand and she says she's finished. If I just help push everything back into place and put the mattress back on the bed that's the last thing.

She leaves the room and I wait until I hear her reach the bottom of the stairs. I open the top drawer and take out my makeup bag. Inside there is the woven purse where I keep, currently, one bag of coke, two bags of ket, and the three and a half pills. All still there. I don't know what I was expecting. Would she throw it all out if she found it? Bring it up? Or just treat it as my business and leave me to it? Would she even go through my makeup bag? I zip it closed and put it back in the drawer.

When I tell Declan about the inspection he finds it hilarious. We are eating lunch in town. Loaded vegan fries in red baskets. He wipes red and white sauce away from the side of his mouth with a napkin as he laughs. I talk it up for effect, add details like rubber gloves snapping on and off, make myself sound clammy and panicked and call it the inspection. He asks what she was up to. I say I don't think anything in the end. My panic was for nothing. It was normal nosiness, no more than that; maybe that's worse, in a way. Maybe genuinely just to clean.

God, it's like living in an army barracks. He laughs. *But full of Catholics.*

I ask if he knows any rooms going and he says no. It's a bad time to look; all the students have come back too recently. He'll ask around.

So are you wanting to be moving on soon? Or what? he says. I pick up a chip and put it down again. Pick it up again, stalling for time. I don't know if it will be soon, or if I want to know that there are other options, or if I'm simply complaining.

Nah, not really. Not soon, I say. *I mean, it's not urgent or anything like that. I want to know what there is.* I pick up the chip and put it into my mouth; Declan nods. We finish the chips and throw the paper, slimy with sauce, in the bin, and then go round the charity shops.

A few days later I am in the kitchen making dinner for the boys. I run cold water over a sieve full of spinach. The boys sit at the kitchen table, engrossed in their phones. Their little worlds. The TV in the kitchen is on. They always say they like to have it on in the background. Even when they have headphones in, which they both do almost constantly. I have tried turning it off a few times, on evenings like these. An experiment, to see if they notice. They always do, almost instantly.

The adverts stop and serious music plays to announce the news. The headline story is a series of fires in Australia. The reader is saying place names I don't recognise. She says this is a

174

strip of land which has not had forest fires before. She doesn't explain how it started but she says, in her clipped newsreader voice, that there has been no rain in the area for months. Everything was very dry, all the trees and leaves and bushes, so it's burning quickly.

The screen shows a section of forest engulfed in flames. Trees that look black against bright yellows and darker oranges and reds, then shots of houses surrounded by trees and an aerial view of smoke filling the sky. So much burning I can almost smell it. Smoky and sweet. The screen goes back to the newsreader in her studio and I really can smell burning. The onions and garlic. Brown and sticking to the bottom of the pan. Some of the onions are charred black at the edges. I scrape the pan with a spatula, assessing the damage. Not too bad. Not bad enough to start again. I pour a tin of tomatoes in and stir.

Behind me, the newsreader talks. She lists the number of people who have died and who are missing. The estimated cost of the property damaged so far. The area of forest currently on fire. Only two of these numbers are something I can really quantify: eight dead and fourteen missing, so far.

I turn and look at the TV again. Images of people wrapped in silver blankets. Messy hair and faces smudged with black and grey. The boys have set their phones and headphones down on the table and are staring at the TV. I can see the side of Calum's face and his mouth is slightly open. Rory has his back to me.

Cool, Rory whispers under his breath, stretching the word out into two syllables. *Coo-aaaaal*. The screen cuts to the news-reader in her studio again. She talks about how long the fires are expected to burn for and what local authorities will do to try and put them out.

I stir the pan. The mixture has turned sticky. I turn the heat down.

The TV shows piles of charred animals by the side of a road. Then something that looks like a fox, maybe, lying beside an ambulance covered in one of the silver blankets. Fur matted into black tufts and patches of charred, exposed skin. The way the body is arranged, it looks like a small person.

Wowwwww, Rory speaks again. It sounds like a good wow. Like amazement, wonder. I tell the TV to turn itself off.

What! No! Calum shouts. They both turn to look at me. Their mouths are open and Rory is holding his hands up in the air; it's as if they've seen something unfair happen in a sports match.

That was real, I say. *Those were real animals. Real houses.*

Yes, we know, Rory says, in a strained voice, as if he is speaking to a child.

The fire went pachinnggggggg, Calum shouts, at the room, more than anyone specifically. He makes a gun shape with his hands and points it at the TV. *Powwwww powww.*

Video game noises. Phone noises. Computer noises. They see everything soundtracked to these noises and I don't know how much of this is just because they're young.

Well, how would you like it if your house went on fire? I look at Calum. *Or Granny's dog?*

He shrugs. He doesn't say anything. Rory tuts. *But that wasn't a dog, it was a fox*, he says. *It's not the same as a pet.*

I'm not sure fire can tell the difference between wild animals and pets, I say.

What do you mean? Of course it can't. Fire doesn't think. But it wasn't a pet, he says.

But I mean it could have been, I say.

He narrows his eyes and shrugs. Calum looks at Rory, then at me, then back at Rory. His hands are still in the gun shape but now resting on his knees. I say it doesn't matter. He is right, fire doesn't think. But no more TV before dinner. They only have five minutes of screen time left, so they should use it wisely. They both scramble to put their headphones back in.

19

*J*esus, *those wee boys are sociopaths*, Declan says when I tell him how the boys reacted to the fires. *Absolute sociopaths.* He laughs. *Jesus.* It has been almost two weeks since that evening. Two weeks of chores and helping with homeworks, running, getting drunk, talking to Anne Marie in the kitchen, sometimes going on dates with Mikey or the American, if they would be called dates, and gossiping with Declan. Two weeks of the fires burning, waning, until it all died down. Burned out. Two weeks of normal life.

Tonight it comes up because Declan says he read this morning there are thirty-eight people now confirmed dead. They think that's the end of it. He doesn't mean it like it's gossip. More like god, what a terrible thing to have happened. And I agree it's terrible; I hadn't seen that number yet, but it's terrible. What else can you say? I could talk more about how it made me feel. Shock, guilt, and then more guilt for being shocked; it's not shocking, this is the way things are now. I could try and find good words for that. I know Declan. He would feel the same, I think. But what then?

And tonight is Friday night. The first Friday Declan isn't

working in weeks, maybe months. And we are sitting at the bar of Madame George's, drinking nicer bottled beers than the ones we would if we were paying. Some of his other friends he hasn't seen in a while are going to join us in a bit. It should be a good evening. So I tell him about the boys, and we laugh about them being sociopaths. *They have the brains rotted out of their heads by those phones, as well,* I say. *Absolutely rotted.*

I ask Declan how it went the other night, with a boy from one of the apps he was meeting for a drink. He says it was an all right evening. They had a few drinks out. He was all right craic. They slept together. Declan didn't stay over.

We wouldn't meet up again. Or not like that. I'll say hello if I see him around, like, he says. *He's a nice boy and all the rest of it. But no spark.* He says he doesn't know if he even wants to see anyone anyway at the minute. He's liking being single. This is true. If he's saying it, it's true. Declan isn't self-conscious about admitting when he wants something. And he likes his independence. But that independence can be a problem with him, the whole time I've known him. He's almost too self-sufficient.

He'll tell you what he wants, and who he wants, and he'll go after the things and the people he wants too. He was the only person out in his year at school, and several surrounding years, from when he was fourteen. Him studying art when he easily had the grades for medicine; that went down terribly with his parents, and he would have none of it. *Well, have another child then!* he used to say when they'd argue about it. *If you want a son who's a doctor, because it won't be me.*

The problem is it can be hard to tell when he needs anything, if he does. He'd never be one to ask for help, and I have to actively remind myself that doesn't mean he never needs it. I remember a few months ago, he'd been paid late and only let slip when he mentioned he couldn't afford to come out for a drink. I transferred him a few hundred quid and messaged to say just to return it when he was paid. He replied, *Thank you, angel xxx*. We never discussed it in person. He returned it two weeks later in full, of course.

But here, how's it going with your love triangle then, anyway? he asks. He takes a sip of his beer.

My love triangle. Is that what we're calling it?

Sure, that's what you call it when you're seeing two people, he says, raising his eyebrows and laughing. The kind of laugh that doesn't mean something is funny, exactly. But more that the nature of his enquiry is friendly, rather than truly probing.

Am I seeing them both? I don't know if I'd call it that? I say, but I'm laughing. He's right.

Well, what would you call it? There's not a more casual way to say it, is there? One of his eyebrows is raised.

No, no. You're right. You're right. I hold my hands up. I tell him it's the same as it has been. Not much is going on. He asks if they know about each other and I say not really. *But, you know, it hasn't come up*, I say. *I don't think it would be a big thing if it did.* The eyebrow goes up again.

Well, of course it hasn't, how would it come up? he scoffs. *You're meaning you haven't brought it up.* He shakes his head. *But I suppose keep going as you were then.*

Other people start arriving. Not Declan's friends yet. A pair of girls with shiny black hair and fringes, dressed in black, straight-legged jeans and dark tops, order a bottle of wine and take it to one of the tables. They look similar, like they could be sisters even, but I can't tell how much of that is the matching hair and clothes. A group of three girls and two boys arrive just after; they gather around a table and hang their scarves and coats on the backs of chairs while they discuss what drinks to order.

Declan gets up and drags a few of the other bar stools over to ours. We arrange our jackets across the seats to reserve them. It looks like it will be a fairly busy night. The friends arrive soon after. Liam, Catherine and Rose. Declan and I stand up to greet them. Hugs and waves. Friendly hellos: *Great to see you, man.*

Erin, it's been ages, I love that jacket. Did it rain while yous walked down? Looks busy enough in here tonight. I'm getting a drink, does anyone want one? They were at the art school with Declan. I don't know them well but I have met them before, mostly at pre-drinks or afters. They've always been friendly, easy to talk to and funny, every time I've met them. Declan doesn't really have any friends I don't like.

We don't sit back down; we all stand around the stools. All the bags and coats are perched on top of them as if they're a table. We stop drinking beer and swap to rum and cokes instead. The bar fills with people, laughter and other conversations. Some girls are dancing but most people are still at the talking stage of the night. It's loud enough for us to have splintered off into smaller groups.

I am talking mostly to Liam. He has lots of good stories about rude customers and his horrible manager at his retail job in Victoria Square. He rolls his eyes dramatically, conspiratorially, at the punchlines. And he puts on voices for the customers and you almost feel like you're there with him.

So there was me, hiding in the stockroom behind a box full of coat hangers, he says, finishing one story. Laughing between each sentence and some of the words, and I'm laughing even more. *My manager comes in and finds me. Literally walks around the room looking and then spots me. And he knows, like, that I've been hiding. And I was just looking at him as if to say: As if I was doing that. I'm not doing that.*

The stories might not even be that good. It could just be the way he tells them. It could be that I've had two rum and cokes, after my two bottled beers. But I have that feeling, like I am enveloped in a cloud of stories and laughter. Warm and separate from everything else.

At one point he tells me about a new tattoo he might get. He lifts up his t-shirt to show me his last one. Thin, intricate blue lines on his ribs trace an abstract shape. A curved wire. It looks like a slash against his very pale skin. He has that fair colouring. Hair that is more mousey than blonde, with a bit of red in it. He doesn't have red hair, exactly, but you can see he has red hair in his family. Freckles on his nose and cheeks, but not on his arms.

I tell him it looks great. It does. He says he went to Paris to get it from someone with a big internet following. Flew there in the morning and back in the evening. He shows me their profile, going through some other designs, and I take my phone out to follow them myself. To show how much I liked his tattoo. The screen is full of notifications. Emails, messages in group chats, notifications from platforms and software updates. I can see there are messages from Mikey. I ask Liam what he's drinking and say I'll get the next round on my way back from the bathroom.

In the quiet of the bathroom, with the sterile lighting and the smell of bleach, I feel drunker. Giddy and light. I stand by the sink and swipe the other notifications off my phone screen before opening Mikey's messages. One from about half an hour ago. *Are you about tonight!* And then another three minutes later:

??.

Why did he send that correction? And three minutes later? But why at all? Does it mean he was opening the message again, checking for a reply?

I look at myself in the mirror. *Yes, it is pathetic to give this amount of thought to a question mark*, I say. *Totally pathetic.*

I open the chat again. He is online. I want to say something casual, maybe a bit mysterious. I don't want him to see I am typing for a few seconds, spending time crafting a response.

Hiii, yes I will be I'll be free later

I can give you a ring then?

I can see he is typing. I put the phone down beside the sink to fix my makeup. Bronzer on my cheeks. I close one eye and then the other to apply fresh grey eyeshadow over the earlier coat which has gathered in the crease of my eyelid. One coat of lipstick. I rub my lips together to smudge it and smile at myself. Too much makeup in this light, but it will look good in the bar.

I check my phone. New messages.

Oh I meant now sorry, haha. For a drink? Lol

The full stop and the haha. Formal or awkward? I'm not free now. He surely doesn't expect me to just immediately drop what I'm doing? Although, does my message make it clear that I'm not free?

Actually I'll give you a call, I type. *Give me two minutes.*

I gather my makeup back up into my bag and walk outside, where it is dry but cold without a coat. I stand by the group of people smoking under the glow of the heater.

Mikey answers more quickly than I expected, on the second ring. I tell him I'm out already, with some friends. *Well, some of Declan's friends, really*, I say. *But they're all sound.* I tell him he can come if he wants. He doesn't answer immediately. Then he says he doesn't want to interrupt, but if nobody minds.

We can just meet after, or whatever. Like if it was a planned thing, he says.

I laugh. *I mean, it was planned. It's not as if we all just bumped into each other. But you are still welcome to come.*

He laughs and says sure. He'll be down shortly.

Inside, the four of them are talking in a group. I nod at Liam on the way past to say I'm still getting his drink. I get two rum and cokes, bring one back to Liam and apologise for the wait. *No bother*, he says, touching my wrist. *Are you all right?*

Yes, totally fine, I say. I explain there's no problem, it's just a friend of ours is going to come down and join us.

No, he's not, Declan says, laughing as he shakes his head. *He is not.*

You two get on! I say. He shakes his head. *You do, admit it.*

Liam asks who it is and Catherine asks what we're talking about. A friend of mine and Declan's is going to join us, I explain. Declan rolls his eyes dramatically, as if to say I want nothing to do with this. Catherine asks if I'm seeing him and I say sort of but tell her not to act like we are. *Oh sure.* She laughs. *One of those ones.* All girls know those ones. Still, as we're talking, before he arrives, I keep feeling that maybe I should explain more. That when he comes he might be wearing naff clothes, but just to ignore it. Or how long it's been going on for. That even if we seem different there's a lot of history there. But then how to explain what the history is? What is it I feel like I have to explain? In the end I say nothing.

I force myself to resist checking my phone for the time, or messages with updates about how close he is; I face away from the door, so I won't be craning past whoever I'm talking to, watching it. I know it would be obvious to Declan what I was doing. I'm notified of his arrival by a tap on the shoulder, thrilled to have been caught deep in conversation. I turn around and I can feel my smile stretching my face.

All right, he says. *Good to see you.* We hug.

When he gets talking to everyone I don't know what I was worried about. He gets on with everyone. Is friendly, polite. He isn't even wearing naff clothes. Black, straight-legged jeans, a white t-shirt with a thick hem at the neckline, a brown belt, black trainers and a dark jacket. Not the height of fashion but not bad either. Now he's here, dressed like this, I sort of can't say what he normally wears. Small differences. No belt, or a jacket with a bad collar? A t-shirt with a thinner hem? Or a shirt tucked into jeans? Small differences, but I think he has done it on purpose. A slightly different person for a slightly different crowd. This is what he's like though. He just adapts. Fits in everywhere.

You never know how much he's trying, how intentional it is, or what he's like when he isn't adapting.

Everyone is on good form. We all keep drinking rum and cokes and buying each other rounds. Talking over the music and the background buzz. Mikey talks to Catherine about the restaurant where she works. He knows someone who used to work there too, it turns out. He vaguely knows some of the people who still work there. They talk about that while I mostly talk to Declan. At some point they get on to her art and she shows him the social media page. I half watch him and I can see he is zooming in on the photos and commenting on certain details.

He asks questions, doesn't talk too much about himself, takes an interest in whatever anyone is talking about. Impeccable manners. I overhear part of a conversation with Liam. Liam is asking about the hospital where he works. *I basically spend all day talking to old people. I'm not complaining, like, but there's no glamour to it*, Mikey says. Liam laughs and says rather you than me.

He taps me on the shoulder at one point, says he's going out for a smoke if I want to come. I say I'll come for air. I might have one. Outside we stand in the orange glow of a patio heater. I sip the end of my drink, deciding whether I want a cigarette after all. The drink's more melted ice than anything else at this stage, a watery sugar taste.

He says thanks for inviting him tonight. Everyone's sound. *I needed to get out of the house anyway*, he says. *My dad and Matt were doing my head in*. He starts explaining about another argument, about the same things they always argue with Matt about, but this one was supposed to be worse because the intervention was recent. *It's just endless chaos with him*, he says. *I forget about it when I'm not here but it really is just one thing after another*. He draws on his cigarette and smoke fills the space between us; the cold keeps it hanging in the air. He squints slightly and his jaw looks square. It's a good light for him.

I feel the smell of it in my nose. The woody danger of burning tar. I put what's left of my drink down on the ground and ask for a cigarette. He lights it and I ask about Matt's eye. It was a little while ago now, but I can't think of anything else to say. *How long did that take to die down then?* I say.

Well, exactly, he says. *That's the other thing. As you say. Getting into this fight the other night. Just chaos.*

No, I didn't mean it like that. I really just meant about the eye, I say.

He raises his eyebrows and looks at me as if to say don't ask stupid questions. I say Matt seems to be having a hard time. He goes to say something and stops. He shakes his head. He looks up at the sky without really moving his head, but it's not exactly like he's rolling his eyes either.

Why are you annoyed? I say.

He laughs. *I'm not,* he says. *It's fine.* He tries to smile but his face contorts like he's tasted something unpleasant.

I laugh now. *Say whatever it is you want to say.*

I don't want to say anything, he says. *Anyway, since when have you and Matt been such good friends?*

We've always been friends, I say, forcing breeziness. *You know, I sometimes think he's nicer than you are. Fuck off.* He laughs and shakes his head. But his mouth doesn't have that sour look any more.

Back inside I get a glass of water at the bar. They've already called last orders. It seems like the place is closing very suddenly, like we've barely been here for an hour or two.

We're herded out to the smoking area. Rose is saying she's going to call it a night. But everyone else is standing talking with their hands in their pockets or is taking an extra layer out of a bag to arrange under their coat or checking their phone. We say our goodbyes to her. Liam starts saying people can come back to his if we want. Well, not his, really. He is cat-sitting for his sister who lives in a new-build apartment on the Ormeau Road. She is a solicitor at the Belfast office of a big firm in London, and lives alone except for the cat.

Catherine looks up from her phone and says she is talking to some of her friends from work and can they come too. They can. She says they're going to get some coke in if anyone else wants to go in too. People agree, start arranging going to the cash point and sending money to each other. Mikey has a gram of coke already which he says people can share. It's been sitting around for ages. He has a twenty on him too which he's happy to chip in. I would prefer ket but I don't want to buy a whole gram or have to marshal support and money for one so I don't bring it up.

20

At liam's sister's flat we all have to leave our shoes in a black metal rack by the door as we come in. A wooden sign hanging above it, shaped like a heart and painted red, says *SHOES* in swirly black letters. I am drunk enough to think it's one of the funniest things I've seen in my entire life. I am laughing so much as I try to unzip my boots, leaning against the wall to support myself, that I veer to the side and almost topple over. After that I sit down on the floor with my back against the wall to take them off. Declan rolls his eyes at me. He had the sense to sit on the floor before trying to take his trainers off, of course.

Everything in the hall except the *SHOES* heart is white, silver or purple. The colour scheme extends into the kitchen-living-room area. Liam takes a bottle of prosecco out of the fridge and pours us all glasses.

Here, we might as well drink the nice bottle before the others get here, he says, as he bends down and squints at the pale liquid in each glass to check which of them needs topped up. Watching him sway, almost losing his balance as he crouches, I can see how drunk we all are. I open cupboards, find glasses and pour everyone water so we can sober up a bit before the prosecco. *Aye, good idea*, Liam says, passing them around.

The flat buzzer rings and I can hear Liam trying to explain which floor the flat is on over the intercom before he tells Catherine to go down and meet them. *They can't hear a word I'm saying, this thing's always fucked, she should get it replaced*, he says. *And here, Catherine, make sure they're quiet coming up the stairs.*

I look around the room. Silver kitchen appliances, white cupboards, white sofas and purple cushions. Horrible. I notice a pile of white fur stirring in a grey fleece basket on the sofa. The cat stretches its body out and sits up. It lets out a little scream and I walk over to say hello. I put my hand out to it and it looks up at me and screams again. I make the same noise back at it and it sniffs my hand. *It's nice to meet you*, I say as I stroke the long white princess hair. It looks up at me with yellow eyes.

Liam laughs. *He'll wander round here for a wee bit and then go into his other bed. He has a basket in the bedroom. Caspar, you call him, but I don't think he knows his name. Bronagh says he does.*

Caspar, I say, looking into the yellow eyes. He screams at me once more and wanders off.

Can I have a nosy around? Declan asks and Liam says of course. *Just don't spill anything in her room or whatever*, he says.

I walk over to where Mikey is standing, looking out the giant window. It runs almost the entire length of the room, leaving about a hand span of wall at each end, and from waist height to the ceiling, like something out of an aquarium. I can't help but laugh at the view. The convenience shop across the street, with half the lights on its sign out, ***Fuck IRA scum*** spray-painted in black on the red-brick wall. Red, white and blue kerbstones and orange and purple flags further down the road. An Ormeau Road flat pretending it's a penthouse suite.

He asks what I'm laughing at. What am I? This thing of everything in the world having to be the same. And the way some things never change, at the same time.

Hard to explain. It's just that the view doesn't match the rest of the flat, I say.

Yeah I know what you mean. He laughs. *It has that Manhattan meets Belfast vibe.*

Right. Exactly that. That's exactly what it is. That's a great description.

He takes a sip of his prosecco and I can see he is smiling.

I turn to look back at the room. Every fitting and piece of furniture is either gleaming or stiff, as if it's all never been used. The entire room could have been fitted this morning.

Liam sits down on one of the sofas. The thing is so rigid, for a second I think it might bounce him back up onto his feet again. He looks back at me. *Here, should we do a line of coke before they get back?* he says. *Catherine hasn't texted or anything to say they're stuck outside. They're maybe meeting the guy before they come up.*

Aye, good thinking, Mikey says, from behind me. *Do you have a book or anything? I'm scared to even leave fingerprints on that coffee table.*

Liam laughs. *Yes, one second,* he says. He goes into the bedroom and comes back with something A4-sized, with a black shiny hardback cover. It looks like a manual. Liam sets it down on the table and Mikey sits down on the rug, just beside the table, and pours his coke onto the cover. He uses a card to spread it across the surface. Doesn't look like a bank card, probably a loyalty card or a gym pass or something; he has always been a one for the gym. He places a banknote over the powder, followed by his card, and then presses his fingers down firmly on the card, rolling them up and down to crush the powder until it's very fine. I have done this myself hundreds of times, but the ritual of it, the smoothness of the movements is hard to look away from.

The memories of it too. The first time someone explained this was a better way to do it than jerking a card all over the place in that slicing motion. Times when it kept sticking together and you realised too late that something involved in the process, the book or the note, was slightly wet. Holes in bags and times when someone tripped and sent the powder flying off the book and you had to negotiate it off the end of the table. Or worse, if it ended up on the floor.

When Mikey divides out the lines he leaves one for Catherine. Thoughtful. He drags her line over to one side of the book, away from the others. Liam, Declan and Mikey do theirs, and then Liam passes me the rolled-up banknote. I sit down by the table and I can see what the book is: the values and culture annual for a law firm. The one where his sister works, no doubt. I see the words DIVERSITY and EXCELLENCE.

What, is this the only book she has? I ask Liam, laughing. He says it is, or it was the only one he could find at least. He laughs too. *Like, she might read other stuff on a Kindle or whatever. It's still ridiculous.*

There is noise from the hall of the flat. Voices and laughing. Catherine explaining about the shoes. She comes back into the room with her work friends and explains they didn't meet the dealer. He won't be here for another half hour; they took longer because they went around the corner for wine.

The work friends are two boys and a girl. One of the boys, who says his name is Seamus, starts to organise the money. I take my chance to ask if anyone wants to get ket as well. If it's not annoying to ask the guy. If anyone else wants to go in on it. Ket is much better; it doesn't make you talk about yourself the way coke does. Mikey says he will and Declan says the same. *Yeah, I'm more in that mood than coke to be honest, actually*, he says. He has some cash. Seamus texts the guy. He replies quickly, grumpily, but says yes, that's fine.

Seamus and one of the other work friends go to meet the guy. Half an hour seems to have passed quickly. The rest of us sit on the sofas and the floor. Mikey directs Catherine to her line. I ask the other work friend her name; she is sitting on the other sofa, at the corner closest to me. She is called Brenda. She has straight orange hair tucked behind her ears, and freckles. Her eyes are almost orange too. She is wearing big gold earrings and a gold top. I want to tell her I really love the gold and orange together. And that I bet everyone says her eyes are brown but I know they're orange. But I know it's the coke talking. Or it's me talking, but it's the coke that would have me say it. Catherine has dark, thick eyebrows and a slightly protruding jaw. Not bad looking, exactly. But no Brenda.

I tell her my name is Erin, smiling as I say it. Mikey introduces himself. She's met Liam and Declan before, but only a few times. The other guy, the one who went with Seamus, is called Peter, she tells us.

Catherine sits on my sofa, between me and Brenda, and asks her how work was. They talk about the certain manager everyone hates, the unfairness of his shift patterns. The worst customers they've both had that week. She asks what I do, and I say I'm a nanny, kind of. For the meantime. Between real things at the minute. I get up to refill my glass as Seamus and Peter come back in. Seamus arranges lines of the new coke and Declan does the ket.

I pour my glass, let it fizz and then top it up, put the teaspoon back into the prosecco bottle to keep it fresh and put it back in the fridge. As I go back to the sofas the conversation has become about how expensive ket is now. Everyone loves talking about that. Everyone has their own stories. When it used to be cheaper than getting drunk, in the first years of university. When it cost less than a third of what it costs now. It hasn't been that way for about half a decade, but everyone talks about it like it's a recent change, like we aren't always having this conversation.

Nobody tells the bad stories. The people you know who grew up in certain places, where it was easier and cheaper to buy ket than a bottle of cider, so they would do that from when they were thirteen or fourteen and by the time they were eighteen they would easily do a whole gram in one line. And then sit there, glazed over. But everyone knows those ones too. It's just we only talk about how good it used to be.

Liam does a line as well as me, Declan and Mikey. We sit back down on the sofas. Mikey is saying the flat is very nice and Liam's sister must do very well for herself. I want to say I think it's horrible, but there's no point. Liam knows it's horrible, Mikey knows. Liam is saying, well, she became an associate very quickly, and is at a training course in London this week. *Then, of course, more pressure for me. She's the golden child. If I even need to say it, like.* He laughs.

He rolls his eyes. In the corner of my eyes certain areas of the room twist and fold, but then when I look directly at them they're straight. The twisting has moved to the new corner of my eyes. I look around, trying to catch it, even though I know it will keep moving. Liam laughs and I look back at him and laugh.

The golden child, I say. *The golden goose.*

Goose. He laughs. *She is like a fucking old goose.*

Is that a thing? An old goose? I laugh. Mikey says it's not. He laughs too.

Giddiness, lightness and warmth. I ask Liam what the other word he said was. He says which one. Mikey says associate. Yes, the word associate. Business associate. Please meet my associate. Spies. I ask Liam if she's a spy and Mikey giggles. A real giggle. Like a teenage girl. I turn to look at him and mess his hair up. He touches my hand for a second. *Aye, stop that,* he says, but gently. He touches my nose with his index finger. He asks Liam who she would be a spy for. Liam says the Corporate Governance Regulation Body.

I pick the book up to look at the cover properly. White residue is scattered across the cover. The D and E from DIVERSITY and EXCELLENCE make two letters of the word SUCCEED. It's designed to look like a crossword puzzle. I hold it up like I'm exhibiting it. Declan laughs at it and shakes his head.

D is for Diversity, D is for Declan, he says. I have to put the book down again because I'm laughing so much.

Liam is talking about his brother now. He is on an eternal gap year. He spent almost a year in China recently. The edges of the room aren't churning any more. I need to do another line.

Declan gets up to refill his glass and gives me the bag of ket. I arrange four lines. The ket people all do one. *So, China?* Declan says. The laughter is back, quicker on the second line because it's almost like it tops up the first. Or maybe that's a placebo.

Seamus asks if Liam's brother noticed much surveillance while he was out there. Declan looks at me and we burst out laughing. Seamus laughs politely. It's not funny to him because he's on coke. But that makes it funnier to us. Surveillance. Spies. SUCCEED.

Liam answers him. He says he doesn't know how different it really was. *I mean, I think he mostly went out drinking with other people teaching for the same school. You can't get any drugs out there. Or he couldn't, maybe you can if you live there. I dunno, like. How different is anywhere, really?*

Seamus is nodding. The coke people are talking about how different anywhere can really be. Different politics, different cultures. Liam is trapped in the coke conversation like a hostage. I hear Peter say he studied International Relations. That's always a bad way to go. When you're saying you studied International Relations, that's when you're losing. Declan is twisting strands of the rug together into a plait. Liam says about another line and stands up, escaping the coke and International Relations. Declan starts to arrange the lines.

Then I am sitting back on the sofa, talking to Mikey. I want to touch his hair again, but I'm sober enough to know it's a ket thing. He is scratching the nail of his thumb against the nail of one of his fingers. There are long strands of the cat's white princess hair all over his black jeans.

Ghostly wisps. I check my phone and it is after four. When

did that happen? When did I sit back down on the sofa? What were we just talking about?

I look around the room and see Declan is playing with the cat. The cat is lying on its back and Declan is scratching its stomach. I peel one of the hairs off Mikey's jeans. *Strange-looking animal, isn't it?* Mikey says. *He's just a wee ball of fur.* He asks if I want another drink. He's getting one. I want something. Another drink, another line, to be more sober, for it to be earlier. All those things.

Yeah, get me one too, I say.

When he gets up I move to the end of the sofa. To Catherine and Brenda's conversation, on the next sofa. The boy who Catherine had been seeing recently isn't replying to texts. Or he is but with one word, two days later. She hasn't seen him in about two weeks. She's reading Brenda the last texts, asking if she should start the conversation up again. Not now, but tomorrow. *What would you say?* says Brenda. *Like, would you have it out with him?* Catherine doesn't know. Maybe she would ask something else first and see how the conversation went.

I agree, I say. *Don't let him waste your time.* We all nod.

Catherine offers me a line of coke and beckons Seamus over to arrange them. I don't know if I want any but I agree out of politeness, camaraderie. Declan has one too. *I'll be asleep on that beanbag over there if I don't.* He laughs.

Then I am in the bathroom. The immaculate bathroom. The mirror doesn't even have any toothpaste speckles. I look so good. Flushed cheeks. But not red. Apple pink. Pink Lady pink behind my freckles. Huge, silky pupils. I was going to top up my makeup but now I don't think I need to.

Back in the living room Declan is sitting on the beanbag,

holding court. The cat seems to have excused itself. He's telling a story I've heard before. When he was seeing some boy and he matched with the boy's dad on one of the apps.

What did you do? I hear one of the girls ask. *Did you tell the son or what?*

What do you mean, did I tell him? scoffs Declan. *As if I'd be getting myself involved with any of that! If he wants to carry on like that in secret, it's his own business, and his own mess he's making, I'll tell you that!* He pauses. *And besides, I wanted to keep seeing the son, didn't I?* He cackles and everyone else joins in.

I look around the kitchen for a drink. I pick up empty wine bottles and put them back down again. Liam notices me poking around and comes over to get a bottle of gin out of the cupboard. *No tonic, but you can use that orange juice in there.* He takes the carton out of the fridge.

I sit back on the sofa with my gin and orange juice, in the seat beside Peter and Seamus. Seamus smiles at me. They are in the middle of a conversation. I turn around to join, but then I hear Peter say: *But you know what? People always underestimate me.* I turn to the other side and lean over the edge of the sofa, but it's Catherine showing the same texts from earlier to Liam.

I turn around to look out the window. The light outside is grey. You can't see the sun properly but there is a trace of it in the sky. Probably after seven. I don't want to check my phone. Liam says does anyone want another line. Seamus says he has to go soon because he is working later today. I say the same. It's late enough. Mikey agrees, he has things to do for his mum tomorrow.

Will we share a taxi? he says to me, from across the other sofa.

It's too late, I say. *I should go back to Anne Marie's to be around there for at least some of tomorrow.*

I'm wrecked, still in a weird place from the coke and the ket, and I don't know what I'd do if we were on our own together, what I'd say. I don't really trust myself to keep it together.

Right. Yes, of course, he says. *No, of course, but share a taxi anyway?*

21

TROUBLE IS AFOOT AT ANNE MARIE'S. There were signs. The spring clean of my room. Whistling and humming around the house. One night, on a Thursday, Rory said he wanted delivery pizza for dinner. *Well then, let's order it!* she said. Just like that, breaking the most sacred house rule about only having delivery on Fridays. The boys looked at each other with giant eyes.

I didn't put it together myself. It was through Mikey I heard. We were sitting in his kitchen having coffee. Pretending that was the sort of thing we did. He was off till a night shift at the hospital. I had an afternoon of running errands and killing time. I don't know who suggested the coffee.

He asked if I wanted to know some gossip. Or maybe if I had heard it. *I don't know,* I said. *Don't tell me if it's going to get me in trouble.*

What would that be? That would get you in trouble? Why would I get you in trouble? he said, laughing. I said fine, tell me. Well, he said, he had heard they were getting back together. Her and Gerard. The news came via his mum's friendship to Anne Marie's sister. Whatever way he said it, I couldn't work out what he meant at first. Gerard and who? Then I realised. Then I started thinking about what that would mean for our arrangement.

I said something like no way. I wanted to say: For god's sake, why did I have to hear this from you? But then, of course this would be how I heard it. And maybe I even did say that about why I had to hear it from him. I don't remember the rest of the conversation well. I was thinking about looking for a new flat, a new job. I remember he said Gerard's new woman had left already. He had been phoning Anne Marie, asking to come back. The sister said that she thinks Anne Marie and Gerard are currently agreeing to the appropriate conditions for his return, and that it's all a terrible idea. Mikey's mum agrees. Why do I remember that bit? Anyway, after I was told, it was obvious.

I don't bring it up with Anne Marie though. I can't think how to. Also, it seems like bringing it up might make things worse. Accelerate the change. But it does make me refocus on my job hunt.

I apply for jobs in call centres. I get a first-stage interview for one providing customer support for a bank. The job title is Executive Chat Bot. If I get it, I will be trained in a centre in Newtownards for two weeks. Then I will work remotely. My contract will be for three months. Then we will have a review to decide if my contract will be extended for another three months. I will be classed as a temporary worker so I will not accrue holiday or be eligible for sick pay. My shift pattern will be four days on and three days off, with different working hours each week. It's a crap job, but I need something. Hard to do better on short notice.

For the first stage I have to record myself answering questions about the bank: why I would be well suited to the culture, the team and the role.

One afternoon while the boys are at school I sit at the kitchen table with a notepad, scrolling through the bank's website, making notes of its slogans. *Champion of enterprise. We pride ourselves on our frictionless service. Supporting your life decisions.* When I start recording my interview I try to use the same words. I say things like: I am a people person. I think the job will be challenging and fast-paced. I love time management. I love to provide a frictionless service. I feel grimy when it finishes recording. Then I have to fill out a questionnaire about the experience. I get an email saying I'll hear back by a certain date. If I don't, to assume I have been unsuccessful this time.

I am with the American when I get the email informing me I have graduated to the next round. The next round is a person-ality test, it says, to find out how you react under pressure and with different types of people. *Ah, great news. Brilliant,* I say out loud when I open the email, surprising myself with the enthu-siasm of my response. It is a Friday, early afternoon. A crisp, bright freezing day. We are sitting on the bench in the back garden of the house he stays in. The ground is solid with the cold. The grass is curled over and grey with frost; it's almost the same effect as if it were wearing hair gel.

He's smoking. He can do that out here when the family upstairs is away, as long as he uses an ashtray and empties it out after. He sets his cigarette down in the ashtray. *So what's the good news?* he asks.

It's not good. It's just news, I say. He asks if it's bad news. I say no. It's not bad. It's just not good. Just the next interview for a job I applied for. *Well, that's good, isn't it?* he says. I tell him it's

202

a crap job. Call centre stuff. Temp contract organised so you don't get holiday or sick pay type thing. One of those ones. His mouth becomes a straight line; the lips almost disappear. *I know*, I say. *I know*. Why apply for a crap job? But it's a stop gap. It will have to do. He asks what is happening with my course and I say I don't want to make a decision yet. I need time to think. I need something in the meantime.

Sure. I understand that, he says. He is nodding, looking off into the distance instead of at me. He asks what's happening with my au pair job and I say maybe nothing. *Fair enough*, he says. A bird with speckled brown feathers lands on the grass and pokes around. He watches it. When it flies away his eyes follow it up into the air. Then he looks back at me.

He opens his mouth and licks his lips and closes it again. *Hmm*, he says. *Right*. I can tell he has something else he wants to say. What? Will he explain how temporary contracts work? Ask if I have checked if it's zero hours or not and then explain what that is?

OK, so, he says, again looking away. *Anyway, I was going to ask if you'd thought about what you're doing for Christmas?*

What? Christmas as in Christmas? I catch my face, eyes narrowed and frowning, and force a smile instead. But that was my reaction. If he saw it, he saw it. What to say? What am I doing? I won't be working. We haven't discussed it, but Anne Marie will take the kids to her parents in Dublin for their extended family Christmas; that's what they do every year. I've heard all about it. All three of Anne Marie's siblings and twelve grandchildren. Old feuds re-enacted via arguments about who gets which room. And through giving expensive presents to each other's children. Stockings with names sewn onto them. Rules about when presents are opened. Stress drinking.

I tell him I'm not working. Anne Marie has a big family thing. *They all go to Dublin, that's where she's from,* I say. *Everyone gets the chance to regress, let's put it that way.*

Ah yes, he says, laughing. *One of those. I know all about those.* He says he usually has one. The years when they have it at his dad's, his new wife uses her grandmother's grandmother's recipe for dessert. They have a schedule for the day. Walks in the snow and board games. Stepbrothers and sisters.

Do yous go to mass? I say.

What? he says. *Oh, church, right. No.* Anyway, every year the same arguments. His sister will get drunk and say his dad started a new family too soon. I ask how long the dad has been married and he says it must be more than fifteen years now. I nod. I want to ask what age his sister is but I also don't want to push too much. He hasn't said much about his family before and he is talking so animatedly now. His hands are flying around the air.

Do people bring partners? I ask.

He pauses. *Yeah, sure. People do. Kids too.* His drops his hands and coughs. I think about the swimming pool photo. I imagine he's thinking about it too, in a sense. What it represents. I look at his face. What did that pause mean? Did you exchange furtive calls on Christmas Day? Fly to the in-laws together, talking about how annoying your brother was going to be? Roll your eyes across the counter while helping peel vegetables? How long since you had a Christmas alone?

Anyway, he says, breaking my train of thought. *So what I was going to say was, well, if you don't have other plans, if you aren't working. We could do something together. Like, a lunch or something.* I don't answer immediately. I don't know what to say. He goes on to explain that it's expensive to fly back.

There's not much point in going for a few days. Besides, he's barely been here any time at all.

Sure, that makes sense. Great idea, I say. What else to say? I don't have other plans. None are likely to materialise. Spending Christmas together seems like it means something. But does it have to? And alone, both separately alone, seems like it means something too. *I mean, if you don't end up flying back in the end,* I say.

Well, I have basically already decided I won't, so that's great. He laughs. An awkward, nervous laugh. I feel like I've been asked to the prom. But then, I suppose I've just agreed to go. I laugh too.

My hands are pink in the cold. I blow into them. I tell him I need to go, sort some things out. *Sure. Yes,* he says. *Of course.* He has to do the same thing. I crunch over the gravel. When I get out into the street I feel like I'm going to laugh again. I feel hysterical. But I hold it in till the end of the street. I don't know how far the sound will travel. Then I kind of squawk to myself. It's a stupid noise. We're doing Christmas together? Why are we doing Christmas together? What do I normally do?

On the walk back to Anne Marie's I think about my normal Christmases with my mum. What do we actually do? Fight, a lot of the time. In the days around it. And then I might go out the night before, get in too late. She'd sulk about that. But there's nowhere open on the day so we'd sit in the house together, watching TV. Drink wine. She's not a big drinker, but she will on Christmas. We'd have a roast dinner. We might argue while we cook, but it sounds like everyone else does too. Watch one of the end-of-year quizzes. One year a neighbour invited us and the rest of the street for a glass of champagne and salmon on crackers and we went to that, which broke the day up.

By the time I get to Anne Marie's street I am thinking: Is it such a bad day? Or was it? It's no worse than anyone else's from the sound of it. I keep coming back to it as I make the dinner and do the homeworks and at night when I'm lying in bed.

In the morning when I go for my run I am still thinking about it. It's dark when I leave the house. Purple darkness broken, at intervals, by orange streetlights. The cold on my ears as I walk down the drive, before I start running and warm up, makes it feel like they're being pulled away from my head. It's bruising. But I warm up quickly. By the time I can smell the river I don't feel it at all.

As I turn onto the towpath the sky is still purple. I know it will be pink soon and the sun will be up. But in the purple dawn, the smell of grass and water is more potent. The wet tarmac feels slimy and oily. Small shifting shapes just ahead on the path could be leaves, but make me think of rats: webbed feet and long serrated tails. Base fears that thrive in the dark. I try to ignore them. I focus on my memories of Christmas.

Are they so bad? What's so bad about them? That's what I'm thinking about when I turn the corner and my mum's dog comes charging towards me, drenched in muddy water. The shock of it makes me stop running suddenly. My feet confuse themselves and I trip over. When I fall to the path, he jumps on top of me, covering my legs in a wet, freezing layer of dirt. He brings his face close to mine, panting. His breath is hot and rancid.

Down, down! she shouts, running after him. I scramble to get back to my feet. She catches up with us, panting, cheeks slightly pink. I ask her what she's doing here and she gestures at the dog. He growls at nothing, turns to face her and barks, turns towards me and barks, then jumps into the water.

I'm sorry but that's not the real reason, I say, shaking my head. I feel my back teeth grind together.

Oh, is it not? she says. *You tell me what the real reason is then.* She speaks in a clipped, official voice. She turns her head away from me and looks at the river, where the dog's head is speeding through the water towards a plastic bottle. She turns back to me. *It's a nice morning, isn't it? Just checking he wasn't going for a family of ducks.*

A nice morning? I say. *What? It's still dark. It's pitch-black.*

She looks around, as if to say: Well, is it? I hadn't noticed.

You've followed me out here, I say. *Can you tell me why?* She doesn't say anything and looks back out at the river again. What does she want? To have the last word? To attempt a reconciliation? Well then, why not just say that? Why come out here like this and make us interact, unless she's willing to follow through on whatever it is she's doing? I can feel a ball of anger forming, growing, starting to roar. At the weirdness of it, the pointlessness of it.

OK, well, goodbye then, I say. I try to copy her tone; I try to sound official, like I'm in charge. *Enjoy your walk. I'm going to head back now because I'm covered in mud.*

I turn and start to run. I focus on breathing. On my feet. My arms. Trying to shrink the anger, picturing it radiating out of my body. Imagining it turning from red to blue. Counting backwards from ten. Basic emotional management strategies. Cheap tricks. I can hear her shout behind me. I start to turn but decide against it. What good would it do?

This roaring feeling is the thing I can't imagine when I think of old memories. I only feel it in the moment. I run the whole way back to Anne Marie's and I still haven't shaken it; it clings to me. I run past the house and on up the street. I stop at the end and stand there, breathing. I could scream. The footpath is covered with muddy slime; there is a flattened plastic bottle in the gutter. I pick it up and throw it at a car parked across the street. Harder than I intend to, and it sets an alarm off. I panic and start to run again, out to the road. Then I start walking, in case one of the neighbours sees me and it's obvious why I'm running.

22

THE WAY I FIND OUT it's Kate's birthday is from my phone; I don't know what to think about that. I don't even see the notification first thing when I wake up. But instead, while the boys are eating bananas and butter on toast for breakfast, arguing with each other about what a certain teacher's first name is, and I'm standing by the sink without much to do, I check the notifications out of boredom.

I look at the new things people have posted. Photos to show someone's life updates, or that they are having fun, that they have friends they go out with, wear good clothes, go to bars. Photos that are deliberately ugly, to show the same things but trying to say, at the same time, that the person posting doesn't care what you think of them. Photos of books and celebrities. Captions making jokes about song lyrics, about the content of the photo, about the act of posting the photos. Self-consciousness that's supposed to look like self-awareness. In the background the boys are listing which fruits they hate to each other. Arguing over whether grapes are nice or not. They both agree apples are not.

I open the notifications for birthdays. A list appears on my screen with three names and their photo and a cartoon birthday cake with a single candle beside each name. Kate's name isn't even at the top. The top name is Rebecca Johnson, a girl I worked with in a call centre many summers ago and used to eat lunch in the park with but haven't spoken to since. The other is Theodore Martin, a boy from my university halls who played a lot of sports and wore a navy blazer with gold buttons to the sports socials.

My stomach lurches. The taste of salt fills my mouth. The boys are talking about apples and grapes and bananas and strawberries in the background, but it seems to be happening in another room of a different house or in a memory or a dream. I want to grip the counter to steady myself, but I feel like if I put my hands down, it might vanish, or I might stretch them out forever and never reach it.

It's so mundane. There with Theodore Martin. Theodore Martin who hosted beer pong tournaments with his friends who all looked just like him. Theodore Martin who kept telling me and everyone else to call him Teddy instead, and I would say, sure, of course, and then always call him Theodore. And Rebecca Johnson who would buy tuna sandwiches and then sit in the park, peeling out each cucumber slice with great precision before eating them. Horrible that it's so mundane. And if I hadn't checked this, would I have known?

I put my phone down and look around for something to focus on, to bring me back to the room, keep me there. My eyes land on a tea towel with the word for breakfast in five different languages printed again and again and again in rows. **Breakfast. Petit-déjeuner. Desayuno. Frühstück. Prima Colazione.** I whisper the syllables to myself, all wrong probably, but I concentrate on doing it. Again and again until the rest of the room comes back.

The boys are arguing about the characters in a game, about who's the worst enemy. I tell them they have to get their bags, we have to go soon, and they both run upstairs, taking the argument with them. I go to the downstairs bathroom and splash water on my face and gargle mouthwash. I say the breakfasts to myself in the mirror and then splash water again. *Breakfast. Petit-déjeuner. Desayuno. Frühstück. Prima Colazione.* I dry my face off and smile at myself.

More arguments on the way to school. About which girl is the tallest in the school, about who is the smallest, about which of the boys is the best at playing piano. When I drop them off I head towards town. To the big church behind the department store, with the mesh cages over the stained-glass windows and the statue of Jesus painted yellow-gold, the tapestries of baby Jesus with the Virgin Mary and the snake whispering to Judas Iscariot, the glittery mosaic tabernacle and the purple velvet upholstery.

When I get there they've set up a nativity scene in the garden leading up to the door. Well, it is December. There is a cave-like structure with a thatched roof and the outside walls painted to look like stone. Four life-size figurines, which look like they're made of plastic, are clustered around a wooden crib. They're adorned with props to tell you which character from the birth of Christ they are. All wearing tattered robes, their paint covered in chips and scuffs. The faces are blank of any features. I can make out Mary, wearing a dark blue robe and stationed right beside the crib, which is empty. The other three are men. One shepherd in a grey robe, with a toy sheep propped up in the crook of his arm. The other two are wearing gold robes and crowns. Wooden boxes have been arranged at their feet. Wise men? But why only two of them? The third one must have gotten lost over the years. The back of the cave is painted navy with silver stars, to clarify that the scene is at night. Although it's as if the night is happening inside the cave. A sorry scene. I shake my head and walk past it into the building.

The heavy metal door closes behind me and my eyes settle into the darkness. I adjust to the heavy, wooden smell of incense. I dip my right hand in the Holy water and touch my forehead, the centre of my chest, then my left and right shoulder. *The Father. The Son. The Holy Spirit.* The place is empty. I sit in the first pew at the front; I never do that, but today I do. I stretch my legs out and look up at Jesus, pinned to the cross with his arms spread out and his legs neatly folded. Plain, painted wood Jesus on a simple cross. The only plain, simple object in this place. Straining ribs carved into his beige chest, a grey loincloth affixed around the waist, head tilted to one side.

I bow my head. So today is Kate's birthday. Why didn't I remember? I never committed the day to memory. Why would I? I'd know it was happening anyway. It would have come up in conversation, or there would be something planned. I knew it was in December. Too close to Christmas, she hated that. And the cold, and the fact it was often raining meant her birthday night out was always disappointing.

There would be pre-drinks in the flat and people would arrive with pink cheeks and wet hair or, if it wasn't raining, wearing scarves and coats with hoodies under them and carrying ruck-sacks to store all their layers cheaply in the coatroom. Two pounds for a bag or one for each layer; it's a no-brainer.

Our flat was never really warm in the winter. Victorian insulation and single glazing. But people would go out to smoke and leave the back door open, and make it freezing, and I would say close the door after you, or Kate would get up to close it, but it would always be open again soon. Everyone would sit with their coats on, hunched over their drinks. Certain people would text last minute to say they couldn't come. Some people hibernate the whole winter. Then taxis or the bus to whatever night it was. Always a nightmare to organise. Everyone was too drunk to remember their bags and phones which they had borrowed chargers for and left on the floor.

I look up at the cross. Simple, plain. The fingers of his hands curled towards the palms. A black dot in the centre of each palm for the nails. *Going out in the winter is the worst, isn't it, Father?* The face doesn't change. I smile and bow my head.

I remember a night we had last summer. The summer before last. The last summer. An excursion more than a night, really. We took the train to Brighton for a party. A boy Kate had met the summer before had invited her up and she wanted to go but didn't want to go by herself. Well, not a boy really, he was older, but not by a lot. A few years. They met at a festival in Poland. I hadn't been there because I was working and couldn't get it off. His tent with his friends was near her tent with our friends. Or someone had to borrow something from them. Something like that. Either way they all ended up drinking together on the first night and kind of went around as a group after that. She hit it off with this one guy, Stephen. He had a girlfriend who wasn't there but he was flirting anyway.

They slept together, but only once, during the day when everyone else was seeing a certain set. One of those sets everyone spends the whole festival talking about how you can't miss. I remember when Kate told me she said it was kind of a secret, she didn't think anyone else knew. *Don't mention it to the others who were there*, she said. *I think some of them still chat to his friends.*

I bet they all knew, I said, laughing. *Of course they did.* She maintained they didn't. But I smile remembering it now. Of course they did. They'd all have known.

She kept chatting to him online after. I would hear dispatches about Stephen, and then his name changed to Steve. *Is that secret boyfriend Steve, do you mean?* I would say. She would shake her head and laugh. *Shut up*, she would say. I didn't see what the fuss was about from the pictures I was shown of him but some people do have an energy. I assumed he was one of those. Then he broke up with his girlfriend and they were talking more and more and he invited her to his friend's party in Brighton, where he lived.

I remember we were sitting in our grotty living room when she told me the girlfriend was out of the picture. It was almost a year after they had met. *But you know they did live together, they were sharing a room*, she said. *I think that's the reason it took so long.* Trying to explain it to herself more than me. I said I thought she was probably right. That's what she needed me to say so I said it. Sometimes when your friend is being stupid you just have to go along with it.

On the day of the party we took the train to Brighton in the afternoon, to make a day of it. It was a warm day, even for the south of England. Temperature was in the early thirties. I remember the felt seat of the train was warm and scratchy on the back of my legs from the minute we sat down. I was wearing a short dress over a white t-shirt and she had a skirt on. Maybe her plaid one? We definitely both wore white socks and trainers. I can't remember which of us started that look but we both wore it all that summer. And we'd both been on the sun beds so we had tans that matched the weather. We had four cans of gin and tonic each for the journey. We'd brought tights and jumpers for the evening, in case it got cold. It was going to be a beautiful day.

Brighton was like a dream place. I'd never been before and I've never been back. The brightness of the sun made long strips of white light stretch along the surface of the sea, and made it glitter. There was a children's birthday smell of candy floss and popcorn. We got in around three; sat on the beach, drinking more. It was so warm people were even in swimming. We got scampi and chips. Drank bottled water to sober up between more gin and tonics and talked. We discussed what time we should go to the party. What it would be like. We'd already decided it would be very cool before coming, but we furnished the details. There would be an arty crowd. They were older so there wouldn't be hundreds of people; it wouldn't be like a student party, but at least fifty. They'd have interesting jobs. Sophisticated wouldn't quite be the right word for it. That word was deemed to be too fusty, but it would almost be that.

The thing was meant to start at seven but we decided you wouldn't go for then. Kate sent Steve a message that said something like *I'll be there in a bit* when he asked what time she'd be down. We thought that was aloof but not outright cold. We decided we'd leave the beach at eight, probably find the house around half past. But Kate put the wrong address into her phone, and then we had to stop for the bathroom in a pub with carpet and slot machines because she didn't want to get there and immediately need to use the toilet. I smile at that memory. Fair enough, it would have been mortifying.

That whole detour meant it was after nine when we got there, which meant it wasn't really early enough for that to be the excuse for how bad the party was when we arrived. Was it even a party? There were no more than twenty people. Slightly more boys than girls. The clothes were terrible. I remember one boy was wearing a black trilby with silver pinstripes. Tinny music played from a tiny speaker propped up on a coffee table where there were also packets of crisps, party rings on a plastic plate and fizzy drinks.

And Steve. My god. He looked worse in real life. His proportions were . . . odd. A long body or short legs. He wore a knee-length long-sleeved top. It was beige; I'd never seen anything like it. It looked like a medieval tabard. I remember a wooden charm on a necklace too. They greeted each other and I went to the drinks table to pour myself a lemonade. I looked back to check her facial expression as they hugged. Yes, it was horror.

I didn't know why she'd liked the idea of him so much if he was this bad. If it was one of those ones where you talk to someone for so long without seeing them that they become something different in your head. If she'd just been out of her mind basically the whole time when they'd met, at that festival. But I knew we had to go. We couldn't even stay an hour for politeness.

I said hello to him and he hugged me. He smelt musky, like unwashed hair. I told them both I had to use the bathroom and he showed me. I locked myself in for a while. I timed it for ten minutes, fixing my makeup and playing with my phone. When I came back out I announced I had food poisoning. *Oh my god,* said Kate. *We have to get back home.* Steve flapped about. I pretended to wince in pain. We both hurried out of the house, clattering down the steps.

We ran down the street and collapsed into laughter at the end of it. She said he didn't look the same as in photos. He basically did, but I said he looked totally different. *You're right,* I said. She looked at me and said, *No, he looked bad in photos too, didn't he?*

I said yes and burst out laughing. So did she. We ran back to the beach, got some beers in the shop over the road and sat on the pebbles talking about how silly we'd been. The sun had set and the promenade was lit up. It looked like something out of a film. It was like that was what we'd come to see the whole time, from the start.

Where were we going to sleep? I remember asking her at one point. We hadn't discussed it, probably expecting a solution both cool and glamorous to present itself.

Literally where? she said, laughing. *Oh god, his necklace.* His necklace was the worst. The embarrassment of it all. But it was shared, the embarrassment. And that made it seem not embarrassing. It just seemed funny. Already it seemed like a good story.

I can remember her face on the beach, glowing orange in the light from the promenade, like I am there right now. Little nose, round cheeks. Big dark eyes and long dark eyelashes.

I didn't forget about your birthday. I didn't forget about you. I've been busy. That's not an excuse, but it's life. I think I have to get a new job soon and move, but maybe you know about that already. And I've been seeing two boys, sort of. Mikey again. I know, bad idea. I smile, thinking about her rolling her eyes.

I never told you, but you were so easy to be around. You probably knew I thought that. You knew I could be prickly. You were good at making fun of that. You made everything fun. And another thing, I don't seem to have any girl friends any more. When did that happen? I met two recently who seem cool and maybe we'll end up being friends, maybe you know about that too. And my mum is stalking me. I think we need to finally have it out. You always said therapy, but good luck with that.

You took a lot of things with you when you left, you know. It's harder to have fun. I don't know what I want any more.

I let myself cry in the pew, really howl, until my body is exhausted from it.

I felt like I knew the way I wanted my life to go, and then with what happened to you, I saw the world a different way and now I don't know any more. I want to make the most of everything but I don't know what that means. I want time to be sad. I miss you.

I want to remember you like that day at the beach. Like the way you were, not anniversaries or birthdays or a tragic event. We were so young. Well, happy birthday.

I sit in the silence for a while with my head bowed. I don't know how long. Then I look up at Jesus on the cross. The loincloth reminds me of Brighton Steve's medieval top; it's the same kind of garment, the same early civilisation vibe. I smile and shake my head. *Brighton Steve. What were you thinking?*

Will you pass that on to her for me, Father, if you're speaking? Jesus's face remains the same. I nod at it and slide to the end of the bench. I light a candle on my way out. Happy birthday.

23

I SEE MIKEY THE EVENING AFTER for a drink. Mulled wine that's too sweet and not alcoholic enough, in the pub near the hospital he works in. The barman is wearing a Santa hat with clumps of the white fur trim missing. He ladles drinks out of a vat and adds an orange peel to each one with a flourish. The place is full of teenagers, all but wearing their school uniforms. One of those places that doesn't card anyone and then gets known for it and becomes a haunt for everyone from a certain school. A crowd of girls stand, doing their best to look like eighteen-year-olds in full faces of makeup, just beside the booth where we sit down. I keep glancing up at them. The full face of makeup is actually the easiest mistake for an underage girl to make. Most eighteen-, nineteen-year-olds simply wouldn't wear smoky eyeshadow to a casual bar in the early evening.

So, here, Mikey says. I look away from the girls and back to him. *It was Kate's birthday yesterday?*

Oh yes, I say, surprising myself with the calm in my voice, the way nothing comes to the surface. I didn't expect him to bring it up, and I wouldn't have expected myself to remain composed if I had expected it. I would have thought that memory from yesterday would fill the room again, and then my howling. And then what? How would he react? Is there an instinct which stops any of that from surfacing because I still don't know what the answer to that question is? *Yes, it was. How did you remember?* I ask.

He squeezes the soft skin on the inside of my elbow and runs his finger down the inside of my arm until he reaches my wrist. He got a notification about it, he says. I tell him me too.

Well. Right, he says. He goes to hold my hand but I don't anticipate it so my fingers are curled into a fist and he ends up clasping his hand around the outside of that. Our hands fumble around until they are holding each other. *Did you do anything for it?*

Went and lit a candle. Just to mark the day, I say.

He nods. *Yes.*

I mean, I don't know what you're supposed to do, I say. *What a person is supposed to do.*

Right. Yes. No. That sounds like the right thing to do. To have done, he says. There is the feeling of him scrambling to say something appropriate and tactful. Maybe not. I smile at him.

I mean, there's no rules, I say.

Of course. Yes. Exactly, he says. *Well, and how do you feel about it?*

It's hard to explain, I say. *I'm getting there.*

OK. Yes, he says. *Right.* He nods; there is a stern, serious look on his face. It's alien; he never has an expression like this. I don't think we can talk about it any more. I ask him what age he thinks the girls behind are. *Don't make it obvious you're looking,* I say. He pretends to look at the drinks menu behind the bar. *I dunno,* he says, *like nineteen or twenty.* He shakes his hand in mid-air. *About that anyway?* I laugh and shake my head.

We don't talk about the birthday again for the rest of that evening. I drink five pints, and he does me the courtesy of keeping pace almost exactly. He pretends not to notice when I pour my fourth down my chin while trying to talk and drink at the same time. I wipe it with my sleeve.

Later that night, in his room, I am drunk enough to say thank you, as I'm stumbling around, trying to get my shoes off standing up.

Thank you, Mikey. I mumble it, as if to allow myself to have said it without him having heard it.

Thanks for what? he says. He is sitting on the edge of the bed.

My shoes are finally off. *Don't make me say any more*, I say. I meet his eyes and force a smile.

I didn't mean it like that, he says. *I meant more, it's nothing. Well, you're welcome, anyway.*

Right, I say, squeezing my eyes shut. *Well, thank you.*

Come here? he says.

He stands up and we hug. With my face buried in his chest I feel a current of emotion wash through me. I let myself sit there, in that, for a few seconds. And then I start kissing him.

I can't tell if he's hard or not. I stroke his neck; that always turns him on.

When I start to undo the button of his jeans he doesn't protest, which means he will be hard. I pull his jeans and boxers down and I kneel and run my tongue over his dick before putting it in my mouth. I really, really don't want to cry; I need to not cry; I need action. He doesn't say anything but he strokes my hair. He starts to groan, lets me continue for a few minutes and then takes my hand and pulls me back to my feet.

He sits back on the bed. *Sit on my knee*, he whispers. We fuck like that, facing each other. My legs are spread out behind him, and my arms are wrapped around his back. He holds onto the bedframe to support himself. He doesn't say anything, and neither do I, except *Jesus*, when I cum. *Fuck*, he says, a little later.

The minute we lie down I know this is something we'll never speak of ever again.

It's the next afternoon, as I am standing in Anne Marie's laundry room, folding the dry washing and organising it into different piles for each member of the household, that I am thinking about why that is and what it means.

I try to picture myself, crying like I was in the church, but with Mikey. I can't decide if it would feel invasive or reassuring. And what does it mean to expose yourself like that to someone? Would that mean we knew each other any better? Maybe we have our own way of doing that anyway, being vulnerable.

There is a knock on the laundry-room door. *Yes, come in*, I shout. Anne Marie appears, smiling widely. In a chipper voice she says we should have a cup of tea and a catch-up when I'm finished. *A biscuit and a bit of a gossip, eh*, she says.

She bounces out of the room and then off down the stairs. I hear her singing the words of one pop song to the tune of another. Dread washes over me. I'm going to be sacked, or as sacked as I can be. Gently let go. I have no new job yet. I haven't found anywhere to live. I'll be in my overdraft again when I pay the deposit for rent. If I even find a place. God. I open the cupboard beside the washing machine and stuff all the clothes I haven't folded onto the top shelf. I slam the door behind them and follow her down to the kitchen. No point prolonging it.

She is sitting at the kitchen table. There are biscuits arranged on a plate in a circle, and a teapot. As if she's her own HR department. When did we even get a teapot? She gestures to the seat opposite her. I sit down. She asks questions about my Christmas plans, who I'm going to have round to the house on the day. I lie, and say some friends, Declan and some other people. *And what a fabulous idea to have them here*, she says. *And this weekend? What have you on?*

I can't tell where the conversation is going. If it is still small talk or if I'm being sacked yet. My stomach is alive with panic. I say not much. The usual.

Well, so I was going to ask if you would mind — and you can definitely say no — but if you would mind staying in this Friday to babysit?

Sure, I say. *No problem*. As if I'd say no. *Where are you off to? Anywhere nice?*

Again she smiles widely, very widely. So widely that her mouth seems drawn out beyond the boundaries of her face. The boundaries of the whole room. She and Gerard have been talking about getting back together for a little while, she tells me.

Oh wow, I say. I try to look surprised but pleased. A big smile from me.

But, you know. I'm not about to rush into anything, oh no. We're going to continue living separately for a while, and go on dates. We need to get to know each other again.

Not going to rush into anything. I feel the tightness in me loosen. *You're being very sensible about it*, I say. I don't want to sound too pleased, or too much of anything, but there is a touch of hysteria in my voice.

She says that's good to hear, good to get my perspective on it. *I worry anyone would think getting back together with a man who had an affair is a terrible idea*, she says; she whispers the word affair. *And when the divorce hasn't even gone through!* She whispers the word divorce and then laughs a very fake laugh.

She jerks the plate with its circle of biscuits towards me. *A Hobnob?*

My stomach is still dancing, with relief and residual panic. Adrenaline. I can't eat but I take one anyway and set it down beside my mug. A gesture of intent.

I tell her I'm flattered she values my perspective. It's true; if she really does, I am. She says I'm a sensible girl.

But you don't think it's a terrible idea? she says, laughing the fake laugh again. *You know it's always useful to get the opinion of someone who hasn't a dog in the fight.* She explains that her sister has been a great help during this, but that does colour her views on things. She trails off. I'm guessing to avoid addressing the sister's disapproval directly. I know what I'm supposed to say.

Well, I wouldn't say I have no dog, I say. *You've been very good to me the whole time I've known you, ever since you first got me in housesitting and babysitting.* I smile. *But you're right. I don't know Gerard well.* I tell her I think it is only a bad idea if she is unprepared for the prospect of the same thing happening again. She says that's a good way of looking at it.

You're right, he definitely won't do it again, she says. *He's seen how it all plays out, hasn't he?* Not exactly what I meant, but I don't think I need to point that out. She knows that's not what I said, probably. If she wanted real advice, she wouldn't ask me.

Yes, I say. I say something about last straws.

Absolutely, she says. *And with the boys and everything, I have to think of what makes their lives easiest as well.*

I agree that it would be less disruptive for them, and that I'm sure they would appreciate the stability. I decide I might as well put in an argument for my own position too, if we're having the conversation anyway. *I think these dates are a good idea for a while too*, I say. *To sketch out your terms, you know.*

I break my biscuit in half and then break one half in half again. She says thank you for the conversation. *It's good to get a picture of how things look from the outside, you know*, she says. A picture from the outside. That isn't what she wanted, but then I don't think I'd ever want that either. Who would want to know how their life genuinely looks to someone else? I would only ever want a sympathetic observer.

I think of her saying I'm a sensible girl. Does she think that or did she feel she had to say that?

We talk about the street after that. One family has a new dog called Fidor. *Very formal name, don't you think?* she says. There's a house on the next street over up for sale. She might go to the open day to look around. I tell her I noticed that; I ran past it. I eat my biscuit eventually and when she has to go for an appointment she gives me the rest of the day off for Christmas shopping.

My position is secure for now. Maybe not long, but I have time. I feel like I should celebrate. It's the afternoon, but I could have a drink. Why not? I call Declan and he has to do Christmas shopping. *I don't know what to get for my mum*, he says. *Whatever I get her, she'll hate it. It's doing my head in.*

But he says if I want to come around town with him we can get a drink after. We can meet at the Christmas markets at the City Hall in an hour.

I put my long black winter coat and scarf on and head into town. It's a sharp winter day, the sun low in the sky, and dry. I arrange the scarf to cover the bottom of my face, to keep the cold off my cheeks. I walk fast and I'm ten minutes early to the City Hall. Declan is always late so he might well not be here for another twenty or thirty minutes. I stand by the black-painted iron gate at the entrance to the grassy area where the market is set up, tapping around on my phone. Photos of friends. Photos of people I barely know. Internet jokes.

I don't realise how absorbed I am until I feel a hand on my shoulder. I look up. *All right, good to see you.* It's not Declan but Matt. Not American Matt but Matt Matt. He is wearing a Santa hat and a red apron with sticky black markings to make it look like a Santa suit. A black band at his waist and black buttons. A white matted beard hangs around his neck on a grubby stretch of elastic.

It's good to see you too, I say. I decide to get the obvious things out of the way first and ask him why he's wearing a costume.

Oh, this? He looks down at himself and laughs, as if he hadn't realised he was wearing it until I pointed it out. *It's actually my uniform.* He is working at the stall that sells hotdogs and mulled wine. *It's good craic actually, easy work. In an ideal world I wouldn't wear the suit, but,* he says.

I laugh. *You can't have everything.* He smiles. I tell him I'm waiting for Declan. He says he's on his break till half past so he can keep me company while I wait. He catches me up on himself. He's doing well. He has paused whatever course it is, this time for a year. His dad agreed to that as long as he goes back. His Santa beard swings from side to side in the wind as he talks.

Although I might just save up and go travelling, you know, he says. *What will your dad say about that?* I laugh.

You know, I might not tell them until I leave. Sure, what can my da really do if I'm sat on a beach somewhere? he says, scratching his neck below the beard. This makes me burst out laughing. Their dad's face when he finds out. Matt lying on a beach towel, rejecting call after call. *They'll have got over it by the time I get back as well, like*, he says, with marked uncertainty.

My phone rings and it's Declan. He gives me an earful because he's been waiting for half an hour at the other gate, around the side of the City Hall. Matt has to go back to work but says to bring Declan to his stall and he'll give us free wine. Declan and I argue about which gate is the front as we walk around stalls selling jewellery made out of wooden beads, stretches of fabric that aren't quite rugs but also aren't blankets, and misshapen handmade candles. There's a barbecue smell in the air from the food stalls.

God, it's all shite, isn't it? Declan says as he picks up a set of wind chimes with the wooden base painted in zebra print. *And thirty-five quid.* He sets them back down on the table beside handheld mirrors with painted frames and necklaces bearing first names. The woman behind the stall pretends to busy herself straightening chimes on the adjoining table.

I mean, I did say it would be like this, I say. *It's like this every year.*

It's not this bad, he says. *This is depressing. Well, sure, let's just get a drink and some food.*

There's a queue at Matt's stall and only two people working but he brings us mulled wine in paper cups anyway. He says if we wait half an hour until his shift ends he can sort us with food then. We sit at the German beer hall benches, set up over a strip of fake grass and under a marquee, with our wines.

So give us the update on the un-divorce then? says Declan. I tell him there isn't much more to it. It's moving, but slowly. I need a new place to live for sure. But not immediately. *So we're drinking to that*, I say.

Well, here, we have something else to celebrate too, he says. One of his paintings has won one of the competitions, which means money and that it will be displayed in a gallery in London.

Well, we'll have to go over and see it, I say. *That's such brilliant news, man.*

He smiles and nods. *If we can find it. I'll bet they're showing hundreds in the same room. It'll be in the hall in the bottom right corner, or wherever, won't it?* He laughs, looking away, embarrassed at the idea he's being seen to show off.

Don't do that, I say. *It's brilliant news.*

He shows me a picture of it on his phone. I've never seen it before; he's cagey about showing me or anyone else anything that's not finished. It's his usual style. Bold, dark colours. Brush strokes that look vivid and energetic at first, but incredibly precise on closer inspection. You can see it in the way he captures shadow and light, with tiny strokes of white. It's always scenes of people communicating or interacting, at a table with food, in a bar, walking, rendered from a perspective a little distance away, so the scene appears as a whole, and at a slight remove. Like you're watching them from the outside.

This one is a man at the end of a bar, during the day. The taps are blurs of yellow. There's no barman in sight. I know better than to ask if it's a customer of Declan's. I can tell it's a different bar. And anyway, it's rude to impose him on to his work like that, as if he's so straightforward.

Matt brings us hotdogs when he's finished. He suggests going for a pint in the Cathedral Quarter. He has taken off his hat and apron. He must have changed clothes too, because he doesn't even smell like fried food. We get pints of Guinness in a bar full of Christmas decorations. Stuffed to the rafters with them, really. Mini Santas and tinsel and plastic mistletoe. Matt drinks two pints before Declan and I have finished our first.

He downs his glass and then, a few seconds later, picks up the empty glass, goes to finish his drink and realises it's empty. *Another round?* he says, waving his empty glass at us. Declan offers to get them but Matt insists. Again, he drinks his pint at twice the speed of us. He swaps to diet coke when I get the next round, which he tops up from a hip flask. Declan and I alternate rounds from then on because the diet cokes are so cheap, despite Matt's protests. I taste a sip at one point when he goes to the bathroom and my body has a convulsive, retching reaction. The same as if I'd smelt chemical cleaner.

Look at the state of your face! Declan laughs. *Is it stinkin'? How strong is it?* He smells it himself and recoils. *Christ, that's not even rum. It's fucking whiskey.*

I sort of can't help but be impressed by how coherent Matt remains, and for how long. Troubling, yes, but undeniably impressive. He tells us all the stories he has gathered from the people working in the surrounding stalls. About his potential travelling plans. Everything. I get pint glasses of water for everyone at one point. Declan and I take cursory sips but Matt just glances at the glass.

Then he is saying a friend of his is having some people round tonight. If we don't have anything on tomorrow, we should come, we could all get some coke in. Declan doesn't have anything tomorrow. I have the school run, but I can go back to bed after. Why not? Matt starts texting numbers for coke.

I go to check my phone and it's gone. We look around the table, the floor under the table and all the coat pockets but it doesn't turn up. While we are looking, Matt reaches across the table, knocks over a glass of water and then stands up quickly to try and sort it out and knocks over his chair, sending it clattering to the floor. He doesn't seem to notice and goes to sit back down on the toppled chair, falling back on top of it. *When did that happen?* He laughs, looking around at the floor. I exchange a look with Declan. I don't know when it happened but Matt is too drunk. I go to the bar to look for my phone while Declan helps him off the floor. Matt pretends to start breakdancing when Declan bends down.

The barman knows what I've come for the minute he sees me; he has my purse too. He gleefully informs me that I emptied my pockets on to the counter and then walked off with my drinks. *I thought you'd be needing these*, he says, waving the bag in the air, thrilled at the chance to tell me off. I check the time and it's around eight. Too early for us all to be in this state.

At the table Matt is back on his chair. I say I feel too drunk to stay out. Declan agrees. Matt says he feels fine and he doesn't mind going to his friend's by himself. Declan shakes his head behind him and mouths no. It doesn't seem right to just leave him to go off and do his night; he's already a state.

We talk him into going back home under the pretext of food and he agrees. Declan is going the other way. Matt and I share a taxi. He lolls about the back seat, singing one or two lines of songs and occasionally saying random sentences to himself. *See, this is the fucking problem. Nobody can fucking chill out. Mikey doesn't know what he's talking about. What will we do with you? What will we do with you!* At one point the driver turns around to ask me if he's going to be sick and I say no. He says there's a fine if he is sick and I say thank you for letting me know.

I get out at Mikey's house, well, Mikey and Matt's house, with him. I think, for a second, as we approach the door, about texting to see if Mikey is in and dismiss it. If he's there, he's there. It seems like the right thing to do. Matt tries his key three times, drawing his face up to the door to peer at the lock when he can't get the key to go into it. He gives up and gives it to me and I let us in.

In the kitchen he pours us both a drink. There's no sign of Mikey; all the lights upstairs seem to be off. *Are you even hungry?* he says. *I'm not sure I am.* He isn't ready to let the night go. The possibility of it glows before him. The infinite possibility. I know that feeling. I tell him I need a drink of water before I drink anything else. We should both have one. I pour glasses of water and we go through to the living room. He forgets the drinks so he does drink the water. He tries to turn the TV on and the remote doesn't work. He puts an old Beats In Space mix on, on his phone – I haven't heard it before but I recognise the opening theme music – and sets it on the mantelpiece. Then he lies back on the sofa with his trainers up on one of the arms and hums along, totally out of tune, while drinking his water. After a while he starts to snore. I get a blanket for him before I leave.

24

Technically rory and calum still both believe in Santa. I doubt they truly do, and I doubt Anne Marie believes they do, but they haven't said they don't so we all carry on as if they do. They make extravagant wish lists of presents, and the practicalities of arranging their gifts have to be conducted in secret.

I am wrapping their presents and the presents for their cousins while they are at school. Two different types of paper, one for the boys' presents and another for the cousins'; the inference being that Santa used one and Anne Marie the other. Everything was ordered to Gerard's apartment; he drove them over for me to wrap and later he will collect the boys' but not the cousins'. That way there is no chance of the boys finding their own presents hidden around the house before. Then, in the morning before they drive down to Dublin, Anne Marie will go to Gerard's to pick the presents up and store them in the car boot.

I nodded along when Anne Marie explained it all out to me. *Does that all make sense? You look confused*, she said. I realised I was squinting. *Perfect sense*, I said. *I'm just concentrating.*

In between wrapping a designer hoody and a wooden puzzle

I check my phone. There is an email from the recruitment company for the call centre job, or chat bot operative, or customer service executive, or whatever it's calling itself. The response to my personality test.

The personality test which was what felt like hundreds of multiple choice questions about how to handle certain situations in an office environment. You got twenty seconds for each question, and if you didn't answer in the twenty seconds, it would automatically go to the next one, and you'd get zero. Sometimes you could tell what you were supposed to say, sometimes every option seemed like the wrong answer and sometimes you didn't really even know what it was asking. Half an hour of that, so by the end you were barely reading the question.

I click into my emails. I can see the word regret in the first line. Oh god. Oh no. I didn't even want the stupid job. Jesus. I resist the overwhelming urge to throw my phone: at the floor, at the wall. *Don't make a bad thing worse*, I whisper. *Don't make a bad thing worse.*

I sit down on the floor and remind myself of all the reasons why this is not that bad. *There are other jobs*, I say, out loud, as if to convince myself I believe it. *You'll get one soon. You don't need something right away anyway, just soon. You didn't even want it anyway, remember that. Isn't that worse though? Maybe it is. You'll get something. Something will come up. You'll get something. You have skills. There are jobs.*

Breathe in. Breathe out. I open the email to read it properly.

Hello Erin,

We regret to inform you that you have not been selected for the position of

Executive Chat Bot. Due to the large volume of applications we are unable to tell you why your application was unsuccessful, although we can inform you that your application did not progress beyond the Personality Suitability Assessment stage.

However, we do have another opportunity which we think may be suitable for your qualifications. We have a vacancy for a Data Inspection Agent. This shares some of the same responsibilities as the role which you applied for, but without the customer-facing component. If this is of interest, please reply YES to this email and we will send further information.

Regards.

Ha, I say out loud. Not all bad news. Maybe not even necessarily bad news at all. I laugh with relief. I imagine the woman from the coffee chain I applied to, ages ago, saying that there was a wee problem with my wee personality and that really makes me laugh. I reply with the YES and carry on with the present wrapping, humming tunelessly while I work.

They send through the information in response a little while later. The company is changing a system they use to store customer data. Upgrading, streamlining, reorganising. The data they have stored can't be moved over to the new system automatically so they are hiring workers on a temporary basis to manually transfer it. Endless copying and pasting. Fine. As well as the manual transfer, we will check each other's work, to minimise errors. Endless copying and pasting beside rows of things that have been copied and pasted and then comparing the different rows. Fine. They will send me a new test in the coming days.

This one tests attention to detail and problem-solving skills. Fine. Great. Wonderful. Perfect.

They email the test the next day. No video, thank god. More multiple choice questions. This time patterns and puzzles. Choose the next shape in the sequence. What is $4 + 7 \times 8 \div 2$? How many manholes would you guess there are in Manchester? The email response comes the day after. My score was eighty-four out of ninety. High enough for me to have obtained one of the positions. I can start at the end of January. We'll have a call to discuss the details. Wow. Great. All sorted then. Perfect. I have a new job!

Christmas is in full swing by now. There are wreaths on doors and Christmas trees in living-room windows. Trees with multi-coloured lights and trees with white lights and trees with red lights. Certain houses maintain their tradition of covering the entire front of their building and garden with ornaments that light up: plastic sleighs and elves and reindeers. And everyone takes pictures when they drive past and speculates about the electricity bill. In Botanic Gardens there is a grotto, and affiliated men dressed as elves stand smoking at the entrance, constantly, because technically the park is their place of work so licensing laws say they aren't allowed to smoke inside.

The Loyalist shop on the way into town displays tree ornaments which say **Snow Surrender** and **Ulster Says Snow** in its window. Christmas songs play, but particularly Fairytale of New York by The Pogues plays, in every shop and bar and pub, everywhere, all the time. If people are drunk enough, they'll sing along about it being Christmas Eve in the drunk tank and rivers of gold and Broadway and the boys of the NYPD choir singing Galway Bay. Everyone knows all the words but none of us sound like Kirsty MacColl.

There are Christmas drinks with people from school, those who left as well as those who stayed. Reunions of people who famously hate each other but pretend not to, competitively buying rounds and returning from lines of coke in the toilets to boast about their courses or careers or partners. Reunions of people who always secretly liked each other, each hoping the other will finally say something. Reunions of friends who have gone in different directions, forced to confront the distance between their old and new lives. There aren't enough pubs for anyone to avoid old ghosts.

I debate whether to get Mikey a present. Are we doing that? Is that a thing we would do? Is it worse to get him one and then he doesn't get me one, or the other way around?

Anne Marie is easy. She announces that she doesn't need anything multiple times, so I buy a bottle of nice wine. I buy each of the boys a C.S. Lewis book, for her benefit too. I choose a pair which follow each other in the series so theoretically they could share and read both.

In the end I buy Mikey a black scarf. Useful. Unisex. I can give it to him or I can keep it. Or give it to someone else if I don't want to keep it. While I'm queuing to pay I decide to buy one for Declan too. Buying two seems more casual than buying one. Just getting scarves for everyone. Mikey messages to meet for a drink on the twenty-third. *A Christmas whiskey or something?* he says. *Before the cousins and aunts and uncles arrive and I'm locked up*. His is another family which does the extended family Christmas.

I agree to meet for the drink. The Christmas whiskey. Then I have to decide whether to bring the scarf and, if so, whether to wrap it. If I don't wrap it, I can easily pretend it's not a present if he doesn't have one. I can just wrap it around my own neck. But then, will it look like a present at all if it's not wrapped and he has brought a wrapped one? I toss a coin. Heads for don't bring it. Tails for bring it. I get heads but decide to wrap it and bring it anyway. I wrap Declan's too.

It's too bulky to hide in a bag so I carry it under my arm to the pub. He's sitting there already when I arrive, at a circular table just to the right of the door, with a pair of drinks on the table in front of him. He smiles and waves when I turn around and see him.

It's obvious he'll have seen the present already so I can't hide it. I can't see any packages on the table. I can't tell from his face what he thinks of mine. I don't have enough time to decide what to do about it, whether to pretend I'm intending to give it to someone else later, or what. Well, I'll just have to give it to him. I smile back, as widely as I can.

Right. Good to see you, he says as I sit down. *Happy Christmas then*. He raises his glass.

I set the package on the table immediately. Just to get it out of the way. *I got you this. Just a small thing*, I say, forcing nonchalance. *I was in the shop anyway.*

He smiles. He has something too. He takes a small rectangle wrapped in gold paper out of his pocket. We open at the same time. Mine is a leather notebook. Well made. Useful. Unisex. We say the same kind of thank you, polite and relieved.

237

We talk about Christmas Day over the whiskeys. His mum will have a fit about the number of people she's cooking for. They'll go to mass and do presents after. He asks if I'm going to see my mum and I tell him maybe, I might just watch TV and enjoy my day off.

25

CHRISTMAS DAY ITSELF IS AWKWARD from the start. What did I expect? American Matt stayed over at Anne Marie's on Christmas Eve, which he has never done before. When I wake up and he is lying there in the bed beside me, this bed which he has never slept in until now, enmeshed, suddenly, in this new area of my life, it feels surreal.

Today crept up on me; I don't think I really believed it would happen. I didn't tell anyone except Declan about it, and he only made fun of it once, and didn't mention it again. Maybe he sensed that the arrangement was the sort of thing that had the potential to quickly become depressing, rather than funny, if talked about too much. Maybe he didn't want to seem to high-light my lack of other options.

Even with the American I barely spoke about it. One evening he mentioned his dad was sending wine, and then qualified it by saying it was a Christmas present. *You know, for Christmas Day*, he said, looking down.

Oh yes! I said. *Well, isn't that thoughtful?*

The actual logistics of the day we arranged by message last week. He would stay the night before; getting a taxi with the wine on Christmas Day itself would be too difficult; it was a box and so awkward to carry.

Even then I still wasn't totally convinced of the impending reality of the day. It seemed like something might intervene and put a stop to it, right up until he pulled up at Anne Marie's house in his taxi. He stood in the drive waving, wearing a knitted Christmas jumper with pom-poms sewn on as Christmas decorations, and holding the box of wine, with two bags at his feet, as the taxi reversed out of the drive. He was smiling widely; he seemed too pleased.

I sit up and turn to face him. His eyelashes pulse but his eyes don't open. His mouth is slightly open but not enough to show his white teeth. However long this has gone on now, between us, he still looks like a one-night stand. Like someone I don't know any better than whatever we told each other last night to end up here this morning. I watch his face. His mouth opens slightly and closes again. His breath catches and he splutters, but doesn't wake.

I get up and go to the bathroom in the hall, taking my phone with me. I leave the tap running after I wash my hands and sit on the white wicker chair facing the sink, reading my messages to Kate from this day last year. I've always wondered what the point of this chair is, why it's in the bathroom. I thought it was decorative, but now I wonder how many situations like this it has served.

My messages to Kate are about me and my mum bickering over dinner. About her wanting to make frozen roast potatoes from Iceland, saying she likes them better, and me wanting to make them from raw potatoes, saying that's the proper way to make them. An argument we have every year, that we arguably prepare to have by buying both types of potato in advance.

A message from me just after 3 p.m. *I'm drunk already.* Then from her a description of a cocktail an aunt had made for everyone in batches in a blender. Kate was another person with a huge extended family, despite being English. In Belfast that tends to mean mums and dads with seven brothers and sisters, all with four children themselves, but for her it meant divorced aunts and uncles with second families. It has to be said that English families broadly seem less insane. But maybe that's just because I haven't seen many up close.

More messages from Kate, about how she was surrounded by bratty cousins. Cousins who got brand new phones for Christmas even though the ones they had were barely six months old, who kept talking about how they wanted to be fashion designers or social media personalities when they grew up, who called their parents by their first names. No Belfast cousin would dare. From the sound of it these cousins would make Rory and Calum look like angels.

I smile at the messages about the cousins. In other messages I say what film I'm watching and she talks about their meal, dessert, sandwiches in the evening. Normal messages. My last message from that day is one I don't remember sending. *Goodnight my dear, and I can't wait to see you at New Year.* I close the messages and open the picture she had chosen for this platform. One of us together at a party, with our arms around each other's waists. I've seen it countless times, but the easy intimacy of it is still disarming.

Happy Christmas, I say, to the photo. *I miss you. I am about to have the strangest Christmas, I can tell. Wish me luck. I miss you.*

I put my phone down on the floor and breathe in and out. What a difference a year can make. I splash my face with water and go back into the bedroom. The American is awake. Sitting up in the bed, propped up against two pillows. A position that emphasises the slight softness of his upper body. The incongruous softness. The sign that he drinks more than he used to. Plays less tennis, or whatever it was he played.

Good morning, he says. *Merry Christmas.* He is smiling. His white teeth are showing. He is smiling so much it looks as if every single one of them is showing. I try to imagine how I will remember this day next year, the year after, ten years from now. Tell myself it will make a good story sometime.

OK, he says. He bounces up and down in the bed as he talks. *So I know we said we wouldn't do gifts, but I did get you a small thing.* He produces a square package, wrapped neatly in dark red paper. So much about it baffles me. Where was it hidden? How is it so neatly wrapped?

Right. Wow. Thank you so much, I say. *You know, I actually got you a small thing too.*

He laughs. His eyebrows turn down at the side. Bashful almost. *You didn't have to,* he says. *Open this first.*

There is no way to tell if he is finding today as strange as I am. As totally surreal and bizarre as I am. If he is, he is doing an excellent job of hiding it. Maybe too good a job. His cheerfulness seems fake, or at least as if it can't possibly be real. But then, it does always seem slightly fake. Nobody is really like this.

I sit on the bed to open the package, unpeeling the corners without ripping the paper. It is a notebook with my initials on the front of it. I smile down at it and flick through the pages, feeling their thickness between my fingers. Why does everybody seem to think I need a notebook? *This is brilliant, thank you,* I say. I turn it over in my hands. I know the initials are meant to be the thing that makes it seem personal but they don't, really. Even someone who has never met me would know my name.

I get Declan's scarf out of the wardrobe. Mercifully there is no tag or card to tear off. I hand the package over to him and when he unwraps it he also says brilliant. *Very warm*, he says, rubbing the fabric between a finger and thumb.

Breakfast is prosecco and cheese on crackers. After a glass and a half I almost suggest we go to mass to break the day up. It's the one day I like to go when there's mass on, not just by myself. Mostly for the songs, and because the priest usually says as short as possible a mass to let everyone get back to their dinner and presents, so it's less than an hour, hardly such an imposition. And besides, that is the whole point of Christmas, after all, celebrating the day Jesus was born. It would give me the upper hand today too, to be in an environment he would, no doubt, find confounding.

If he said yes and we went, I could pretend the hymn booklet makes it obvious when you're supposed to sit and stand, and feign surprise at his confusion over the practicalities of communion. In reality the instructions are all misprints or printed to accord with the whims of a priest who left the parish long ago. Seasoned attendees know to ignore them. If he said no, I could pick a fight about how godless it is to not go to mass on Christmas day, say things like: the birth of Christ, for god's sake, and, you see, this is the whole problem with Western civilisation. But I don't think I want to deal with the long-term consequences of mass becoming a topic of conversation between us.

We start cooking early instead. With Christmas food there's so much peeling and chopping and organising baking trays to fit beside each other in the oven that you can really spend a whole day doing it. Even just for two people. It's the sheer number of ingredients. He tells Anne Marie's speakers to put a certain Christmas playlist on. *It's the best one*, he says. *No filler.* I ask about The Pogues and he laughs and says of course. *Literally the second or third song.*

We swap to drinking red wine as we cook. His dad sent a case with six expensive bottles. It seemed like overkill yesterday, but as I start my second glass while peeling carrots, it crosses my mind it might not be enough. That's the thing with Christmas Day, you just drink and drink.

We get into a rhythm as we peel and chop, drink more wine and try to figure out when each component has to go into the oven so they're all ready together. We're having pie, potatoes, carrots, sprouts, parsnips and gravy. More ingredients I keep remembering as we cook. I write a list with timings on it and it gets so wet and greasy it's hard to read. He burns his hand taking a tray out of the oven with a tea towel instead of the oven gloves.

I go out to the back garden for fresh air at one point and the coldness of it, after the clamminess of the kitchen, reminds me of getting out of a plane in a hot country, somewhere in Europe. The opposite sensation but the same feeling. I stand in the cold looking up at the sky. It's not dark yet, but almost. What a day.

When we sit down to eat we gently make fun of the symbolism of having Christmas together. We pull two crackers before we eat, one with our right hands and one with our left. He taps his glass before saying a toast. *To the least stressful Christmas I can remember having*, he says, *in years.* We clink our glasses.

To stress-free Christmases, I say. We start to eat.

So, talk me through your normal day. What would it look like up to now? he says. He is holding his fork with a roasted carrot skewered on it, in mid-air.

I tell him we'd go to mass in the morning. He asks if that's something my mum likes to do. I know I can just say yes but I tell him I like going too. I take a sip of my red wine. I know I can fill the silence by saying it's tradition, or it breaks the day up, or you see people you know. I know I can say something non-committal and move the conversation along. Maybe it's because we're on our second bottle of red wine, but I don't want to.

Huh, he says. *Yes.* He nods. *What do you like about it?*

It's hard to say. Maybe I mean it's hard to explain, I say. *It's the ritual of it. Space to think.* I find myself telling him I don't just go on Christmas, but other times. *Not to mass, like. Not regularly. But the odd time. Just to think*, I say.

Maybe I am trying to be provocative, hoping to goad him into accidentally calling me provincial or backwards, or maybe I feel some kind of lapsed, but still god-fearing, Catholic loyalty, or guilt. He nods. I notice a change in his face. His eyebrows are slightly closer together, slightly higher. His mouth seems tighter. I read it as disapproval. It could be surprise. He smiles. *Like, think about what?*

The big questions. I laugh. *Obviously, what else?*

The big questions, right. You mean like praying? he says.

Not praying exactly. I'm not sure if that's the right word.

I tell him it's not as committed as that, not as religious. That here you don't have to be religious to go to church the odd time and light a candle. It means something different. Or maybe it doesn't. I don't know how to explain it properly; the wine isn't helping. *You know, almost nobody I know would say they're religious*, I say. *But they'd still go to light a candle.*

He smiles politely and takes a sip of his wine; I can see he is unconvinced. I tell him, not knowing what I am trying to prove exactly, that I have even known priests who aren't religious. I sound so defensive, so ridiculous, almost as if being a priest is something I would want to do myself.

I go on about the priests anyway. *Old men, obviously, nobody my age*, I say. *Well, of course it's old men. I mean, it's not like I know anyone my age who's a priest.* But I explain that with the older generation, say two generations, or one-and-a-half ago, it was common. It used to mean something different. For people who were very poor it was a way to do something with your life or get away to somewhere else. I start talking in more general terms. I say not everyone ends up doing what they love; most people make compromises of some sort. If you think of it that way, it's not so different from a lot of other jobs. *Or it didn't used to be*, I say.

He laughs at that. He asks about the celibacy thing and that makes me smile but I manage not to laugh. When people talk about priests and celibacy they think they're showing themselves to be very worldly, transgressive even, when really they're showing themselves to be naive.

Well, I don't know how well it was enforced, the celibacy thing, back in the day, I say. He frowns, a confused frown. *You know, say if you worked as a missionary or whatever. And it was just you living out there, wherever it was, halfway across the world. Or a pair of you. And you would write letters back occasionally.* I stop. He still looks confused, somehow. I go on. *So, well, who would know what you were up to? If you see what I mean? You could take up with someone who lived out there. Or the two of you could get together. I mean who knows.*

He looks surprised. *What? Right, like, how do you know that?*

Now he says that, I think there was a story I was told some time, or something I overheard adults talking about, about a great uncle or a second cousin, some older relative, with dementia. He had been a priest and they had retired him. He lived in a home and he would tell these inappropriate stories, or in the middle of talking to someone he would forget who they were and start to go on in an inappropriate way. I don't remember the details of it, if I ever knew them. Or if anyone said what the inappropriate thing was. Maybe I just heard that word and decided for myself. Still, there was something. But it's not my story to tell.

I think it's just something that is known, sort of? I say, fobbing him off. *I don't know exactly. It's just one of those things people know, I think. I mean, is it so hard to imagine?*

Sure, I guess not. He laughs. *Yeah, I wonder if there's a book or an archive or something about it.*

Good lord, I think. Why would there be an archive of it? Why can something not have happened unless there's a formal record of it? But then he has moved the conversation on to the abuse scandals, and a film and a documentary about them which both got a great critical reception and awards. Away from the weirdness and mysticism of spirituality, or what religion can mean when you're talking about more than just the arcane rules that can go with it, and on to the sorts of things that everyone knows what you're supposed to think about.

I get up to open a new bottle of wine. *How did we get on to this anyway?* I ask. *Oh yes. Our normal days. What would you be doing now?*

Oh. Let me think, he says. *Hmmm. Talking to my uncle about my*

*cousin who went to law school. My cousin, as in his son. He always
has a new apartment or a car or some other shiny thing.*

That doesn't sound fun, I say.

*Yes, and my cousin, Toby he is named, would always seem to be
standing slightly away from us, but just within earshot*, he says. *And
he kind of jumps out at the opportune moment and waves his phone
at me with photos of whatever his dad was talking about. And then
they would ask me about the academic job market. And say it must be
very stressful.*

He moves his hands around in the air as he talks, drawing
the scene. *And maybe my sister is standing in the corner having a
whispered argument with her husband, or my dad*. He gestures to the
corner, which makes me laugh. *We haven't eaten yet, but everyone
is drunk.*

Then I'd go for a walk, to smoke outside, he says, pointing towards
the doors. *There's trees, a little wood almost, behind my dad's house.
Me and my brother would put hiking boots on and go out there.*

He fills up his wine glass, splashes some on the table as he
does so. I ask if his brother is his ally for the day. He takes a sip
of wine.

*Yes, basically. Although that doesn't mean we won't argue about
something stupid later. One of us might say someone else had always
been something.*

Like what? I say. I'm enjoying this scene.

Selfish, maybe. Or stuck-up, that's a popular one, he says. *Or maybe
that someone has always been impossible. My sister likes to say that,
that someone is impossible. Or she likes to start an argument with me
and then say I'm petrifying if I respond.*

How would she describe these arguments? I ask.

She would say I snap at her and make her cry so I can accuse her of acting the martyr, he says. *Or she might point at me and say I'm a cruel person and storm out of the room.*

He hangs his head in mock shame. We both laugh.

OK, yes, I say. *This sounds like me and my mum's arguments. She likes to say I attacked her and I'm selfish. Things like that.*

He takes a sip of his wine. *You never see each other, right?*

Maybe because I'm drunk I tell him that we sometimes see more of each other, that I saw her the other week. And that we're in an argument at the minute because I don't think she supported me when I was going through a change. But her part of the argument is that she feels like I abandoned her. Did I even know that until I said it? Well, there it is now. *We're both stubborn,* I say. And, maybe because I am drunk, I say that she's had a hard life and that she had to be a parent by herself and nobody told her how to do anything and that we're very different and maybe that's part of it too.

I don't even mention any of the other stuff, about her life. There's too much to unpack there, and god knows what narrative he'd put over the top of it. That everything about the Troubles was a terrible thing that should never have happened, as if people don't have the right to live as they choose, or only some of them do. As if 'one man, one vote' isn't the starting point of a decent life for any of us. As if it didn't do any good at all, didn't give me a life with freedoms and opportunities my grandparents could never have imagined.

Or as if there was no bad to it at all; it never went wrong. And if he'd been there, well, he'd have risked his life no bother. Dead easy. So what of whoever was left behind?

He starts talking about unhealthy patterns of behaviour, unhealthy dynamics, and that makes me laugh.

I'm sure that's what they would say in therapy, I say.

What's wrong with therapy? He laughs.

Well, what good has it done you? I ask.

He really laughs at that. So much he has to set his wine glass down on the table. *Fair point*, he says. *Fair point.*

You know what, I don't even have anything against it. Against therapy, I say. *It's just. It just is what it is. Here, do you think there are any families that aren't like this?*

He laughs. *Not that I know of.*

After dinner we watch a comedy quiz round-up of the year. Teams of comedians make jokes and perform skits about news events from the year and there are clips and sound effects from buzzers and special guests. Trash TV. The tone of it is hysterical. People running around the studio and wearing novelty bow ties and shoes. The audience booing and hissing as if they're at a pantomime.

Each round is introduced with a short reel of the year's big news stories. Ostensibly separate from the comedy and so over-laid with serious music. I should expect it, but it takes me by surprise when the news story about Kate comes up on the screen. The food poisoning outbreak, the other victims, the changes in farmed salmon standards because of it. Bigger tanks, less crowding. Stringent hygiene rules. She isn't named, none of them are; it's a short reel. It closes on a positive note, highlighting how few fatalities there were compared to how many there could have been, and summarising the advances made in research into similar potential incidents since. Really, not just since, but almost thanks to that happening. As if to say progress sort of cancels out destruction.

God, remember that. The American points at the screen, his entire arm extended. He is saying it is hard to believe that was this year. It feels like it was about a decade ago. *And they did a salmon purge, remember?* he says. *With all the supermarkets.* I could tell him now. What would he say? What can you say?

I get up to get a glass of water. I say I remember, but it feels recent to me. I think about the texts from this morning that I didn't remember sending. *Well, long ago in some ways, short in others.* I ask if he thinks the tone is strange. Of the show.

Oh yeah, it's terrible, he says. *Just like incredibly crude and morbid. This is a stupid show though, at the end of the day. What do you expect?* He laughs from the sofa. A better response than I expected. *British humour is supposed to be smart, but it's always so fucking stupid,* he says.

You know, I'll always agree that everything British is stupid, I say, grateful to get away from this topic. He changes the channel. I bring back another bottle of wine. Today could have been worse.

We climb into bed too drunk and overfed to have sex. He wraps his arms around me, lying behind me and I feel very conscious of how much space he occupies in the bed.

I check my phone before I fall asleep and there is a text from my mum. **Happy Christmas.** No more than that. **And to you**, I reply.

26

I GET A MESSAGE FROM MATT on the afternoon of the twenty-ninth saying we should go for a drink tonight. Not American Matt, Matt Matt. It strikes me as odd. The twenty-ninth is not a big Christmas drinks night. And even if it was, why should the two of us go as a pair?

The style of the message is odd too. *Erin, we should get a drink in tonight?* it says. He could well be drunk and bored at home, messaging everyone he's spoken to recently, looking for something to do. The oddness of it makes me want to go more.

Sure, when were you thinking? I reply.

Well tonight if you were free? Or whenever? Tomorrow?

Tonight is fine. I meant what time?

He says six and I say sure. He suggests a pub I've only been to once or twice, on the way into town. I remember it being dingy, full of old men in brown leather jackets and mauve furniture. I'm supposed to be meeting Declan and Liam, but I can join them after. I saw Declan on the twenty-seventh, for a few drinks which turned into so many, with him venting about his mum's tantrum over the presents this year; I was sick several times the next day.

It's not about the thing itself, it's about what it says about what you think about me! his mum had said. *She's getting nothing next year!* Declan kept saying. *Spare us all the hassle.*

I was supposed to meet Mikey on the twenty-eighth but couldn't stomach drinking again so soon after that. Christmas does that to you.

Depending on what Matt's up to, we can both meet them after. I tell Declan I'll be late because I have to meet Matt first.

I get to the pub at ten to six. Inside it's as dingy as I remembered, maybe more so. The mauve furniture is dusty and faded. There are yellowed posters curling off the walls. The coloured lights of slot machines and a quiz machine flash in one corner. The place smells like bleach and whiskey. There's almost nobody else here. Two old men with red faces and oily strands of hair slicked across their bald heads like kelp, sit at the bar, cradling their pints. A pair of teenage girls drinking clear fizzy liquid are talking in one of the booths.

I order a Guinness and a packet of crisps and take them to a booth. I click around on my phone while I wait, looking at the Christmas photos people have posted, opening an article, reading the start of it and then closing it again, replying to group chats. I took my jacket and scarf off when I sat down but I put them back on after a few minutes. It's cold. I can tell it's one of those pubs which never feels warm.

I've almost finished my drink by the time Matt arrives. Cream foam coats the bottom of my glass. I look up from my phone and he is waving at me from the bar. He gestures at my glass and I nod. I put my phone away and he brings two Guinnesses over to the table.

Right, he says, as he sits down. *Good to see you, thanks for coming down.* He nods briskly at me. *And how are you getting on? How was your Christmas?*

It wasn't just the message that was odd. He is acting oddly. Too formal or too much eye contact. Nodding briskly at me. The way he is getting on reminds me of when you'd go to someone's house and meet their dad who barely speaks and he would ask gruff questions about what you were doing with yourself and say it was very good, whatever it was.

I want to ask what's going on, why he is acting this way. But I just say my Christmas was good, quiet. I ask why he suggested this pub.

Ah, I love it in here, he says, looking around and smiling. *I never get to come.*

I look around too, at the dusty mauve furniture and the slot machines. I can't help but laugh. *What do you like about it?* I ask.

He says it's authentic. Cheap pints. An interesting crowd. He scratches his nose. *Right, so, but anyway,* he says. *So I was thinking, after the other night. I can't remember most of it. Or the end of it at least. Like, I do remember being in the living room.* He trails off and looks to one side.

I wait for him to continue and he doesn't. He doesn't even look back at me. What is going on? Then I realise where he is going. The fact he is not looking at me. The trailing off. He's worried he tried something the other night. And he was too drunk to remember. Or he remembers us sitting in the living room and then nothing after that and he's put it together, jumped to conclusions. Oh god.

Oh no, Matt, I say. I want to reach out and touch his hand. I want to say that nothing happened, he didn't do anything wrong, there's nothing to worry about. It's all OK. Really I sort of want to give him a hug and say, not just about this, but in general, that it's all going to be OK and I really want to mean it. *Nothing happened. You were just drunk and tired*, I say.

He looks back at me, cocks his head to one side. *What do you mean?* he says. *Yeah, I think I remember that. Thank you for taking me back and everything else.*

He scratches his nose again and draws a deep breath. *I was thinking about it*, he says. *I don't mean to be annoying, and maybe you know this already. But if you don't. Well, you have been seeing a lot of Mikey recently, and I thought you might not. I was going to make sure you knew that he was sleeping with that Catherine.*

He says it all quickly and winces, slightly, at the last bit. I nod, slowly, taking it in. My face is hot and my mouth is very dry. I don't say anything for a few seconds or who knows how long.

Oh right, I say. *I see. Which Catherine?* I want my voice to sound even but it goes screechy at the last bit. It sounds like I'm going to cry, but I'm not. It's more like the sheer embarrassment of it has broken my voice. Or maybe I am going to cry.

I don't actually know her well, but I think she knows Declan, he says. *I only met her once.*

I lean forward and rest my face on one of my hands. My left cheek feels hot to the touch. *I know who you mean*, I say. *I didn't know that, actually. Thanks for telling me.*

Now it has sunk in and I'm angry. Furious, really. I could throw my pint over Matt, just for telling me, just for being the messenger. And I know if I did, he wouldn't even be

255

annoyed and he would probably say sorry and not even bring it up again another time. He's just like that, I guess, because he's kind.

I tell him I'm just going to the bathroom for a minute. I stand up from the booth too quickly and bang my knee on the table so I have to hobble to the bathroom. Inside the smell of bleach is stronger, laced with urine and old perfume. The soap dispenser has fallen off the wall and is sitting in the sink. There is an over-flowing bin just below the sink, with toilet paper and wrappers scattered on the floor around it. There are two toilet cubicles. The door of one doesn't lock and the door of the other is oddly short. Could Matt have chosen a worse pub for this meeting?

I put the toilet lid down in the cubicle with the short door and sit on top of it. When did he even do it? And why? Why does he ever do it? What did I expect? What did she even look like? I barely remember. And her talking about her ex-boyfriend or online dating or whatever it was. And me listening to it. I shake my head. I count to ten and back down, over and over. Until my face isn't red and I don't want to throw a pint over anyone.

I open the short toilet door. I look at myself in the mirror. *You know it's his loss*, I say, without conviction. I don't want to splash water on my face because I have makeup on. I didn't bring my bag to the bathroom with me so I can't top it up. I can't think of anything else to do to make myself feel fresh. I breathe in and out, a few more times, and open the door.

When I get back to the table there is a fresh pint waiting for me. Matt has got rid of the old one too. He was right to do that; it would have looked grotty, depressing. The thought-fulness of that gesture catches in my throat. I sit down and take a sip.

Don't feel you have to stay, he says. *If you need to go, don't worry. I'll drink both of these. I needed to get out of the house anyway.*

Thank you. Really, thank you, I say. *Do you know when it started?*

No idea really, you can never tell with him, he says, smiling. *Maybe a month, maybe less than that? Sorry, I don't mean to be annoying. I don't know all the details.*

No, it's not annoying. Thank you for telling me, I say. *You know the worst thing?* I laugh.

What's that? he says.

She wasn't even the hot one, I say.

He laughs too. *Who was the hot one?*

I shake my head. *There was a red-haired girl there that night. It's a long story. She was the hot one.*

Oh yeah. Is she single, do you think? He raises his eyebrows which makes me laugh again.

Thank you for telling me, I say.

It's no bother. I would have wanted to know, he says.

I tell him he did the right thing, and that he's a kind person. He says I can tell Mikey he told me if I want to; he doesn't mind if they have an argument or whatever. I want to get up and hug him again but I don't. I do reach across the table and squeeze his hand though, and he squeezes back, tightly.

I take my hand back after a few seconds and raise my glass. *You're a good friend, Matt, cheers.* He raises his too. I sip my pint. It crosses my mind that the one thing I could do that would annoy Mikey more than anything else would be to sleep with Matt. And that maybe I even could tonight, after a few drinks. But what good would it do any of us? And Matt might not even want to. How would I come back from that? There's been enough humiliation today to last me a good while. I smile to myself.

257

I ask him to tell me about his Christmas. It was the same as it always is. His mum was stressed, snapping and hissing as she cooked. His dad didn't help with cooking, but castigated everyone else for not doing more. One cousin is applying to do medicine and would talk of nothing else. Another had finished their accountancy exams and was likewise. She has started running marathons and she even ran on Christmas Day. We finish our pints and I get a new round.

You know. I'm thinking to do dry January, he says. *But I was hoping to squeeze in a few more benders before the New Year.* I tell him that's a great idea.

While I drink the next pint I ask him to tell me any gossip from the market. I just want to talk about anything else. He has collected stories of people seeing each other behind each other's backs, someone seeing a manager to get better shifts, a turf war between the two paella stalls and counterfeit merchandise from the woman who sells wind chimes.

It's only when we're on our fourth or fifth pint – I notice Matt seems to have paced himself to drink at the same rate as me – that I ask if he thinks I've been stupid and deluded. He says no. *God, no! Of course not.* He might just be saying it, but I need to hear it. Whether it's true or not, it's what I need to hear.

My phone rings and it's Declan. I'm too drunk to answer or explain. I reject the call and send him a message saying I won't make it, I'll call tomorrow. *OK!!! Hope everything's all right xxxx* he says.

Yes dw, talk tomorrow, I reply.

I have more pints with Matt. More gossip. At one point I ask him if he thinks it's worse that it wasn't even the hot one.

Aye, he says. *It probably is, isn't it.* I laugh because I don't know if he even knows what I'm talking about. I don't know if I even know.

I wake up and don't remember getting back. There is a dull pain in my head. My eyes are crusted with mascara, and I never go to bed with my makeup on. It hurts to open my eyes but it hurts only slightly less to keep them closed. I pick my phone up and it says it is just after eight. I notice a chip in the bottom right-hand side of the screen. I think I remember a taxi. But was that last night? Or another time? I have the thought that maybe it wasn't Matt drinking at the same rate as me, but me drinking at the same rate as him.

I lie in bed, picking the mascara off my eyelashes. I remember about Mikey, and asking Matt if he thinks I'm stupid. I pull the covers over my head to get away from the memory of it. It's too much. But of course, I can't get away from it. I give myself a few minutes and then get out of bed.

I take two paracetamol with a can of coke and ice and sit out in the garden. I'll text Mikey to meet later today. The grass is wet but the sky is clear. I tell myself it's going to be one of those bright winter sun days. Cold but beautiful. And I tell myself that when the paracetamol kicks in in half an hour my head won't feel so bruised. And I'll meet Mikey and have this conversation and it will be bleak but then tomorrow will be a new day.

27

I ARRANGE TO MEET MIKEY IN Botanic park just after three. I could have said a pub, and when I leave the house and the cold hits my face, I think I should have. But on the walk down, past the river with its grass smell and the red-brick terraces, the cold fades. It's a beautiful winter day, just like I told myself it would be, and I know we should be sitting out in it.

I walk up through the rose gardens, with all the flowers dead for the year, past the bandstands where teenagers will be drinking later, and towards the glass roof of the tropical ravine, which I said we should meet just outside. The grass looks fresh, the air is smoky with frost. I know I've chosen the right place to meet.

I can see he is already sitting on the bench as I approach. I make out the back of his head and that he is sitting with his hands by his sides. One hand drums on the bench. For a second I think I could just turn and walk back the way I came. Have the conversation some other time, or even not at all. Keep going the way we are. That we're not done yet. That even the fact that I'm thinking that has to count for something. But I told myself it would be a bright winter sun day and I told myself I would have this conversation, so I'm going to do it.

I tap his shoulder before I sit down.

Hi, Erin, he says. He squints in the sunlight. But he still looks good. His square jaw and slightly crooked nose can hold a squint better than a lot of other faces. He is smiling. Does he know why we're here?

Impossible to tell.

I don't know how to say it. I just say hello and sit down. He asks how I'm doing and I say fine. I ask about his Christmas and he says fine. Then neither of us says anything.

So, here, I say, breaking the silence. *I know about Catherine by the way.* I look at him and he looks away and then back.

Ah, right, he says. *How much do you know?*

Enough, I think, I say.

He opens his mouth and licks his lips but doesn't say anything. After a few seconds of silence he says it's not serious and I say doesn't that make it worse and he says probably, yes. I say it's humiliating, it's made me look stupid, why does it have to be someone I know. He says she instigated it, she messaged. It only happened a few times. They only slept together twice. He makes a grab for one of my hands and I say don't touch me. We're saying the things you have to say, having the argument you have when this happens. It doesn't even sound like us. It could be anyone. I think the fact we don't have a better way of talking to each other about it, our own way, makes me sadder than what happened.

Do you ever mean anything you say? I ask him, at one point.

What do you mean? he says. *You mean conversations we had? Yeah, I meant things I said, I was being serious.*

I don't even know what this means. Why *things*? Why not *the things*? Is this on purpose? A slip of the tongue? I shake my head

261

and look forward, towards the tropical ravine. The building is made of glass. I can see the black outline of tall rainforest plants pressing up against the inside of the windows. I let my eyes trace the outline of the shapes for a while. He doesn't say anything.

OK, so, he says. I keep looking at the plant outlines; I don't turn around. *What did you do on Christmas Day?* The way he says it, I can tell he knows how I spent it. Fuck. How does he know? What to say? I close my eyes for a second. Hot blood runs to my face. I can feel it in my cheeks.

Well, I say, *I was at Anne Marie's house.* My voice doesn't sound like my voice. It sounds high and far away.

Right. And who with? he says.

A man called Matt, I say. *He's American, he works at Queen's.*

Yeah, I thought that, he says.

I ask how he knows and he says it doesn't matter. I say he isn't anyone, he's just some guy, and he says maybe that makes it worse. I say he's got me there. I don't know what to say after that.

Did you do this on purpose? I ask, after a pause.

What do you mean? he says.

I mean did he sleep with Catherine to get back at me. But I also sort of mean did he somehow make this whole situation happen. Is it his fault I was seeing the American, because I thought he might do something like this? Can I tell myself that? That's a question he can't answer.

I don't know, I say. I shake my head.

I don't think this is my fault, he says and he looks away. I could ask what he means but I think I know.

I don't think it's mine, I say.

You don't think I have any feelings, he says.

262

There is something in his voice. I don't know if it's anger or frustration. I don't know if it's sadness. I don't know if it's an act to make me feel bad, but I want to believe it's not. I could say a retort. I could say you're spoiled and entitled. The real problem is you think your feelings matter more than anything else. I could say I don't even know what I'm doing here. You just waste my time. I could say you both got me the same Christmas present and it was generic. From both of you, it was generic. I could say everybody thinks you're bad news. Kate always said that, you know. I could say are you just a good fuck, is that all you are? Something defensive that would be true, but would also hide how I really feel. Sad, disappointed, in myself as much as him. And I want this conversation to be better than that.

It's not that, I say. *I just don't know what they are.*

Fair enough. He laughs. *What do you want from this?*

Honestly? I don't know, I say. *What do you want from this?*

I asked you first, he says.

I laugh at that. *Fair enough.*

I know we're different, he says. *But I just find you interesting. The way you go about things.*

I don't know if I believe that, I say. I laugh, but not to make it a retort; it's a real laugh.

He laughs too. *I know*, he says. *We don't trust each other, do we? Like, that's it, at the end of the day.*

I lean my head on his shoulder and he puts his arm around mine. *No, I guess we don't*, I say. *At the end of the day.* I trace the dark outlines of plants in the tropical ravine with my eyes and breathe in his smell. Wood and cigarette smoke.

You've always been so stubborn, he says, after a few seconds.

263

You're worse. I laugh.

This is the end for a wee while, isn't it? he says.

I think so, I say. *For a wee while.*

We sit like that for a few minutes. I am thinking about what a year this has been, and that it's New Year's Eve tomorrow, and what a time for fresh starts. I don't know what he's thinking about. If I ever did.

I stand up first. We hug goodbye and tell each other to look after ourselves. He says he'll see me around.

You will, I say. *I think I'm friends with your brother now.*

Christ, that fucker. He laughs. *He needs to make his own friends.*

I laugh. *He's nicer than you are.*

Probably, he says.

We hug once more and then part ways. I walk towards Botanic Avenue, past more flower beds with dead roses, past more red-brick terraced houses. The black outlines of birds fly overhead. Jet-black specks in the sky. I shield my eyes and look up at them. I'm dazed. I don't even know where I'm going until I sit down under the heater, at a metal table outside the old man pub in the middle of Botanic Avenue. I call Declan.

What was going on last night? he says, when he answers.

It's a long story. Are you about today? I need a drink, I say.

He is. I tell him where I am and he says he'll be half an hour. I get a Guinness while I wait, watch people bustling around the road on their way to or from post-Christmas sale shopping, carrying those big stiff cardboard bags with the string handles that always bang into your legs as you walk, tightly gripping coffees in paper cups because sale shopping really does take it out of you.

When Declan arrives and I tell him about Catherine, he says

264

which Catherine. I laugh at that. I explain which one and he just says right and shakes his head.

Did you know? I say.

He doesn't say anything for a few moments. *If you're asking if I knew, I didn't. But if you're asking am I surprised, then no.*

Right, I say.

So where have you left it? he says.

I think we've left it, I say. *For now.*

Right, he says. *And how do you feel about that?*

I don't know, I say. *Sad. But, we'll see. Life goes on. I'll get over it.*

I want to talk about something else so I ask for the Christmas gossip, the fights. His mum is still not over this year's present tantrum. He has good news too. He's a finalist in another competition, a different one. I get us a round for that.

28

I N THE MORNING I SIT out in Anne Marie's garden. There
was torrential, biblical rain last night; it smells like sodden
grass. Water has collected in empty plant pots and sunken-in
dents in the patio furniture. I'll be moving on from this soon,
from this garden and this other family, to my own room in a
shared house. To my new temporary data entry job. To whatever
I do after that, back to my course or on to something new. I
know I'll probably be back to babysit and housesit, but this stage
is ending. The new year is starting.

I feel hollowed out by yesterday, but cleansed, at the same
time. Like I'm moving forward in some ways, like I'm getting
back on my feet, like I need my own space for a while. I know
I have to end things, whatever they are, with American Matt.
Arrange to collect my things. Let it go.

Yesterday wasn't his fault, but it feels like it was. I can't
blame him, but I do. And I know he's not a bad person. He's
basically a decent guy. And he's lonely. And maybe he's scared
of getting older. But I don't think I can help with that, even
if I wanted to. I call to see if he's around and he says sure,
come over. I can't help but find his voice shrill, and I don't

really know what I'll say when I get there, but I need to get it over with.

On the walk over I think about things to say. *We're different people. It's because you always patronise me. This whole thing was a way of me distracting myself from the sad death of a good friend of mine. I was seeing someone else and now I'm not any more and it's basically your fault even though it isn't. I'm thinking of becoming a priest.* I smile to myself. It's another clear day; the rain from last night lingers on car bonnets and hedges, but today looks like it will be dry. White bundles of cloud stretch out in the pale blue sky. The kind of clouds which are flat along the bottom, like they've been sliced in half.

By the time I am crunching across the gravel, around the house on the way to the granny flat, I still don't know what to say. I knock on the door and he lets me in.

I look around the place and think back to the first night I came here. Some things haven't changed. The suitcase is in the corner now, and the clothes have been housed elsewhere, but that bag of plugs and cables has never been unpacked. You can see them spilling out of it. There is still a pile of clothes on the sofa, but it is less random. The sofa is where the clean laundry goes now. There are big stacks of pages printed out, sitting on the desk and the floor. Research for the book I don't think he'll write. But maybe he will.

I don't know where to start. He is his normal cheerful self, smiling, looking sort of bashful. He asks if I want a drink. Tea? Coffee? A beer?

Yes, a beer would be great, I say. I go to sit on the sofa. He goes into the kitchen and there is a knock at the door. I shout that there is someone at the door and he goes out to answer it. It's the dad of the family upstairs. He says hello to Matt and he moves his head to the side and says hi to me too.

Hi, nice to meet you, I say. He smiles.

He says there's something for Matt at the door; Matt asks if it's a package.

No, it's not. It's actually someone from the States to see you, he says. I can only see the back of the American's head, but I can see the dad from the family open his eyes very wide and nod slowly.

I think it seems like a personal thing, so it is probably best if Matt comes up by himself. He smiles at me again.

Matt turns around and smiles too; I detect a nervousness in his eyes. They dart about and don't meet mine. He tells me it will only take a second. *I think I know who this is,* he says. *I'll be back shortly.*

They both leave and close the flat door, and I hear the gravel crunching as they make their way round to the front of the house. I can tell something is going on, something I'm not supposed to know about. I wait until the crunching stops and then get up, open the door and then close it behind me very slowly, holding the handle up until the door is in the frame so it doesn't slam.

I walk slowly along the side wall of the house, placing my feet down on the gravel carefully with each step. At the edge of the wall I stand, grasping it to steady myself, the bricks scratching the palms of my hands, and then crane my head around it so I can see what's going on at the front door.

He's there, with his arms spread out, an imploring gesture, talking to the brown-haired woman from the swimming pool photo. Her teeth are just as white and her hair is just as shiny in real life. All that's missing is the pool. A little toddler stands between them, holding an elephant in his chubby hands. He has brown hair and is wearing a stripy top with a boat on it and red trousers. I can't hear what they're saying, but she is pointing in the air with one finger. His stance looks imploring.

I draw my head back behind the wall. Fuck. God. So that's what he's been up to. That's what he's running away from. I want to think I saw the signs, even in hindsight. I have to be honest with myself that I did not. Is the biggest surprise that he could be cunning enough to do this? Maybe. I wouldn't have thought he'd have it in him.

I stand by the wall of the house, hidden, deciding what to do. I could creep back to the flat, pretend I didn't see it and have the conversation as before. Or I could say I did see it and pretend that is the reason for having the conversation. A third option occurs to me.

I doubt she knows I exist. Even if she'd tried to keep tabs on him, after he left, there's no photos of us together anywhere. It's possible he's told her about me, but I doubt it. I could just walk past them and leave. I could be something to do with the house – a resident, a babysitter or a neighbour. I weigh it up. Would she know? What would she do even if she does? If she tried to talk to me, I could just run away down the street. It would surprise her so much that, even if she did give chase, she'd never catch me.

I emerge from behind the wall and stride purposefully across the gravel. They both turn to look at me. His face is contorted with horror. His mouth is open.

Oh, hello, Matt, I say. *Ian said just to use the back door because you were out here. I have another tutoring lesson so I'm just heading off.*

He looks confused. *Oh, great, hello. Sorry if we were in the way. Of the door.* The woman looks exhausted but she smiles at me and nods.

No problem, I say. His eyes cast around wildly. In that moment his ceaselessly chipper manner seems recast as the giddiness of someone who can't quite believe they're getting away with something: a man on the run. I realise I've had that impression of him before, the look of a man on the run, when I arrived to find him sat in Madame George's one evening. I suppose I presumed it had more to do with me than it did.

Well, have a good day, guys, if you're going sightseeing. I wave at them all and head out of the gate and down the street.

I walk aimlessly, past parked cars sparkling in the winter sun, detached yellow-brick houses and terraced red-brick ones, tall trees with no leaves, cafes and milkshake parlours. Always so many milkshake parlours here, for the Christian teenagers who don't drink.

I want to put distance between me and whatever was going on back there; beyond that I'm not sure what I'm doing. Do I need a drink or to go to church? Maybe not church right now. But I'll light a candle for her when I do go, that woman from the swimming pool photo with the baby and the exhausted smile. And for him, the American, who might not be a basically decent guy after all, but still seems lonely and lost.

Running away from his life, his responsibilities. Looking for what?

I've reached Botanic park. I walk up to the front of the Ulster Museum, a grey stone building with a front of glass. I try the doors, but it seems to be closed for the holidays, so I sit on the bench outside and watch the Santa's grotto on the stretch of grass nearby being dismantled. Depressing to still have it up in January, I suppose: a reminder that it's all over for another year. Men in green work outfits wrestle red tarpaulin off a metal frame and then start on the red velour furniture that was arranged inside the grotto.

So what for American Matt now? He might call. I'll answer if he does; I need to get my things sometime. He might go back to his old life or he might try to make a new one. I don't know. I know even less about him than I thought I did. I want to be able to say to myself that I sensed what he was up to, but I know I didn't. I wonder how much of his apparent enthusiasm about whatever we were doing, about that strange Christmas and helping to store my things, was really about what he had left, and about finding a way to make the fact he had done so mean something. I'll never know.

The men have started on the metal frame of the grotto now. Taking it apart is more involved than I would have thought. Poles need to be unscrewed and detached from each other and one man has to hold the bottom pole while the other lifts the top one, and they keep sticking together.

29

I OPEN THE HEAVY WOODEN DOORS of the church I used to go to when I was young, very young, in primary school. Before I understood all this the way I do now; when I really might have understood it better. I sometimes think that, anyway. The incense here smells sweet like it does nowhere else, like they're burning fresh roses in the basement.

I know that smell so well, from such a long time ago, that I can barely stand it. The smell, the whole place, is full of ghosts and dreams. Memories of when the priest was talking and I was imagining the way everything was going to be, before anything had ever gone wrong, before I had failed at anything, when it was all endless. Possibilities, choices, life. The distance between the way everything was going to be and the way it is keeps me from coming back here, most of the time. But it has to be this one today.

I dip my fingers in the Holy water, let the coldness coat the tips, and then touch my forehead, my chest, and then my left and right shoulder. *The Father. The Son. The Holy Spirit.*

The place is the way it always was. Red and purple velvet on chairs at the altar and on the seats in the crying chapel.

Scenes from the crucifixion and the ascension into heaven carved into slate tiles, with certain details outlined in gold and silver, every few metres along the walls. Stained-glass windows depicting scenes from the birth of Christ in jewel colours. Judas Iscariot in the garden, Jesus on his way to be crucified under Pontius Pilate, Jesus on the cross. Mary, the manger, the three wise men. There are pillars leading the whole way down the centre of the church, between the middle two aisles, and each one has a Celtic cross carved into it.

I walk to the third pew from the front. There are two Jesuses nearby. Hanging on the wall to the right is a tapestry of baby Jesus being cradled by the Virgin Mary; standing on the altar there is a statue of Jesus on the cross. The Jesus on the cross stands on a concrete plinth. The cross is tall, about ten foot. Shiny mahogany. Jesus is carved out of wood too, with his details filled in in rich, oily paints. But not jewel tones, normal colours. This Jesus on the cross is understated, as they go.

I bow my head and think of that day in Brighton. The children's birthday smell and the funfair lights on the promenade when the sun went down. Kate smiling and laughing about Steve. Brighton Steve.

So, happy New Year. I whisper. *I don't know if you know, but I have a new job starting soon. That all got sorted out. Some boring data entry thing, but it'll do for now. I don't have a new place, but I'll get on it. Declan is keeping his eye out. Some hole probably, four flatmates and no living room. But it'll do. Declan keeps winning competitions too, I think this is going to be his year.*

What else? So you were right about Mikey. Bad idea. One of those girls I told you might be my new friends too. I smile. *I know, can you believe it? But I don't know where we left it, really. I think we're getting somewhere.* I can hear her groaning. I laugh. *I know, I know, I need to leave that one alone for a while. I will. I promise.*

And the American, what was going on there? He was the worst of us all in the end. He was just the best at hiding it. But, you know, he did make me think. About my mum. I'm going to talk to her, or try to, properly. That's one of my New Year's resolutions, so we'll see where we are this time next year. Spend the next eleven months putting it off, probably. I smile. *But I don't want to be doing what he was. Running away from everything. Can't live like that.*

Anyway. Happy New Year. I miss you.

I open my eyes and look up at the cross again. The painted face hangs, expressionless, at the top of the cross. *Will you pass that on, Father, when you get a chance?* The face doesn't change. I smile and bow my head again.

Forgive me, Father, for having no patience with my mum, and for being an antagonist, sometimes the main antagonist, even, in the arguments we have, because I can't let certain things go from when I was a child, even though I know that's not a good excuse because I'm hardly a child any more; and for not making the best out of opportunities I've had that a lot of other people would have done almost anything for, my mum certainly being one of them; and for being distrustful of people and giving them reasons to be distrustful of me; for wasting other people's time, and my own. Because time is the one thing, Father, I know that.

That's what it's all about, this place: the idea that there might be something outside time, or some way to get around things ending, or somewhere beyond the end of things. Something, or somewhere, so good you can't even imagine, where you would be perfect. But you would still be yourself. Or else what's the point? And even that part, really the smallest part of it, is too hard to imagine.

Because you could glow like an angel and wear white, and be young, or an age where you were very happy, forever, the way they make it in some films and children's books, but that obviously wouldn't be it. Everybody knows that wouldn't be it, just like everybody knows they only show it that way because nobody knows what it would look like.

And everybody knows how to be better, more perfect. But that isn't it either. Because you could stop lying and scheming; stop drinking too much and doing drugs, or party drugs at least; never lose your temper or snap or start shouting for no reason; never feel jealous; never do anything out of spite; love your neighbour, whoever they are, as yourself; stop being lazy but, at the same time, not do things out of a craving for status and special treatment; never worship false idols like money, respect, or people who you know are no good for you, or even people who you think are good for you in their own way but who everyone else thinks are bad news; never give into, or lead others into, temptation; give up instant gratification; give up your vanity; and give up your pride. But who would you be? Would you recognise yourself?

I look up at the tapestry of the baby Jesus being cradled by the Virgin Mary. Gold stitching traces the outline of their features; their faces are deliberately abstract: warped, neckless ovals with half circles for eyes. Both heads are encircled by glittering gold halos to say they are angels or saints, and to allude to eternity: a circle never ends. I can never pray to the baby Jesus, even one that isn't cartoonish like this. It doesn't feel right. I can't imagine anyone does, but I know why this version of him is so well represented: the purity and innocence of a little boy born in a manger, in a barn. The unlikeliness of that. What a story.

I nod at the tapestry, the pair of blank, beige faces shaped like spoons, and turn slightly to the left to face the altar, and the statue of Jesus on the cross hanging above it. I think of a line from mass, a line that comes into my head sometimes, from one of the only prayers I know well enough to say by myself. *He will come again, in glory, to judge the living and the dead, and his kingdom will have no end.* The living and the dead, together: the distinction collapsed, time collapsed. In the kingdom that has no end.

I look at his face, hanging near the top of the cross, tilted to the left slightly, but still looking straight ahead rather than down. The slightly open mouth, the head bearing its ring of thorns. *What will your kingdom be like, Father? When you come.* The face continues to stare passively forward. He looks peaceful. His eyes don't meet mine; of course they don't. I smile and bow my head.

Father, what would I be like? In that place, if it exists. Whatever it is. Who would I see again? Would I know them? Would we be people, in the way I think of that word now, or something else? And what about the rest of it, Father? Why is it so hard to imagine? And why do any of us look to this thing, your kingdom, if we don't know what it is? Why have so many people, forever, wanted something they can't imagine?

I think about when I first moved back. I was running away from my life, and what had happened, from the sadness of it. From the way the world is now. But I was running towards something too. I don't know if it was a time I was trying to get back to, or a person, or a feeling I don't have the words for, and maybe don't even know how to feel. Whatever it was might not exist, or might be something that would always have been on the periphery of my reality, unreachable, like a flash of something you see out of the corner of your eye that looks different when you turn to face it, or how sometimes you hear a few seconds of a certain song and it seems like you're about to feel some way you'd forgotten how to be, and then in the next few seconds that sense disappears, and no matter how many times you listen to it again it's always the edge of the feeling you have rather than the feeling itself.

Or maybe it was real. A place I could get to, or a person, or a state I could reach. But whether the thing itself is real or not, the instinct to get to it is. That longing. And I don't think that started when Kate died, or just after, before I moved back here. I think back to when I first left this place, how doing so seemed so urgent, how it felt like everything was about to start. What was everything though? What was I trying to get to? Did I ever know? Was it ever not something?

I think of Mikey, always with another girl, then another one, and then going back to the first one, never telling anyone exactly what he is doing, not even knowing himself, probably; and of Matt, both the Matts, with the drinking and drugs, dropping out all the time, moving away, leaving his family and the book he might write one day, maybe; and Anne Marie, with her beautiful house, then houses, and getting divorced to start again and then deciding she didn't want that after all; and her boys always with their screens instead of whatever is going on around them; and my mum, who wishes I was different but can't seem to let me go, even though she must know I can't be; even Declan, entering his paintings into competition after competition, because every new one might be the one which would start it all off. Maybe this is all the same thing. That same longing.

I lean back against the pew and stretch my legs out in front of me. I think about trying to ask any of them, what words I could use, and the impossibility of it makes me smile. I look at Jesus on the cross again, each of his hands bound to an arm of the cross by a single nail, the fingers curled, slightly, into his palms. His peaceful, impassive face, empty and looking straight ahead.

Do they feel the same, Father? Or am I on my own? And that longing. Will that ever go away? Maybe if I get there, to whatever it is. Is that possible?

His face looks forward, still, unchanged; of course it does. What would I do if it didn't? I smile and bow my head. I think of the priest who would come to our class when I was young, who was so good at not answering questions in such a way that you wouldn't notice he hadn't answered them. The way that we were still young enough to ask strange questions that he couldn't answer. And how other people would ask about the things I had been thinking about and we would all laugh, as if that wasn't what we had been thinking about ourselves. Even then, when we were younger and braver, there were things we were scared to be honest with each other about.

Thank you for that, Father. For that memory. For having been so young once. For being young, still. For getting older. For the time I have spent here, trying to put a broken heart back together. For having time to spend. For having a heart that could be broken. For this place, this home for the feeling that there is a way I could be happy and perfect. But still myself, somehow. For that feeling.

For every winter morning when the sun is so bright and the air is so cold that it seems as if the day might crack and turn into something new. For the way streetlights look like golden streaks on the black, oily

278

surface of a river at night. For trees with leaves that turn into red and orange feathers in the autumn, when the air smells like something cold is burning. For the bitter, fresh smell of wet grass against the saltiness of wet pavement in the morning in spring. For evenings when the sky is pink and orange and light grey at the same time.

I nod at Jesus on the cross, then at baby Jesus on the tapestry, and slide to the end of the bench. At the back of the church I dip my right hand into the shallow metal tray of Holy water by the door, let the coldness of it coat the tips of my fingers, and then touch my forehead, the centre of my chest, my left and then my right shoulder. *In the name of the Father, the Son, the Holy Spirit. For the kingdom, the power and the glory are yours. Now and forever.*

At the back of the church I use both hands to push the wooden door open. Outside, the winter sun is bright white. I stand for a few seconds, blinking, in the scalding intensity of it. Then I put my hands in my pockets, away from the cold, and start walking. The air is hazy with frost and my breath appears as a small cloud before me.

ACKNOWLEDGEMENTS

Thank you to my mum Monica Gallagher for being nothing like the mother in this book, for bringing me up to be tough and to hate snobbery, for your integrity and style, and for giving me the freedom, always, to write exactly as I choose. What a gift that is. To my dad Stephen Connolly for giving me that freedom too. To my brother Ryan Connolly for your incredible way with words, your sense of humour and your unfailing loyalty. To my brother Luke Connolly for your kindness and for showing me what real strength and resilience looks like. To my grandma Betty Gallagher for showing me that women don't have to act the way they often do in books and films. For your fight, your cheekiness and your glamour. And for teaching me how to tell a good story.

Thank you to Rachael McK, Jake C, Ravinda G, Alice O, Adam P, Clare C, Amy KS, Elise M and Conor C for making Belfast in the 2000s the best place and time in the world to be a teenager. A part of me still lives there. I wouldn't have written this without your friendship.

Thank you to Ross F for too many things to list here, but mostly for always taking me and my work seriously and for being the best reader. To Rachel McG for your support of my work, your humour, your wisdom, your loyalty and your friendship. To Felix H for teaching me how to be an artist. To Alice O (again) for being the perfect model of a housemate, at a time when a lot of the ideas and characters in this book were forming in my head, and of a friend. To Eve K, for resisting what people expected of you in grief, which has informed this book.

Thank you to Brian O'Flynn for your invaluable feedback and thoughts on various drafts of this book, and for sharing your writing with me, from which I have learned so much. Also for your authenticity. To Sarah M for your endless support and early feedback. To Eliza C and Jess W for the advice, the support and, most importantly, the gossip. To Jason O for helping me stay sane while bringing this book into the world. To Mark O'C for your support of my writing, which means so much to me, and for the best book recommendations.

Thank you to my agent Tracy Bohan for reading all my terrible drafts, for your thoughts and guidance on this book and my work in general, which is so useful to me, and for understanding my vision from the start. To Jackie Ko for your work on this book in the states. To my editor Francis Bickmore for your faith in this book and your brilliant editorial guidance, you made the book so much better. To my editor Gina Iaquinta for the same, and for seeing and helping me to accentuate the tenderness of the book and of Erin, even your smallest suggestions made such a big difference. And to Sarahmay Wilkinson for a truly perfect cover.